The Integral Trees

The Integral Trees

LARRY NIVEN

A Del Rey Book

BALLANTINE BOOKS • NEW YORK

A Del Rey Book
Published by Ballantine Books

Diagrams by Shelly Shapiro

Manufactured in the United States of America

First Edition: March 1984
10   9   8   7   6   5   4   3   2   1
Library of Congress Cataloging in Publication Data

Niven, Larry.
    The integral trees.

    I. Title.
PS3564.I9I54   1984   813'.54   83-15870
ISBN 0-345-31270-8

This book is dedicated to Robert Forward, for the stories he's sparked in me, for his help in working out the parameters of the Smoke Ring, and for his big, roomy mind.

Contents

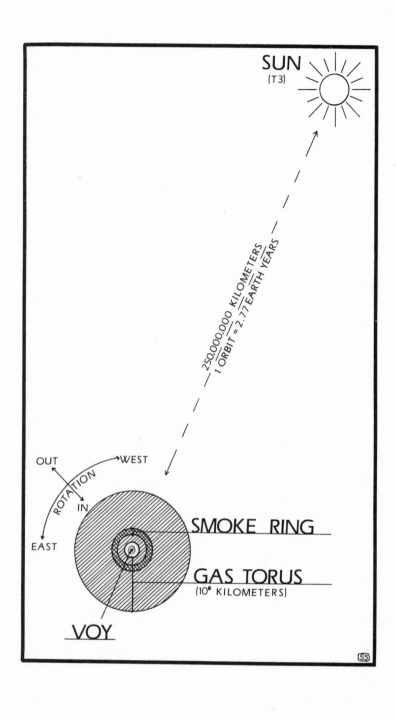

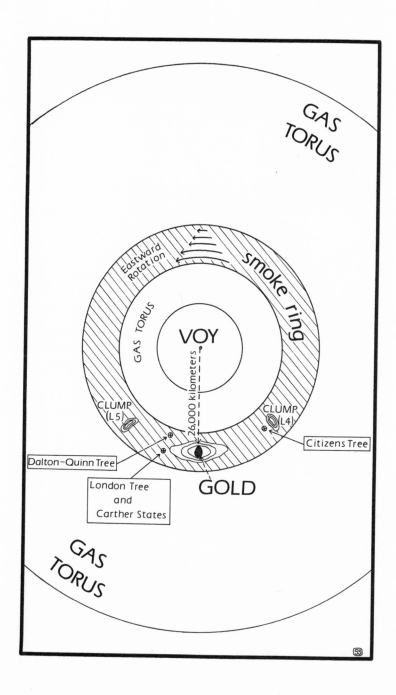

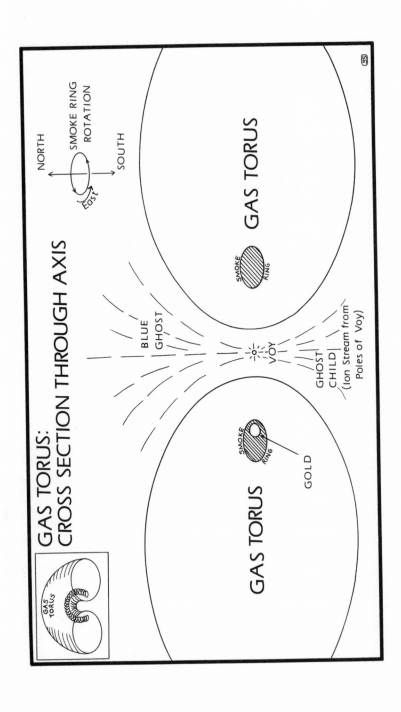

GAS TORUS: CROSS SECTION THROUGH AXIS

GAS TORUS

GAS TORUS

GAS TORUS

SMOKE RING

SMOKE RING

GOLD

BLUE GHOST

VOY

GHOST CHILD
(Ion Stream from Poles of Voy)

NORTH

SMOKE RING ROTATION

SOUTH

East

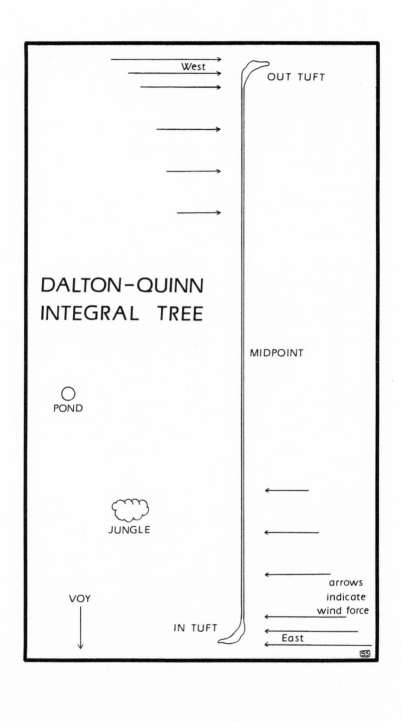

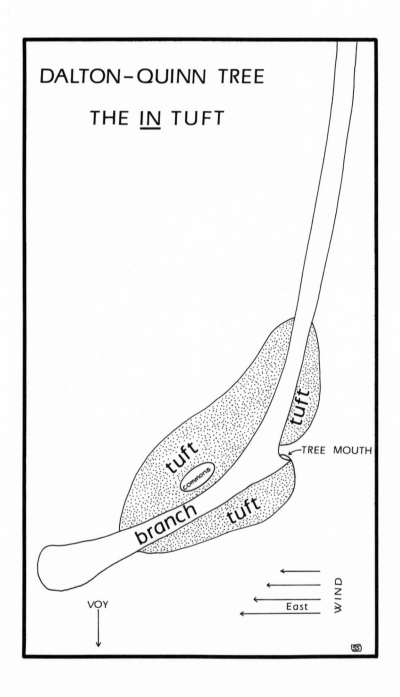

DALTON-QUINN TREE

THE IN TUFT

tuft

commons

tuft

branch tuft

TREE MOUTH

WIND

East

VOY

Prologue

Discipline

IT WAS TAKING TOO LONG, MUCH LONGER THAN HE HAD EX-
pected. Sharls Davis Kendy had not been an impatient man.
After the change he had thought himself immune to impatience.
But it was taking too long! What were they *doing* in there?

His senses were not limited. Sharls's telescopic array was powerful; he could sense the full electromagnetic spectrum, from
microwave up to X-ray. But the Smoke Ring balked his view.
It was a storm of wind, dust, clouds of water vapor, huge rippling
drops of dirty water or thin mud, masses of free-floating rock;
dots and motes and clumps of green, green surfaces on the drops
and the rocks, green tinges of algae in the clouds; trees shaped
like integration signs, oriented radially to the neutron star and
tufted with green at both ends; whale-sized creatures with vast
mouths, to skim the green-tinged clouds...

Life was everywhere in the Smoke Ring. Claire Dalton had
called it a Christmas wreath. Claire had been a very old woman
before the State revived her as a corpsicle. The others had never
seen a Christmas wreath; nor had Kendy. What they had seen,
half a thousand years ago, was a perfect smoke ring several tens

of thousands of kilometers across, with a tiny hot pinpoint in its center.

Their reports had been enthusiastic. Life was DNA-based; the air was not only breathable, but tasted fine . . .

Discipline presently occupied the point of gravitational neutrality behind Goldblatt's World, the L2 point. This close, the sky split equally into star-sprinkled, black- and green-tinged cloudscape. Directly below, a vast distorted whirlpool of storm hid the residue of a gas giant planet, a rocky nugget two and a half times the mass of Earth.

Sharls would not enter that inner region. The maelstrom of forces could damage his ship. He couldn't guess how long the seeder ramship must survive to accomplish his mission. He had waited more than half a thousand years already. The L2 point was still within the gas torus of which the Smoke Ring was only the densest part. *Discipline* was subject to slow erosive forces. He couldn't last forever in this place.

At least the crew were not extinct.

That would have hurt him terribly.

He had done his duty. Their ancestors had been mutineers, a potential threat to the State itself. To reeducate their descendants was his goal, but if the Smoke Ring had killed them . . . well, it would not have surprised him. It took more than breathable air to keep men alive. The Smoke Ring was green with the life that had evolved for that queer environment. Native life might well have killed off those Johnny-come-lately rivals, the erstwhile crew of the seeder ramship *Discipline*.

Sharls would have grieved; but he would have been free to return home.

They'd call me an obsolete failure, he thought gloomily while his instruments sought a particular frequency in the radio range. *A thousand years out of date by the time I'm home. They'd scrap the computer for certain. And the program? The Sharls Davis Kendy program might be copied and kept for the use of historians. Or not.*

But they hadn't died. Eight Cargo and Repair Modules had gone with the original mutineers. Time and the corrosive environment must have ruined the CARMs; but at least one was still operational. Someone had been using it as late as six years ago. And—there: the light he'd been searching for. For a moment it reached him clearly: the frequency of hydrogen burning with oxygen.

He fired a maser in ultrashort, high-powered pulses. "Kendy for the State. Kendy for the State. Kendy for the State."

The response came four seconds later, sluggish, weak, and blurred. Kendy pinpointed it and fine-focused his telescopes while he sent his next demand.

"Status. Tell me three times."

Kendy sorted the garbled response through a noise-eliminator program. The CARM was on manual, mostly functional, using attitude jets only, operating well inside its safety limits. Once it had been a simplified recording of Kendy's own personality. Now the program was deteriorating, growing stupid and erratic.

"Course record for the past hour."

It came. The CARM had been free-falling at low relative velocity up to forty minutes ago. Then, low-acceleration maneuvers, a course that looked like a dropped plate of spaghetti, a mad waste of stored fuel. Malfunction? Or . . . it could have been a dogfight-style battle.

War?

"Switch to my command."

Four seconds; then a signal like a scream of bewildered agony. Massive malfunction.

The crew must have disconnected the autopilot system on every one of the CARMs, half a thousand years ago. It had still been worth a try, as was his next message.

"Give me video link with crew."

"Denied."

Oh *ho*! The video link hadn't been disconnected! A block must have been programmed in, half a thousand years ago, by the mutineers. Certainly their descendants wouldn't know how to do that.

A block might be circumvented, eventually.

The CARM was too small to see, of course, but it must be somewhere near that green blob not far from Goldblatt's World.

A cotton-candy forest. Plants within the Smoke Ring tended to be fluffy, fragile. They spread and divided to collect as much sunlight as possible, without worrying about gravity.

For half a thousand years Kendy had watched for signs of a developing civilization—for regular patterns in the floating masses, or infrared radiation from manufacturing centers, or industrial pollution: metal vapor, carbon monoxide, oxides of nitrogen. He hadn't found any of that. If the children of *Discipline*'s crew were developing beyond savagery, it was not in any great numbers.

But they lived. Someone was using a CARM.

If only he could see them! Or talk to them— "Give me voice-over. Citizen, this is Kendy for the State. Speak, and your reward will be beyond the reach of your imagination."

"Amplify. Amplify. Amplify," sent the CARM.

Kendy was already sending at full amplification. "Cancel voice-over," he sent.

Not for the first time, he wondered if the Smoke Ring could have proved *too* kindly an environment. Creatures evolved in free-fall would not have human strength. Humans could be the most powerful creatures in the Smoke Ring: happy as clams in there, and about as active. Civilization develops to protect against the environment.

Or against other men. War would be a hopeful sign...

If he could *know* what was going on! Kendy could perturb the environment in a dozen different ways. Cast them out of Eden and see what happened. But he dared not. He didn't know enough.

Kendy waited.

Chapter One

Quinn Tuft

GAVVING COULD HEAR THE RUSTLING AS HIS COMPANIONS TUN-
neled upward. They stayed alongside the great flat wall of the
trunk. Finger-thick spine branches sprouted from the trunk, divided endlessly into wire-thin branchlets, and ultimately flowered
into foliage like green cotton, loosely spun to catch every stray
beam of sunlight. Some light filtered through as green twilight.

Gavving tunneled through a universe of green cotton candy.

Hungry, he reached deep into the web of branchlets and pulled
out a fistful of foliage. It tasted like fibrous spun sugar. It cured
hunger, but what Gavving's belly wanted was meat. Even so, its
taste was *too* fibrous . . . and the green of it was too brown, even
at the edges of the tuft, where sunlight fell.

He ate it anyway and went on.

The rising howl of the wind told him he was nearly there. A
minute later his head broke through into wind and sunlight.

The sunlight stabbed his eyes, still red and painful from this
morning's allergy attack. It always got him in the eyes and
sinuses. He squinted and turned his head, and sniffled, and waited

while his eyes adjusted. Then, twitchy with anticipation, he looked up.

Gavving was fourteen years old, as measured by passings of the sun behind Voy. He had never been above Quinn Tuft until now.

The trunk went straight up, straight out from Voy. It seemed to go out forever, a vast brown wall that narrowed to a cylinder, to a dark line with a gentle westward curve to it, to a point at infinity—and the point was tipped with green. The far tuft.

A cloud of brown-tinged green dropped away below him, spreading out into the main body of the tuft. Looking east, with the wind whipping his long hair forward, Gavving could see the branch emerging from its green sheath as a half-klomter of bare wood: a slender fin.

Harp's head popped out, and his face immediately dipped again, out of the wind. Laython next, and he did the same. Gavving waited. Presently their faces lifted. Harp's face was broad, with thick bones, its brutal strength half-concealed by golden beard. Laython's long, dark face was beginning to sprout strands of black hair.

Harp called, "We can crawl around to lee of the trunk. East. Get out of this wind."

The wind blew always from the west, always at gale velocities. Laython peered windward between his fingers. He bellowed, "Negative! How would we catch anything? Any prey would come right out of the wind!"

Harp squirmed through the foliage to join Laython. Gavving shrugged and did the same. He would have liked a wind-break... and Harp, ten years older than Gavving and Laython, was nominally in charge. It seldom worked out that way.

"There's nothing to catch," Harp told them. "We're here to guard the trunk. Just because there's a drought doesn't mean we can't have a flash flood. Suppose the tree brushed a pond?"

"*What* pond? Look around you! There's *nothing* near us. Voy is too close. Harp, you've said so yourself!"

"The trunk blocks half our view," Harp said mildly.

The bright spot in the sky, the sun, was drifting below the western edge of the tuft. And in that direction were no ponds, no clouds, no drifting forests... nothing but blue-tinged white sky split by the white line of the Smoke Ring, and on that line, a roiled knot that must be Gold.

Looking up, out, he saw more of nothing... faraway streamers of cloud shaping a whorl of storm... a glinting fleck that might indeed have been a pond, but it seemed even more distant than the green tip of the integral tree. There would be no flood.

Gavving had been six years old when the last flood came. He remembered terror, panic, frantic haste. The tribe had burrowed east along the branch, to huddle in the thin foliage where the tuft tapered into bare wood. He remembered a roar that drowned the wind, and the mass of the branch itself shuddering endlessly. Gavving's father and two apprentice hunters hadn't been warned in time. They had been washed into the sky.

Laython started off around the trunk, but in the windward direction. He was half out of the foliage, his long arms pulling him against the wind. Harp followed. Harp had given in, as usual. Gavving snorted and moved to join them.

It was tiring. Harp must have hated it. He was using claw sandals, but he must have suffered, even so. Harp had a good brain and a facile tongue, but he was a dwarf. His torso was short and burly; his muscular arms and legs had no reach, and his toes were mere decoration. He stood less than two meters tall. The Grad had once told Gavving, "Harp looks like the pictures of the Founders in the log. We all looked like that once."

Harp grinned back at him, though he was puffing. "We'll get you some claw sandals when you're older."

Laython grinned too, superciliously, and sprinted ahead of them both. He didn't have to say anything. Claw sandals would only have hampered his long, prehensile toes.

Night had cut the illumination in half. Seeing was easier, with the sunglare around on the other side of Voy. The trunk was a great brown wall three klomters in circumference. Gavving looked up once and was disheartened at their lack of progress. Thereafter he kept his head bent to the wind, clawing his way across the green cotton, until he heard Laython yell.

"Dinner!"

A quivering black speck, a point to port of windward. Laython said, "Can't tell what it is."

Harp said, "It's trying to miss. Looks big."

"It'll go around the other side! Come on!"

They crawled, fast. The quivering dot came closer. It was long and narrow and moving tail-first. The great translucent fin blurred with speed as it tried to win clear of the trunk. The slender torso was slowly rotating.

The head came in view. Two eyes glittered behind the beak, one hundred and twenty degrees apart.

"Swordbird," Harp decided. He stopped moving.

Laython called, "Harp, what are you doing?"

"Nobody in his right mind goes after a swordbird."

"It's still meat! And it's probably starving too, this far in!"

Harp snorted. "Who says so? The Grad? The Grad's full of theory, but he doesn't have to hunt."

The swordbird's slow rotation exposed what should have been its third eye. What showed instead was a large, irregular, fuzzy green patch. Laython cried, "Fluff! It's a head injury that got infected with fluff. The thing's injured, Harp!"

"That isn't an injured turkey, boy. It's an injured *swordbird*."

Laython was half again Harp's size, and the Chairman's son to boot. He was not easy to discipline. He wrapped long, strong fingers around Harp's shoulder and said, "We'll miss it if we wait here arguing! I say we go for Gold." And he stood up.

The wind smashed at him. He wrapped toes and one fist in branchlets, steadied himself, and semaphored his free arm. "Hiyo! Swordbird! Meat, you copsik, *meat!*"

Harp made a sound of disgust.

It would surely see him, waving in that vivid scarlet blouse. Gavving thought, hopefully, *We'll miss it, and then it'll be past.* But he would not show cowardice on his first hunt.

He pulled his line loose from his back. He burrowed into the foliage to pound a spike into solid wood, and moored the line to it. The middle was attached to his waist. Nobody ever risked losing his line. A hunter who fell into the sky might still find rest somewhere, if he had his line.

The creature hadn't seen them. Laython swore. He hurried to anchor his own line. The business end was a grapnel: hardwood from the finned end of the branch. Laython swung the grapnel round his yead, yelled, and flung it out.

The swordbird must have seen, or heard. It whipped around, mouth gaping, triangular tail fluttering as it tried to gain way to starboard, to reach their side of the trunk. Starving, yes! Gavving hadn't grasped that a creature could see him as *meat* until that moment.

Harp frowned. "It could work. If we're lucky it could smash itself against the trunk."

The swordbird seemed bigger every second: bigger than a man, bigger than a hut—all mouth and wings and tail. The tail was a translucent membrane enclosed in a V of bone spines with serrated edges. What was it doing this far in? Swordbirds fed on creatures that fed in the drifting forests, and there were few of these, so far in toward Voy. Little enough of anything. The creature did look gaunt, Gavving thought; and there was that soft green carpet over one eye.

Fluff was a green plant parasite that grew on an animal until the animal died. It attacked humans too. Everybody got it sooner or later, some more than once. But humans had the sense to stay in shadow until the fluff withered and died.

Laython could be right. A head injury, sense of direction fouled up...and it was meat, a mass of meat as big as the bachelors' longhut. It must be ravenous...and now it turned to face them.

An isolated mouth came toward them: an elliptical field of teeth, expanding.

Laython coiled line in frantic haste. Gavving saw Harp's line fly past him, and tearing himself out of his paralysis, he threw his own weapon.

The swordbird whipped around, impossibly fast, and snapped

up Gavving's harpoon like a tidbit. Harp whooped. Gavving froze for an instant; then his toes dug into the foliage while he hauled in line. *He'd hooked it.*

The creature didn't try to escape: it was still fluttering toward them.

Harp's grapnel grazed its side and passed on. Harp yanked, trying to hook the beast, and missed again. He reeled in line for another try.

Gavving was armpit-deep in branchlets and cotton, toes digging deeper, hands maintaining his deathgrip on the line. With eyes on him, he continued to behave as if he *wanted* contact with the killer beast. He bellowed, "Harp, where can I hurt it?"

"Eye sockets, I guess."

The beast had misjudged. Its flank smashed bark from the trunk above their heads, dreadfully close. The trunk shuddered. Gavving howled in terror. Laython howled in rage and threw his grapnel ahead of it.

It grazed the swordbird's flank. Laython pulled hard on the line and sank the hardwood tines deep in flesh.

The swordbird's tail froze. Perhaps it was thinking things over, watching them with two good eyes while the wind pulled it west.

Laython's line went taut. Then Gavving's. Spine branches ripped through Gavving's inadequate toes. Then the immense mass of the beast had pulled him into the sky.

His own throat closed tight, but he heard Laython shriek. Laython too had been pulled loose.

Torn branchlets were still clenched in Gavving's toes. He looked down into the cushiony expanse of the tuft, wondering whether to let go and drop. But his line was still anchored . . . and wind was stronger than tide; it could blow him past the tuft, past the entire branch, out and away. Instead he crawled along the line, away from their predator-prey.

Laython wasn't retreating. He had readied his harpoon and was waiting.

The swordbird decided. Its body snapped into a curve. The serrated tail slashed effortlessly through Gavving's line. The swordbird flapped hard, making west now. Laython's line went taut; then branchlets ripped and his line pulled free. Gavving snatched for it and missed.

He might have pulled himself back to safety then, but he continued to watch.

Laython poised with spear ready, his other arm waving in circles to hold his body from turning, as the predator flapped toward him. Almost alone among the creatures of the Smoke Ring, men have no wings.

The swordbird's body snapped into a U. Its tail slashed Laython in half almost before he could move his spear. The beast's mouth snapped shut four times, and Laython was gone. Its mouth continued to work, trying to deal with Gavving's harpoon in its throat, as the wind carried it east.

The Scientist's hut was like all of Quinn Tribe's huts: live spine branches fashioned into a wickerwork cage. It was bigger than some, but there was no sense of luxury. The roof and walls were a clutter of paraphernalia stuck into the wickerwork: boards and turkey quills and red tuftberry dye for ink, tools for teaching, tools for science, and relics from the time before men left the stars.

The Scientist entered the hut with the air of a blind man. His hands were bloody to the elbows. He scraped at them with handfuls of foliage, talking under his breath. "Damn, damn drillbits. They just burrow in, no way to stop them." He looked up. "Grad?"

" 'Day. Who were you talking to, yourself?"

"Yes." He scrubbed at his arms ferociously, then hurled the wads of bloody foliage away from him. "Martal's dead. A drillbit burrowed into her. I probably killed her myself, digging it out, but she'd have died anyway . . . you can't leave drillbit eggs. Have you heard about the expedition?"

"Yes. Barely. I can't get anyone to tell me anything."

The Scientist pulled a handful of foliage from the wall and tried to scrub the scalpel clean. He hadn't looked at the Grad. "What do you think?"

The Grad had come in a fury and grown yet angrier while

waiting in an empty hut. He tried to keep that out of his voice. "I think the Chairman's trying to get rid of some citizens he doesn't like. What I want to know is, why me?"

"The Chairman's a fool. He thinks science could have stopped the drought."

"Then you're in trouble too?" The Grad got it then. "You blamed it on me."

The Scientist looked at him at last. The Grad thought he saw guilt there, but the eyes were steady. "I let him think you were to blame, yes. Now, there are some things I want you to have—"

Incredulous laughter was his answer. "What, more gear to carry up a hundred klomters of trunk?"

"Grad...Jeffer. What have I told you about the tree? We've studied the universe together, but the most important thing in it is the tree. Didn't I teach you that everything that lives has a way of staying near the Smoke Ring median, where there's air and water and soil?"

"Everything but trees and men."

"Integral trees have a way. I taught you."

"I...had the idea you were only guessing...Oh, I see. You're willing to bet *my* life."

The Scientist's eyes dropped. "I suppose I am. But if I'm right, there won't be anything left but you and the people who go with you. Jeffer, this could be *nothing*. You could all come back with...whatever we need: breeding turkeys, some kind of meat animal living on the trunk, I don't know—"

"But you don't think so."

"No. That's why I'm giving you these."

He pulled treasures from the spine-branch walls: a glassy rectangle a quarter meter by half a meter, flat enough to fit into a pack; four boxes each the size of a child's hand. The Grad's response was a musical "O-o-oh."

"You'll decide for yourself whether to tell any of the others what you're carrying. Now let's do one last drill session." The Scientist plugged a cassette into the reader screen. "You won't have much chance to study on the trunk."

PLANTS

LIFE PERVADES THE SMOKE RING BUT IS NEITHER DENSE
NOR MASSIVE. IN THE FREE-FALL ENVIRONMENT PLANTS CAN
SPREAD THEIR GREENERY WIDELY TO CATCH MAXIMUM SUN-
LIGHT AND PASSING WATER AND SOIL, WITHOUT BOTHERING
ABOUT STRUCTURAL STRENGTH. WE FIND AT LEAST ONE
EXCEPTION . . .

THESE INTEGRAL TREES GROW TO TREMENDOUS SIZE. THE
PLANT FORMS A LONG TRUNK UNDER TERRIFIC TENSION,
TUFTED WITH GREEN AT BOTH ENDS, STABILIZED BY THE
TIDE. THEY FORM THOUSANDS OF RADIAL SPOKES CIRCLING
LEVOY'S STAR. THEY GROW UP TO A HUNDRED KILOMETERS
IN LENGTH, WITH UP TO A FIFTH OF A GEE IN TIDAL "GRAV-
ITY" AT THE TUFTS AND PERPETUAL HURRICANE WINDS.

THE WINDS DERIVE FROM SIMPLE ORBITAL MECHANICS.
THEY BLOW FROM THE WEST AT THE INNER TUFT AND FROM
THE EAST AT THE OUTER TUFT (WHERE *IN* IS TOWARD LE-
VOY'S STAR, AS USUAL). THE STRUCTURE BOWS TO THE
WINDS, CURVING INTO A NEARLY HORIZONTAL BRANCH AT
EACH END. THE FOLIAGE SIFTS FERTILIZER FROM THE
WIND . . .

THE MEDICAL DANGERS OF LIFE IN FREE-FALL ARE WELL
KNOWN. IF *DISCIPLINE* HAS INDEED ABANDONED US, IF WE
ARE INDEED MAROONED WITHIN THIS WEIRD ENVIRONMENT,
WE COULD DO WORSE THAN TO SETTLE THE TUFTS OF THE
INTEGRAL TREES. IF THE TREES PROVE MORE DANGEROUS
THAN WE ANTICIPATE, ESCAPE IS EASY. WE NEED ONLY JUMP
AND WAIT TO BE PICKED UP.

The Grad looked up. "They really didn't know very much
about the trees, did they?"

"No. But, Jeffer, they had seen trees from outside."

That was an awesome thought. While he chewed it, the Scientist said, "I'm afraid you may have to start training your own
Grad, and soon."

* * *

Jayan sat cross-legged, coiling lines. Sometimes she looked up to watch the children. They had come like a wind through the Commons, and the wind had died and left them scattered around Clave. He wasn't getting much work done, though it seemed he was trying.

The girls loved Clave. The boys imitated him. Some just watched, others buzzed around him, trying to help him assemble the harpoons and the spikes or asking an endless stream of questions. "What are you doing? Why do you need so many harpoons? And all this rope? Is it a hunting trip?"

"I can't tell you," Clave said with just the proper level of regret. "King, where have you been? You're all sticky."

King was a happy eight-year-old painted in brown dust. "We went underside. The foliage is greener there. Tastes better."

"Did you take lines? Those branches aren't as strong as they used to be. You could fall through. And did you take a grown-up with you?"

Jill, nine, had the wit to distract him. "When's dinner? We're still hungry."

"Aren't we all." Clave turned to Jayan. "We've got enough packs, we won't be carrying food, we'll find water on the trunk... claw sandals... jet pods, I'm glad we got those... hope we've got enough spikes... what else do we need? Is Jinny back?"

"No. What did you send her for, anyway?"

"Rocks. I gave her a net for them, but she'll have to go all the way to the treemouth. I hope she finds us a good grindstone."

Jayan didn't blame the children. She loved Clave too. She would have kept him for herself, if she could... if not for Jinny. Sometimes she wondered if Jinny ever felt that way.

"Mmm... we'll pick some foliage before we leave the tuft—"

Jayan stopped working. "Clave, I never thought of that. There's no foliage on the trunk! We won't have *anything* to eat!"

"We'll find something. That's why we're going," Clave said briskly. "Thinking of changing your mind?"

"Too late," Jayan said. She didn't add that she had never wanted to go at all. There was no point, now.

"I could bust you loose. Jinny too. The citizens like you, they wouldn't let—"

"I won't stay." Not with Mayrin and the Chairman here, and Clave gone. She looked up and said, "Mayrin."

Clave's wife stood in the half-shadows on the far side of the Commons. She might have been there for some time. She was seven years older than Clave, a stocky woman with the square jaw of her father, the Chairman. She called, "Clave, mighty hunter, what game are you playing with this young woman when you might be finding meat for the citizens?"

"Orders."

She approached, smiling. "The expedition. My father and I arranged it together."

"If you'd like to believe that, feel free."

The smile slipped. "Copsik! You've mocked me too long, Clave. You and *them*. I hope you fall into the sky."

"I hope I don't," Clave said mildly. "Would you like to assist our departure? We need blankets. Better have an extra. Nine."

"Fetch them yourself," Mayrin said and stalked away.

Here in the main depths of Quinn Tuft there were tunnels through the foliage. Huts nestled against the vertical flank of the branch, and the tunnels ran past. Now Harp and Gavving had room to walk, or something like it. In the low tidal pull they bounced on the foliage as if it and they were made of air. The branchlets around the tunnels were dry and nude, their foliage stripped for food.

Changes. The days had been longer before the passing of Gold. It used to be two days between sleeps; now it was eight. The Grad had tried to explain why, once, but the Scientist had caught them at it and whacked the Grad for spilling secrets and Gavving for listening.

Harp thought that the tree was dying. Well, Harp was a teller, and world-sized disasters make rich tales. But the Grad thought so too...and Gavving *felt* like the world had ended. He almost wanted it to end, before he had to tell the Chairman about his son.

He stopped to look into his own dwelling, a long half-cylinder, the bachelors' longhut. It was empty. Quinn Tribe must be gathered for the evening meal.

"We're in trouble," Gavving said and sniffled.

"Sure we are, but there's no point in acting like it. If we hide, we don't eat. Besides, we've got this." Harp hefted the dead musrum.

Gavving shook his head. It wouldn't help. "You should have stopped him."

"I couldn't." When Gavving didn't answer, Harp said, "Four days ago the whole tribe was throwing lines into a *pond*, remember? A pond no bigger than a big hut. As if we could pull it to us. We didn't think that was stupid till it was gone past, and nobody but Clave thought to go for the cookpot, and by the time he got back—"

"I wouldn't send even Clave to catch a swordbird."

"Twenty-twenty," Harp jeered. The taunt was archaic, but its meaning was common. *Any fool can foresee the past.*

An opening in the cotton: the turkey pen, with one gloomy turkey still alive. There would be no more unless a wild one could be captured from the wind. Drought and famine... Water still ran down the trunk sometimes, but never enough. Flying things still passed, meat to be drawn from the howling wind, but rarely. The tribe could not survive on the sugary foliage forever.

"Did I ever tell you," Harp asked, "about Glory and the turkeys?"

"No." Gavving relaxed a little. He needed a distraction.

"This was twelve or thirteen years back, before Gold passed by. Things didn't fall as fast then. Ask the Grad to tell you why, 'cause I can't, but it's true. So if she'd just fallen on the turkey pen, it wouldn't have busted. But Glory was trying to move the cookpot. She had it clutched in her arms, and it masses three times what she does, and she lost her balance and started *running* to keep it from hitting the ground. *Then* she smashed into the turkey pen.

"It was as if she'd thought it out in detail. The turkeys were all through the Clump and into the sky. We got maybe a third of them back. That was when we took Glory off cooking duties."

Another hollow, a big one: three rooms shaped from spine branches. Empty. Gavving said, "The Chairman must be almost over the fluff."

"It's night," Harp answered.

Night was only a dimming while the far arc of the Smoke Ring filtered the sunlight; but a cubic klomter of foliage blocked light too. A victim of fluff could come out at night long enough to share a meal.

"He'll see us come in," Gavving said. "I wish he were still in confinement."

There was firelight ahead of them now. They pressed on, Gavving sniffling, Harp trailing the musrum on his line. When they emerged into the Commons their faces were dignified, and their eyes avoided nobody.

The Commons was a large open area, bounded by a wickerwork of branchlets. Most of the tribe formed a scarlet circle with the cookpot in the center. Men and women wore blouses and pants dyed with the scarlet the Scientist made from tuftberries and sometimes decorated with black. That red would show vividly anywhere within the tuft. Children wore blouses only.

All were uncommonly silent.

The cookfire had nearly burned out, and the cookpot—an ancient thing, a tall, transparent cylinder with a lid of the same material—retained no more than a double handful of stew.

The Chairman's chest was still half-covered in fluff, but the patch had contracted and turned mostly brown. He was a square-jawed, brawny man in middle age, and he looked unhappy, irritable. Hungry. Harp and Gavving went to him, handed him their catch. "Food for the tribe," Harp said.

Their catch looked like a fleshy mushroom, with a stalk half a meter long and sense organs and a coiled tentacle under the edge of the cap. A lung ran down the center of the stalk/body to give the thing jet propulsion. Part of the cap had been ripped away, perhaps by some predator; the scar was half-healed. It looked far from appetizing, but society's law bound the Chairman too.

He took it. "Tomorrow's breakfast," he said courteously. "Where's Laython?"

"Lost," Harp said, before Gavving could say, "Dead."

The Chairman looked stricken. "How?" Then, "Wait, Eat first."

That was common courtesy for returning hunters; but for Gavving the waiting was torture. They were given scooped-out seedpods containing a few mouthfuls of greens and turkey meat in broth. They ate with hungry eyes on them, and they handed the gourds back as soon as possible.

"Now talk," the Chairman said.

Gavving was glad when Harp took up the tale. "We left with the other hunters and climbed along the trunk. Presently we could raise our heads into the sky and see the bare trunk stretching out to infinity—"

"My son is lost and you give me poetry?"

Harp jumped. "Your pardon. There was nothing on our side of the trunk, neither of danger nor salvation. We started around the trunk. Then Laython saw a swordbird, far west and borne toward us on the wind."

The Chairman's voice was only half-controlled. "You went after a swordbird?"

"There is famine in Quinn Tuft. We've fallen too far in, too far toward Voy, the Scientist says so himself. No beasts fly near, no water trickles down the trunk—"

"Am I not hungry enough to know this myself? Every baby knows better than to hunt a swordbird. Well, go on."

Harp told it all, keeping his language lean, passing lightly over Laython's disobedience, letting him show as the doomed hero. "We saw Laython and the swordbird pulled east by the wind, along a klomter of naked branch, then beyond. There was nothing we could do."

"But he has his line?"

"He does."

"He may find rest somewhere," the Chairman said. "A forest somewhere. Another tree...he could anchor at the median and go down...well. He's lost to Quinn Tribe at least."

Harp said, "We waited in the hope that Laython might find a way to return, to win out and moor himself along the trunk, perhaps. Four days passed. We saw nothing but a musrum borne on the wind. We cast our grapnels and I hooked the thing."

The Chairman looked ill with disgust. Gavving heard in his mind, *Have you traded my son for musrum meat?* But the Chairman said, "You are the last of the hunters to return. You must know of today's events. First, Martal has been killed by a drillbit."

Martal was an older woman, Gavving's father's aunt. A wrinkled woman who was always busy, too busy to talk to children, she had been Quinn Tribe's premier cook. Gavving tried not to picture a drillbit boring into her guts. And while he shuddered, the Chairman said, "After five days' sleep we will assemble for Martal's last rites. Second: the Council has decided to send a full hunting expedition up the trunk. They must not return without a means for our survival. Gavving, you will join the expedition. You'll be informed of your mission in detail after the funeral."

Chapter Two

Leavetaking

THE TREEMOUTH WAS A FUNNEL-SHAPED PIT THICKLY LINED WITH dead-looking, naked spine branches. The citizens of Quinn Tuft nested in an arc above the nearly vertical rim. Fifty or more were gathered to say good-bye to Martal. Almost half were children.

West of the treemouth was nothing but sky. The sky was all about them, and there was no protection from the wind, here at the westernmost point of the branch. Mothers folded their babes within their tunics. Quinn Tribe showed like scarlet tuftberries in the thick foliage around the treemouth.

Martal was among them, at the lower rim of the funnel, flanked by four of her family. Gavving studied the dead woman's face. Almost calm, he thought, but with a last lingering trace of horror. The wound was above her hip: a gash made not by the drillbit, but by the Scientist's knife as he dug for it.

A drillbit was a tiny creature, no bigger than a man's big toe. It would fly out of the wind too fast to see, strike, and burrow into flesh, leaving its gut as an expanding bag that trailed behind it. If left alone it would eventually burrow through and depart, tripled in size, leaving a clutch of eggs in the abandoned gut.

Looking at Martal made Gavving queasy. He had lain too long

awake, slept too little; his belly was already churning as it tried
to digest a breakfast of musrum stew.

Harp edged up beside him, shoulder-high to Gavving. "I'm
sorry," he said.

"For what?" Though Gavving knew what he meant.

"You wouldn't be going if Laython wasn't dead."

"You think this is the Chairman's punishment. All right, I
thought so too, but...wouldn't you be going?"

Harp spread his hands, uncharacteristically at a loss for words.

"You've got too many friends."

"Sure, I talk good. That could be it."

"You could volunteer. Have you thought of the stories you
could bring back?"

Harp opened his mouth, closed it, shrugged.

Gavving dropped it. He had wondered, and now he knew.
Harp was afraid..."I can't get anyone to tell me anything," he
said. "What have you heard?"

"Good news and bad. Nine of you, supposed to be eight. You
were an afterthought. The good news is just a rumor. Clave's
your leader."

"Clave?"

"Himself. Maybe. Now, it could still be true that the Chairman's getting rid of anyone he doesn't like. He—"

"Clave's the top hunter in the tuft! He's the Chairman's son-
in-law!"

"But he's not living with Mayrin. Aside from that...I'd be
guessing."

"What?"

"It's too complicated. I could even be wrong." And Harp
drifted off.

The Smoke Ring was a line of white emerging from the pale
blue sky, narrowing as it curved around in the west. Far down
the arc, Gold was a clot of streaming, embattled storms. His
gaze followed the arm around and down and in, until it faded
out near Voy. Voy was directly below, a blazing pinpoint like a
diamond set in a ring.

It was all sharper and clearer than it had been when Gavving was a child. Voy had been dimmer then and blurred.

At the passing of Gold, Gavving had been ten years old. He remembered hating the Scientist for his predictions of disaster, for the fear those predictions raised. The shrieking winds had been terrible enough... but Gold had passed, and the storms had diminished...

The allergy attack had come days later.

This present drought had taken years to reach its peak, but Gavving had felt the disaster at once. Blinding agony like knives in his eyes, runny nose, tightness in his chest. Thin, dry air, the Scientist said. Some could tolerate it, some could not. Gold had dropped the tree's orbit, he was told; the tree had moved closer to Voy, too far below the Smoke Ring median. Gavving was told to sleep above the treemouth, where the rivulets ran. That was before the rivulets had dwindled so drastically.

The wind too had become stronger.

It always blew directly into the treemouth. Quinn Tuft spread wide green sails into the wind, to catch anything that the wind might bear. Water, dust or mud, insects or larger creatures, all were filtered by the finely divided foliage or entangled in the branchlets. The spine branches migrated slowly forward, west along the branch, until gradually all was swallowed into the great conical pit. Even old huts migrated into the treemouth to be crushed and swallowed, and new ones had to be built every few years.

Everything came to the treemouth. The streams that ran down the trunk found an artificial catchbasin above, but the water reached the treemouth as cookwater, or washwater, or when citizens came to rid themselves of body wastes, to "feed the tree."

Martal's cushion of spine branches had already carried her several meters downslope. Her entourage had retreated to the rim, to join Alfin, the treemouth custodian.

Children were taught how to care for the tree. When Gavving was younger his tasks had included carrying collected earth and manure and garbage to pack into the treemouth, removing rocks to use elsewhere, finding and killing pests. He hadn't liked it much—Alfin was a terror to work under—but some of the pests had been edible, he remembered. Earthlife crops were grown here too, tobacco and maize and tomatoes; they had to be harvested before the tree swallowed them.

But in these dark days, passing prey were all too rare. Even the insects were dying out. There wasn't food for the tribe, let alone garbage to feed the insects and the tree. The crops were nearly dead. The branch was nude for half its length; it wasn't growing new foliage.

Alfin had had care of the treemouth for longer than Gavving had been alive. That sour old man hated half the tribe for one reason or another. Gavving had feared him once. He attended all funerals . . . but today he truly looked bereaved, as if he were barely holding his grief in check.

Day was dimming. The bright spot, the sun, was dropping, blurring. Soon enough it would brighten and coalesce in the east. Meanwhile . . . yes, here came the Chairman, carefully robed and hooded against the light, attended by the Scientist and the Grad. The Grad, a blond boy four years older than Gavving, looked unwontedly serious. Gavving wondered if it was for Martal or for himself.

The Scientist wore the ancient falling jumper that signified his rank: a two-piece garment in pale blue, ill-fitting, with pictures on one shoulder. The pants came to just below the knees; the tunic left a quarter meter of gray-furred belly. After untold generations the strange, glossy cloth was beginning to show signs of wear, and the Scientist wore it only for official functions.

The Grad was right, Gavving thought suddenly: the old uniform would fit Harp perfectly.

The Scientist spoke, praising Martal's last contribution to the health of the tree, reminding those present that one day they must all fulfill that obligation. He kept it short, then stepped aside for the Chairman.

The Chairman spoke. Of Martal's bad temper he said nothing;

of her skill with the cookpot he said a good deal. He spoke of another loss, of the son who was lost to Quinn Tuft wherever he might be. He spoke long, and Gavving's mind wandered.

Four young boys were all studious attention; but their toes were nipping at a copter patch. The ripe plants responded by launching their seedpods, tiny blades whirring at each end. The boys stood solemnly in a buzzing cloud of copters.

Treemouth humor. Others were having trouble suppressing laughter; but somehow Gavving couldn't laugh. He'd had four brothers and a sister, and all had died before the age of six, like too many children in Quinn Tuft. In this time of famine they died more easily yet . . . He was the last of his family. Everything he saw today squeezed memories out of him, as if he were seeing it all for the last time.

It's only a hunting party! His jumpy belly knew better. Hero of a single failed hunt, how would Gavving be chosen for a last-ditch foraging expedition?

Vengeance for Laython. Were the others being punished too? *Who* were the others? How would they be equipped? When would this endless funeral be over?

The Chairman spoke of the drought, and the need for sacrifice; and now his eye did fall on selected individuals, Gavving among them.

When the long speech ended, Martal was another two meters downslope. The Chairman departed hurriedly ahead of the brightening day.

Gavving made for the Commons with all haste.

Equipment was piled on the web of dry spine branches that Quinn Tribe called *the ground*. Harpoons, coils of line, spikes, grapnels, nets, brown sacks of coarse cloth, half a dozen jet pods, claw sandals . . . a reassuring stack of what it would take to keep them alive. Except . . . food? He saw no food.

Others had arrived before him. Even at a glance they seemed an odd selection. He saw a familiar face and called, "Grad! Are you coming too?"

The Grad loped to join them. "Right. I had a hand in planning it," he confided. A bouncy, happy type in a traditionally studious profession, the Grad had come armed with his own line and harpoon. He seemed eager, full of nervous energy. He looked about him and said, "Oh, treefodder."

"Now, what is that supposed to mean?"

"Nothing." He toed a pile of blankets and added, "At least we won't go naked."

"Hungry, though."

"Maybe there's something to eat on the trunk. There'd better be."

The Grad had long been Gavving's friend, but he wasn't much of a hunter. And Merril? Merril would have been a big woman if her tiny, twisted legs had matched her torso. Her long fingers were callused, her arms were long and strong; and why not? She used them for everything, even walking. She clung to the wicker wall of the Commons, impassive, waiting.

One-legged Jiovan stood beside her, with a hand in the branchlets to hold him balanced. Gavving could remember Jiovan as an agile, reckless hunter. Then something had attacked him, something he would never describe. Jiovan had returned barely alive, with ribs broken and his left leg torn away, the stump tourniquetted with his line. Four years later the old wounds still hurt him constantly, and he never let anyone forget it.

Glory was a big-boned, homely woman, middle-aged, with no children. Her clumsiness had given her an unwanted fame. She blamed Harp the teller for that, and not without justice. There was the tale of the turkey cage; and he told another regarding the pink scar that ran down her right leg, gained when she was still involved in cooking duties.

The hate in Alfin's eyes recalled the time she'd clouted him across the ear with a branchwood beam; but it spoke more of Alfin's tendency to hold grudges. Gardener, garbage man, funeral director... he was no hunter, let alone an explorer, but he was here. No wonder he'd looked bereaved.

Glory waited cross-legged, eyes downcast. Alfin watched her

with smoldering hate. Merril seemed impassive, relaxed, but Jiovan was muttering steadily under his breath.

These, his companions? Gavving's belly clenched agonizingly on the musrum.

Then Clave entered the Commons, briskly, with a young woman on each arm. He looked about him as if liking what he saw.

It was true. Clave was coming.

They watched him prodding the piled equipment with his feet, nodding, nodding. "Good," he said briskly and looked about him at his waiting companions. "We're going to have to carry all this treefodder. Start dividing it up. You'll probably want it on your back, moored with your line, but take your choice. Lose your pack and I'll send you home."

The musrum loosed its grip on Gavving's belly. Clave was the ideal hunter: built long and narrow, two and a half meters of bone and muscle. He could pick a man up by wrapping the fingers of one hand around the man's head, and his long toes could throw a rock as well as Gavving's hands. His companions were Jayan and Jinny, twins, the dark and pretty daughters of Martal and a long-dead hunter. Without orders, they began loading equipment into the sacks. Others moved forward to help.

Alfin spoke. "I take it you're our leader?"

"Right."

"Just what are we supposed to be doing with all this?"

"We go up along the trunk. We renew the Quinn markings as we go. We keep going until we find whatever it takes to save the tribe. It could be food—"

"On the bare trunk?"

Clave looked him over. "We've spent all our lives along two klomters of branch. The Scientist tells me that the trunk is a *hundred* klomters long. Maybe more. We don't know what's up there. Whatever we need, it isn't here."

"You know why we're going. We're being thrown out," Alfin said. "Nine fewer mouths to feed, and *look* at who—"

Clave rode him down. He could outshout thunder when he wanted to. "Would you like to stay, Alfin?" He waited, but Alfin didn't answer. "Stay, then. *You* explain why you didn't come."

"I'm coming." Alfin's voice was almost inaudible. Clave had made no threats, and didn't have to. They had been assigned. Anyone who stayed would be subject to charges of mutiny.

And that didn't matter either. If Clave was going, then... Alfin was wrong, and Gavving's stomach had been wrong too. They would find what the tribe needed, and they would return. Gavving set to assembling his pack.

Clave said, "We've got six pairs of claw sandals. Jayan, Jinny, Grad... Gavving. I'll take the extras. We'll find out who else needs them. Everyone take four mooring spikes. Take a few rocks. I mean it. You need at least one to hammer spikes into wood, and you may want some for throwing. Has everybody got his dagger?"

It was night when they pulled themselves out of the foliage, and they still emerged blinking. The trunk seemed infinitely tall. The far tuft was almost invisible, blurred and blued almost to the color of the sky.

Clave called, "Take a few minutes to eat. Then stuff your packs with foliage. We won't see foliage again for a long time."

Gavving tore off a spine branch laden with green cotton candy. He stuck it between his back and the pack, and started up the trunk. Clave was already ahead of him.

The bark of the trunk was different from the traveling bark of the branch. There were no spine branches, but the bark must have been meters thick, with cracks big enough to partly shield a climber. Smaller cracks made easy grip for fingers.

Gavving wasn't used to claw sandals. He had to kick a little to seat them right, or they slipped. His pack tended to pull him over backward. Maybe he wanted it lower? The tide helped. It pulled him not just downward, but against the trunk too, as if the trunk sloped.

The Grad was moving well but puffing. Maybe he spent too much time studying. But Gavving noted that his pack was larger than the others'. Was he carrying something besides provisions?

Merril had no pack, just her line. She managed to keep up using her arms alone. Jiovan, with two arms and a leg, was overtaking Clave himself, though his jaw was clenched in pain.

Jayan and Jinny, above Gavving on the thick bark, stopped as by mutual accord. They looked down; they looked at each other; they seemed about to weep. A sudden, futile surge of homesickness blocked Gavving's own throat. He lusted to be back in the bachelors' hut, clinging to his bunk, face buried in the foliage wall...

The twins resumed their climb. Gavving followed.

They were moving well, Clave thought. He was still worried about Merril. She'd slow them down, but at least she was trying. She'd find it easier, moving with just two arms, when they got near the middle of the trunk. There would be no tide at all there; things would drift without falling, if the Scientist's smoke dreams were to be believed.

Alfin alone was still down there in the last fringes of tuft. Clave had expected trouble from Alfin, but not this. Alfin was the oldest of his team, pushing forty, but he was muscular, healthy.

Appeal to his pride? He called down, "Do you need claw sandals, Alfin?"

Alfin may have considered any number of retorts. What he called back was, "Maybe."

"I'll wait. Jiovan, take the lead."

Clave worked his pack open while Alfin moved up to join him. Alfin was climbing with his eyes half-shut. Something odd there, something wrong.

"I was hoping you could at least keep up with Merril," Clave said, handing Alfin the sandals.

Alfin said nothing while he strapped one on. Then, "What's the difference? We're all dead anyway. But it won't do that copsik any good! He's only got rid of the lames—"

"Who?"

"The Chairman, our precious Chairman! When people are starving, they'll kick out whoever's in charge. He's kicked out the lames, the ones who couldn't hurt him anyway. Let him see what he can snag when they kick him into the sky."

"If you think I'm a lame, see if you can outclimb me," Clave said lightly.

"Everyone knows why *you're* here, you and your women too."

"Oh, I suppose they do," Clave said. "But if you think *you'd* like living with Mayrin, you can try it when we get back. I couldn't. And she didn't like that, and her father didn't like it either. But you know, she was really built to make babies, when I was just old enough to notice that."

Alfin snorted.

"I meant what I said," Clave told him. "If there's anything left that can save the tribe, it's somewhere over our heads. And if we find it, I think I could be Chairman myself. What do you think?"

Startled, Alfin peered into Clave's face. "Maybe. Power hungry, are you?"

"I haven't quite decided. Let's say I'm just mad enough to go for Gold. This whole crazy...well, Jayan and Jinny, they can take care of themselves, and if they can't, I can. But I had to take Merril before the Chairman would give me jet pods, and then at the last minute he wished Gavving on me, and that was the last straw."

"Gavving wasn't much worse than the other kids I've had to train. Constantly asking questions, I don't know any *two* people with that boy's curiosity—"

"Not the point. He's just starting to show beard. He never did anything *wrong* except *be* there when that damn fool Laython got swallowed...Skip it. Alfin, some of our party is dangerous to the rest."

"You know it."

"How would you handle that?"

It was rare to see Alfin smiling. He took his time answering. "Merril will kill herself sooner or later. But Glory will kill someone else. Slip at the wrong time. Easy enough to do something about it. Wait till we're higher, till the tide is weaker. Knock against her when she's off balance. Send her home the fast way."

"Well, that's what I was thinking too. You are a *danger* to us, Alfin. You hold grudges. We've got problems enough without watching our backs because of you. If you slow me down, if you give *any* of us trouble, I'll send you home the fast way, Alfin. I've got enough trouble here."

Alfin paled, but he answered. "You do. Get rid of Glory before she knocks someone off the trunk. Ask Jiovan."

"I don't take your orders," Clave said. "One more thing. You spend too much energy being angry. Save it. You're likely to need your anger. Now lead off." And when Alfin resumed climbing, Clave followed.

Chapter Three

The Trunk

DAY BRIGHTENED AND FADED AND BRIGHTENED AGAIN WHILE they climbed. The men doffed their tunics and tucked them into their pack straps; somewhat later, so did the women. Clave leered at Jayan and Jinny impartially. Gavving didn't leer, but in fact the sight distracted him from his climbing.

Jayan and Jinny were twenty-year-old twins, identical, with pale skin and dark hair and lovely heart-shaped faces and nicely conical breasts. Some citizens called them stupid, for they had no fund of conversation; but Gavving wondered. In other matters they showed good sense. As now: Jinny was climbing with Clave, but Merril had dropped far behind, and Jayan stayed just beneath her, pacing her.

Jiovan had lost ground after Clave resumed the lead. He cursed as he climbed, steadily, monotonously: the wind, the bark handholds, his missing leg. Alfin should have been one of the leaders, Gavving thought; but he kept pausing to look down.

Gavving's own shoulders and legs burned with fatigue. Worse, he was making mistakes, setting his claw sandals wrong, so that they slipped too often.

Tired people make mistakes. Gavving saw Glory slip, thrash, and fall two or three meters before she caught an edge of bark. While she hugged herself ferociously against the tree, Gavving moved crosswise until he was behind and to the side of her.

Fear held her rigid.

"Keep going," Gavving said. "I'll stay behind you. I'll catch you."

She looked down, nodded jerkily, began climbing again. She seemed to move in convulsions, putting too much effort into it. Gavving kept pace.

She slipped. Gavving gripped the bark. When she dropped into range he planted the palm of his hand under her buttocks and pushed her hard against the tree. She gasped, and clung, and resumed climbing.

Clave called down. "Is anybody thirsty?"

They needed their breath, and the answer was too obvious. Of *course* they were thirsty. Clave said, "Swing around east. We'll get a drink."

Falling water had carved a channel along the eastern side of the trunk. The channel was fifty meters across and nearly dry over most of its water-smoothed surface. But the tree still passed through the occasional cloud; mist still clung to the bark; wind and Coriolis force set it streaming around to the east as it fell; and water ran in a few pitiful streams toward Quinn Tuft below.

"Watch yourselves," Clave told them. "Use your spikes if you have to. This is slippery stuff."

"Here," the Grad called from over their heads.

They worked their way toward him. A hill of rock must have smacked into the tree long ago, half embedding itself. The trunk had grown to enclose it. It made a fine platform, particularly since a stream had split to run round it on both sides. By the time Merril and Jayan had worked their way up, Clave had hammered spikes into the wood above the rock and attached lines.

Merril and Jayan worked their way onto the rock. Merril lay gasping while Jayan brought her water.

Glory lay flat on the rock with her eyes closed. Presently she crawled to the portside stream. She called to Clave. "Any limit?"

"What?"

"On how much we drink. The water goes—"

Clave laughed loudly. Like the Chairman hosting a midyear celebration, he bellowed, "Drink! Bathe! Have water fights! Who's to stop us? If Quinn Tribe didn't want their water secondhand, we wouldn't be here." He worked their single cookpot from his pack and threw streams of water at selected targets: Merril, who whooped in delight; Jiovan, who sputtered in surprise; Jayan and Jinny, who advanced toward him with menace in their eyes. "I dare not struggle on this precarious perch," he cried and went limp. They rolled him in the stream, hanging onto his hands and feet so that he wouldn't go over.

They climbed in a spiral path. They weren't here just to climb, Clave said, but to explore. Gavving could hear Jiovan's monotonous cursing as they climbed into the wind, until the wind drowned him out.

Gavving reached up for a fistful of green cotton and stuffed it in his mouth. The branch that waved above his pack was nearly bare now. The sky was empty out to some distant streamers of cloud and a dozen dots that might be ponds, all hundreds of klomters out. They'd be hurting for food when sleeptime came.

He was crossing a scar in the bark, a puckering that ran down into the wood itself. An old wound that the bark was trying to heal...big enough to climb in, but it ran the wrong way. Abruptly the Grad shouted, "Stop! Hold it up!"

"What's the matter?" Clave demanded.

"The Quinn Tribe markings!"

Without the Grad to point it out, Gavving would never have realized that this was writing. He had seen writing only rarely, and these letters were three to four meters across. They couldn't be read; they had to be inferred: DQ, with a curlicue mark across the D.

"We'll have to gouge this out," the Grad said. "It's nearly grown out. Someone should come here more often."

Clave ran a critical eye over his crew. "Gavving, Alfin, Jinny, start digging. Grad, you supervise. Just dig out the Q, leave the D alone. The rest of you, rest."

Merril said, "I can work. For that matter, I could carry more."

"Tell me that tomorrow," Clave told her. He made his way across the bark to clap her on the shoulder. "If you can take some of the load, you'll get it. Let's see how you do tomorrow with your muscles all cramped up."

They carved away bark and dug deeper into the wood with the points of their harpoons. The Grad moved among them. The Q took shape. When the Grad approached him, Gavving asked, "Why are the letters so big? You can hardly read them."

"They're not for us. You could see them if you were a klomter away," the Grad said.

Alfin had overheard. "Where? Falling? Are we doing this for swordbirds and triunes to read?"

The Grad smiled and passed on without answering. Alfin scowled at his back, then crossed to Gavving's position. "Is he crazy?"

"Maybe. But if you can't dig as deep as Jinny, the mark will look silly to the swordbirds."

"He tells half a secret and leaves you hanging," Alfin complained. "He does it all the time."

They left the tribal insignia carved deep and clear into the tree. The wind was beating straight down on them now. Gavving felt a familiar pain in his ears. He worked his jaw while he sought the old memory, and when his ears popped it came: pressure/pain in his ears, a score of days after the passing of Gold, the night before his first allergy attack.

These days he rarely wondered if he would wake with his eyes and sinuses streaming in agony. He simply lived through it. But he'd never wakened on the vertical slope of the tree! He pictured himself climbing blind . . .

That was what distracted him while a thick, wood-colored rope lifted from the bark to wrap itself around Glory's waist.

Glory yelped. Gavving saw her clinging to the bark with her face against it, refusing to look. The rope was pulling her sideways, away from him.

Gavving pulled his harpoon from his pack before he moved. He crawled around Glory toward the living rope.

Glory screamed again as her grip was torn loose. Now only the live rope itself held her from falling. He didn't dare slash it. Instead he scampered toward its source, while the rope coiled itself around Glory, spinning her, reeling her in.

There was a hole in the tree. From the blackness inside Gavving saw a thickening of the live rope and a single eye lifting on a stalk to look at him. He jabbed at it. A lid flicked closed; the stalk dodged. Gavving tracked it. He felt the jar through his arm and shoulder as the harpoon punched through.

A huge mouth opened and screamed. The living rope thrashed and tried to fling Glory away. What saved Glory was Glory herself; she had plunged her own harpoon through the brown hawser and gripped the point where it emerged. She clung to the haft with both hands while the rope bent around to attack Gavving.

The mouth was lined with rows of triangular teeth. Gavving pulled his harpoon loose from the eye, with a twist, as if he had practiced all his life. He jabbed at the mouth, trying to reach the throat. The mouth snapped shut and he struck only teeth. He jabbed at the eye again.

Something convulsed in the dark of the hole. The mouth gaped improbably wide. Then a black mass surged from the hole. Gavving flung himself aside in time to escape being smashed loose. A hut-sized beast leapt into the sky on three short, thick legs armed with crescent claws. Short wings spread, a claw swiped at him and missed. Gavving saw with amazement that the rope was its nose.

He had thought it was trying to escape. Ten meters from its den it turned with astonishing speed. Gavving shrank back against the bark with his harpoon poised.

The beast's wings flapped madly, in reverse, pulling it back against its stretching nose . . . futilely. The foray team had arrived in force. Lines wrapped Glory and trapped the creature's rope of a nose. Lines spun out to bind its wings. Clave was screaming orders. He and Jinny and the Grad pulled strongly, turning the beast claws-outward from the tree. In that position it was reeled in until harpoons could reach its head.

Gavving picked a spot and jabbed again and again, drilling through bone, then red-gray brain. He never noticed when the thing stopped moving. He only came to himself when Clave shouted, "Gavving, Glory, dinner's on you. You killed it, you clean it."

You killed it, you clean it was an easy honor to dodge. You only had to admit that your prey had hurt you...

Jayan and Jinny worked at building a fire in the creature's lair. They worked swiftly, competently, almost without words, as if they could read each other's minds. The others were outside, chopping bark for fuel. Gavving and Glory moored the corpse with lines and spikes, jut outside the hole, and went to work.

The Grad insisted on helping. Strictly speaking, he didn't have the right, but he seemed eager, and Glory was tired. They worked slowly, examining the peculiar thing they had killed.

It had a touch of trilateral symmetry, like many creatures of the Smoke Ring, the Grad said. A smaller third wing was placed far back: a steering fin. The forward pair were motive power and (as the Grad gleefully pointed out) ears. Holes below each wing showed as organs of hearing when the Grad cut into them. The wings could be cupped to gather sound.

It was a digger. Those little wings would barely move it. Everything in the Smoke Ring could fly in some sense; but this one would prefer to dig a hole and ambush its prey. Even its trunk wasn't all that powerful. The Grad searched until he found the sting that had been in its tip. The size of an index finger, it was embedded in Glory's pack. Glory nearly fainted.

They kept the claws. Clave would use them to tip his grapnels. They cut steaks to be broiled and passed to the rest, who by now were moored on spikes outside. They set bigger slabs of meat to smoke at the back of the wooden cave.

Gavving realized that his eyes were blurry with exhaustion. Glory was streaming sweat. He put his arm over her shoulders and announced, "We quit."

"Good enough," Clave called in. "Take our perches. Alfin, let's carve up the rest."

Clave's team was well fed, overfed. They drifted on lines outside the cave. Meat smoked inside. The carcass, mostly bones now, had been set to block the entrance.

Clave said, "Citizens, give me a status report. How are we doing? Is anyone hurt?"

"I hurt all over," Jiovan said and scowled at the chorus of agreement.

"All over is good. Glory, did that thing break any of your ribs?"

"I don't think so. Bruises."

"Uh-huh." Clave sounded surprised. "Nobody's fallen off. Nobody's hurt. Have we lost any equipment?"

There was a silence. Gavving spoke into it. "Clave, what are you doing here?"

"We're exploring the trunk, and renewing the Quinn markings, and stopping a famine, maybe. Today's catch is a good first step."

Gavving was prepared to drop it, but Alfin wasn't. "The boy means, what are *you* doing here? You, the mighty hunter, why did you go out to die with the lames?"

There was muttering, perhaps, but no overt reaction to the word *lames*. Clave smiled at Alfin. "Turn it around, Quinn Tribe's custodian of the treemouth. Why was the tribe able to spare *you*?"

The west wind had softened as they climbed, but it was still formidable; it blew streamers of smoke past the carcass. Alfin forced words from himself. "The Chairman thought it was a good joke. And nobody . . . nobody wanted to speak up for me."

"Nobody loves you."

Alfin nodded and sighed as if a burden had been lifted from him. "Nobody loves me. Your turn."

Gavving grinned. Clave was stuck, and he knew it. He said, "Mayrin doesn't love me. I traded her in for two prettier, more loving women. Mayrin is the Chairman's daughter."

"That's not all of it and you know it."

"If you know better than I do, then keep talking," Clave said reasonably.

"The Grad can back me up. He knows some tribal history. When things go wrong, when citizens get unhappy, the leader's in trouble. The Scientist himself almost got drafted! The Chairman is scared, that's what. The citizens are hungry, and there's an obvious replacement for the Chairman. Clave, he's scared of *you*."

"Grad?"

"The Scientist knows what he's doing."

"He blamed it all on you!" Alfin cried. "I was there!"

"I know. He had his reasons." The Grad noticed the silence and laughed. "No, I didn't cause the drought! We rounded Gold, and Gold swung us too far in toward Voy, down to where the Smoke Ring thins out. It's a gravity effect—"

"Many thanks for explaining it all," Clave said with cheerful sarcasm. Gavving was irritated and a bit relieved: nobody else understood the Grad's gibberish either. "Is there anything else we should settle?"

Into the silence Gavving said, "How do we cause a flood?"

There was some laughter. Clave said, "Grad?"

"Forget it."

"It'd solve everybody's problems. Even the Chairman's."

"This is silly . . . well. Floods come when a pond brushes the tree, somewhere on the trunk. A lot of water clings to the trunk. The tide pulls it down. Usually we get some warning from a hunting party, and we all scurry out along the branch. The big flood, ten years ago . . . most of us got to safety, but the waterfall tore away some of the huts, and most of the earthlife crops, and the turkey pens. It was a year before we caught any more turkeys."

"And I wish we'd have another flood," the Grad said. "Sure I do. The Scientist thinks the whole *tree*—never mind. You can't catch a pond. We're too far into the gas torus region—"

"There," Gavving said and pointed east and out, toward a metal-colored dot backed by rosy streamers of cloud. "I think it's bigger than it was."

"What of it? It'll come or it won't. If it did come floating past, what would you do, throw lines and grapnels? Forget it. Just forget it."

"Enough," Clave said. "That meat's probably done. Let's get the smoke out and get inside."

Gavving woke in the night and wondered where he was.

He half remembered the sounds of groans. Someone in pain? It had stopped now. Sound of wind, sound of many people breathing. Warm bodies all around him. Rich smells of smoke and perspiration. Aches everywhere, as if he'd been beaten.

A woman's voice spoke near his ear. "Are you awake too?"

And another, a man's: "Yes. Let me sleep." Alfin?

Silence. And Gavving remembered: the cave was just large enough to accommodate nine exhausted climbers, after they flung the nose-arm's bones into the sky. By now the offal might have reached Quinn Tuft, to feed the tree.

They huddled against each other, flesh to flesh. Gavving had no way to avoid eavesdropping when Alfin spoke again, though his voice was a whisper. "I can't sleep. Everything hurts."

Glory: "Me too."

"Did you hear groaning?"

"Clave and Jayan, I think, and believe me, they're feeling no pain."

"Oh. Good for them. Glory, why are you talking to me?"

"I was hoping we could be friends."

"Just don't *climb* near me, all right?"

"All right."

"I'm afraid you'll knock me off."

"Alfin, aren't you afraid to be so high?"

"No."

"I am."

Pause. "I'm afraid of falling off. I'd be crazy not to be."

There was quiet for a time. Gavving began to notice his own aching muscles and joints. They must be keeping him awake... but he was dozing when Alfin spoke again.

"The Chairman knew it."

"Knew what?"

"He knows I'm afraid of falling. That's why the copsik bastard kept sending me under the branch on hunts. Nothing solid under me, trying to hang on and throw a harpoon too...I got even, though."

"How?" Glory asked while Gavving thought, *So did the Chairman.*

"Never mind. Glory, will you lie with me?"

A strained whisper. "No. Alfin, we can't be alone!"

"Did you have a lover, back in the tuft?"

"No."

"Most of us didn't. Nobody to protect us when the Chairman thought this up."

A pause, as for thought. "I still can't. Not here."

Alfin's voice rose to a shout. "Clave! Clave, you should have brought a masseuse!"

Clave answered from the darkness. "*I* brought *two.*"

"Treefodder," Alfin said without heat, perhaps with amusement. Presently there was quiet.

Chapter Four

Flashers and Fan Fungus

IN THE MORNING THEY HURT. SOME SHOWED IT MORE THAN others. Alfin tried to move, grunted in pain, curled up with his face buried in his arms. Merril's face was blank and stoic as she flexed her arms, then rose onto her hands. Jayan and Jinny commiserated with each other, massaging each other's pains away. On Jiovan's face, amazement and agony as he tried to move, then a look of betrayal thrown in Clave's direction.

From Glory, wild-eyed panic. Gavving tapped her shoulder blade (and flinched at his own agony-signals). "We all hurt. Can't you tell? What are you worried about? You won't be left behind. Nobody's got the strength."

Her eyes turned sane. She whispered, "I *wasn't* thinking that. I was thinking I *hurt*. That's normal, isn't it?"

"Sure. You're not crippled, though."

"Thank you for taking care of me yesterday. I'm really grateful. I'm going to get better at this, I promise."

The Grad spoke without trying to move. "We'll all get better. The higher we get, the less we weigh. Pretty soon we'll be floating."

41

Clave trod carefully among citizens who were awake but not mobile. Gavving felt a stab of envy/anger. *Clave* didn't hurt. From the back of the nose-arm's burrow he selected a slab of smoked meat ragged with harpoon wounds. "Take your time over breakfast," he instructed them. "Eat. It's the easiest way to carry provisions—"

"And we burned a lot of energy yesterday," the Grad said. He moved like a cripple to join Clave and began tearing into a meter's length of what had been the nose-arm's rib. It made sense to Gavving, and he joined them. The meat had an odd, rank flavor. You could get used to it, he thought, if your life depended on it.

Clave moved among them, gnawing at his huge slab of meat. He sliced a piece off and made Merril take it. He listened to Jiovan describing his symptoms, then interrupted with, "You've got your wind back. That's good. Now eat," handing him more of the steak. He cut the rest in half for Jayan and Jinny and spent a minute or two doing massage on their shoulders and hips. They winced and groaned.

Presently, when all had eaten something, Clave looked around at his team. "We'll circle to the east and get water half a day after we start. There's no room in here to do warm-up exercises; we'll just have to start moving. So saddle up, citizens. We'll have to 'feed the tree' in the open, and whether you actually feed the tree is up to the tide and the wind. Alfin, take the lead."

Alfin led them on an upward spiral, counterclockwise. Gavving found his aches easing as they climbed. He noticed that Alfin never looked down. Not surprising if Alfin didn't give a damn for those following him—but he *never* looked down.

Gavving did, and marveled at their progress. Two extended hands would have covered all of Quinn Tuft.

They delayed to repair the Q in a DQ mark. The sun had been horizontal in the east when they started. It was approaching Voy before they reached water-smoothed wood.

A rivulet flowed down a meandering groove. This time there was no natural perch. Nine thirsty citizens pounded spikes into the wood and hung by their lines to drink, wash, soak their tunics, and wring them out.

Gavving noticed Clave speaking to Alfin a little way below. He didn't hear what was said. He only saw what Alfin did.

"And suppose I don't?"

"Then you don't." Clave gestured upward, where the rest of them hung. "Look at them. *I* didn't choose them. What do I do if one of my citizens turns out to be a coward? I live with it. But I have to know."

Alfin looked white with rage. *Not* red with fury. There isn't any "white with rage"; white means fear, as Clave had learned long ago. A frightened man can kill...but Alfin's hands were clenched on his line, and Clave's harpoon was over his shoulder, easily reached.

"I have to know. I can't put you in the lead if you can't make yourself look down to see how they're doing. See? I'll have to put you where you don't hurt anyone else if you funk it. Tail-end Charley. And if you freeze, I want to be sure nobody—"

"All right." Alfin dug in his pack, produced a spike and a rock. He pounded the spike in beside the one he was hanging from.

"Make sure you can depend on it. It's *your* life."

The second spike was in deeper than the first. Alfin tied the loose end of his line to both spikes and knotted it again. "And I leave you next to it?"

"You take that chance too. Or you don't. I have to *know*."

Alfin leapt straight outward, trailing loops of line. He thrashed, then threw his arms over his face.

He fell slowly. *We're all lighter,* Gavving realized. *It's real. I thought I was just feeling better, but we're lifting less*—And Alfin was still falling, but now he'd uncovered his face. His arms wind-milled to turn him on his back. Gavving noticed Clave's hand covering the spikes that moored Alfin's line. The line pulled taut and swung Alfin in against the tree.

Gavving watched him climb up. And watched him jump

again, limbs splayed out as if he were trying to fly. It seemed he might make it, he fell so slowly; but presently the tide was pulling him down against the tree again.

"That actually looks like fun," Jayan said.

Jinny said, "Ask first."

Alfin didn't jump again. When he had climbed back up to Clave's position, and both had climbed to rejoin the team, Jinny spoke. "Can we try that?"

Alfin sent her a look like a harpoon. Clave said, "No, time to get moving. Saddle up—"

Alfin was in the lead again when they set out. He made a point of pausing frequently to look back. And Gavving wondered.

Yesterday Alfin had swarmed all over the nose-arm, hacking like a berserker maniac, like Gavving himself. It was hard to believe that Alfin was afraid of Clave, or of heights, or of anything.

The sun circled the sky, behind Voy and back to zenith, before they came to lee again. The water-smoothed wood was soft here, soft enough that they could cross with a spike in each hand, jab and yank and jab. They veered down to avoid scores of birds clustered on the wood. Scarlet-tailed, the birds were otherwise the grayish-brown of the wood itself.

When they reached the rivulet, it was smaller yet, but it was enough: they hung in the water and let it cool them and run into their faces and mouths. Clave shared out smoked meat. Gavving found himself ravenous.

The Grad watched the birds as he ate. Presently he burst out laughing. "Look, they've got a mating dance going."

"So?"

"You'll see."

Presently Gavving did see; and so did others, judging by Clave's bellowing laugh and the giggles from Jayan and Jinny. A gray-brown male would approach a female and abruptly spread his gray wings like a cloak. Under the gray was brilliant yellow, and a tube protruding from a splash of crimson feathers.

"The Scientist told me about them once. Flashers," said the Grad. His smile died as he said, "I wonder what they eat?"

"What difference does it make?" Alfin demanded.

"Maybe none." The Grad made his way upward toward the birds. The birds flew off, then returned to dive at him, shrieking obscenities. The Grad ignored them. Presently he returned.

Alfin asked, "Well?"

"The wood's riddled with holes. Riddled. The holes are full of insects. The birds dig in and eat the insects."

"You're in love," Alfin challenged. "You're in love with the idea that the tree's dying."

"I'd love to believe it isn't," the Grad said, but Alfin only snorted.

They spiraled around to the western side while the sun dipped beneath Voy and began to rise again. The wind was less ferocious now. But they were getting tired; there was almost no chatter. They rested frequently in crevasses in the bark.

They were resting when Merril called, "Jinny? I'm hung up."

A pincer the size of Clave's fist gripped the fabric of Merril's nearly empty pack. Merril pulled back against it. From a hole in the bark there emerged a creature covered in hard, brown, segmented plates. Its face was a single plate with a deeply inset eye. The body looked soft behind the last plate.

Jayan slashed where its body met the bark. The creature separated. It still clung to Merril's pack with idiot determination. Jayan levered the claw open with her harpoon and dropped the creature into her own pack.

When they had circled round to water again, Clave set water to boiling in the small, lidded pot. He made tea, refilled the pot, and boiled Merril's catch. It made one bite each for his team.

They wedged themselves into a wide crack with the shape of a lightning-stroke and moored themselves with lines. Together but separate, head to foot within the bark, they had no chance to converse, and no urge. Four days of climbing since breakfast left them too tired for anything but sleep.

At waking they ate more of the smoked meat. "Let's look for more of those hard-shelled things," Clave suggested. "That was good." He didn't have to urge them to get moving. He never would, Gavving realized, as long as they couldn't sleep where water flowed.

This time Jiovan was given the lead. He took them on a counterclockwise spiral that brought them back to lee within half a day. Again the wood was soft and riddled with holes, and flashers swarmed below them. Alfin and Glory tended to lose ground in the leeward regions. Jiovan remarked on it and earned a look of dull hatred from Alfin.

The thing was that Alfin took more care setting his spikes than the rest did. And Glory didn't, so she lost time slipping and catching herself—

They moored themselves in the stream and drank and washed.

Alfin spotted something far above them: gray nubs reaching out from the bark on both sides of the rivulet. He climbed, doggedly pounding spikes into the wood, and came back with a fan-shaped fungus, pale gray with a red frill, half the size of his pack. "It could be edible," he said.

Clave asked, "Are you willing to try it?"

"No." He started to throw it away.

Merril stopped him. "We're here to keep the tribe from starving," she said. She broke a red-and-gray chunk from the fringe and ate a meager mouthful. "Not much taste, but it's nice. The Scientist would like it. You could chew it with no teeth." She took another bite.

Alfin broke off a piece of the grayish white inside and ate that, looking as if he were taking poison. He nodded. "Tastes okay."

At which point there were more volunteers, but Clave vetoed that. When they departed, Clave veered upward to pick a bouquet of the fan-shaped fungi. A meter-square fan rode like a flag above his pack.

The sun was rising up the east.

It was below Voy—you could look straight down along the trunk, past the green fuzzball that was Quinn Tuft, and see Voy's bright spark at the fringe of the soft sun-glow—and the west wind was blowing almost softly across the ridges of the bark, when Gavving heard Merril shout, "Who needs legs?"

She was holding herself an arm's-length from the bark by a one-handed grip. He shouted down. "Merril? Are you all right?"

"I feel *wonderful*!" She let go and began to fall and reached out and caught herself. "The Grad was right! We can *fly*!"

Gavving crawled toward her. Jinny was already below her, pounding in a spike. When Gavving reached them, Jayan was using the spike for support, with her line ready in her other hand. They pulled Merril back against the tree.

She didn't resist. She crowed, "Gavving, why do we live in the tuft? There's food here, and water, and who needs legs? Let's stay. We don't need any nose-arm cave, we can dig out our own. We've got nose-arm meat and those shelled things and the fan fungus. I've eaten enough foliage to last me the rest of my life! But if anyone wants it, we'll send down someone with legs."

We'll have to be careful of that fan fungus, Gavving thought. He was pounding spikes into bark; on the other side of Merril, Jiovan was doing the same. Where was Clave?

Clave was with Alfin, high above them, in furious inaudible argument.

"Come on, let's get going! What are you doing?" Merril demanded while Gavving and Jiovan bound her to the bark. "Or, listen, I've got a wonderful idea. Let's go back. We've got what we want. We'll kill another nose-arm and we, we'll grow fan fungus in the tuft. Then set up another tribe here. Claaave!" she bellowed as Clave and Alfin climbed down into earshot. "How would I do as Chairman of a colony?"

"You'd be terrific. Citizens, we'll be here for a while. Moor yourselves. Don't do any flying."

"I never thought it could be this good," Merril told them. "My parents—when I was little, they were just waiting for me to die. But they wouldn't feed me to the treemouth. I thought about it too, but I never did. I'm glad. Sometimes I thought of me as an example, something people need to be happy. Happy they have legs. Even one leg," she whispered hoarsely to Jiovan. "Legs! So what?"

Jiovan asked Clave, "How long do we have to put up with this?"

"You don't. Take, ah, take the Grad and find us a better place to sleep."

Jiovan looked about him. "Like what?"

"A cave, a crack or a bulge in the bark . . . anything that's better than hanging ourselves here like smoking meat."

"I'll go too," Alfin said.

"You stay."

"Clave, you do not have to treat me like a baby! I only ate from the middle of the thing. I feel fine!"

"So does Merril."

"What?"

"Never mind. You feel grouchy, and *that's* fine. Merril feels fine, and that's—"

"Alfin, I am *so* glad you didn't stop me from coming." Merril smiled radiantly at him. In that moment Gavving thought her beautiful. "Thank you for trying, though. Feel sleepy," Merril said and went to sleep.

Alfin saw questioning eyes. He spoke reluctantly. "I, I thought I could talk the Chairman out of this idiocy. Sending a, a legless woman up the tree! Clave, I *do* feel fine. Wide-awake. Hungry. I'd like to try some more."

Clave removed a fan from his pack. He tore away some of the scarlet fringe, then offered Alfin a hand-sized piece of the white interior. If Alfin flinched, it was for too short a time to measure. He ate the whole chunk with a theatrical relish that had Clave grinning. Clave broke off the rest of the red fringe and pouched it separately.

Jiovan and the Grad returned. They had found a DQ mark overgrown with fungus like a field of gray hair. "Infected. We'll have to burn it out," the Grad said.

"Suppose it keeps on burning? We don't have any water," Clave said. "Never mind. Let's have a look. Jayan, Jinny, stay with Merril. One of you come get me if she wakes up."

They examined the fungus patch dubiously. Scraping out all that gray hair would be a dull job. Clave pulled up a wad and set fire to it. It burned slowly, sullenly.

"Let's try it. But get some of our packs emptied in case we have to beat it out."

The fungus patch burned slowly. The west wind wasn't strong at this height, and the smoke tended to sit within the fungus "hairs," smothering the fire. It kept putting itself out. Yet it crept around in glowing fringes, restarting itself. They had to back away as foul-smelling smoke built up in the vicinity.

The smoke was dissipating. Gavving moved in and found most of the fungus gone, the rest left as black char. The Q was two meters deep.

Clave made a torch from a chunk of bark and burned out some remaining patches. "Scrape that out and I think we can all sleep in it. Gavving, Jinny, you go back for Merril."

When they started to move her, Merril woke instantly, happy and active and bubbling with plans. They coaxed her across the bark, ready for anything, and presently moored her in the scraped-out bottom of the Q.

Then there was nothing for it but to settle into the Q for early sleep.

Merril slept like a baby, but others shifted restlessly. Desultory conversations started and stopped. Presently Clave asked, "Jiovan, how are you doing?"

"How do you mean?"

"I mean the whole trip. How are you doing?"

Jiovan snorted. "I'm hungry. I hurt a lot, but I'm used to that. I can climb. Do you mean how are *we* doing? We won't know that till we get home. Merril's out of her head right now, but she could be right too."

Clave was startled. "You mean, live *here*?"

"No, that's crazy. I mean go back now. Kill something and smoke it and collect more fan fungus and go home. We'd be heroes, as much as any hunt party that comes home with meat, and I don't mind telling you, I'm ready. I'm treefeeding sick of being one of the—the lames. I used to be the one who *fed* the tribe...and if the fan fungus will grow in the tuft—"

By now the whole troop was listening. Clave knew he was talking for an audience. He said, "Merril could be pretty sick, you know."

"She feels great."

"Oh, let's see how she feels when it wears off. I might want to try it myself," Clave chuckled. He was hoping it would drop there.

No chance, not with Alfin listening. "What about going home? We've got what we came for."

"I don't think so. We sure haven't scraped out all the tribe-marks, have we, Grad?"

"They're supposed to run all along the trunk."

"Then let's go at least as far as the middle. We already know we can feed ourselves. Who knows what else we'll find? The nose-arm was good eating, but we've only found one, and we couldn't feed him in the tuft. We can pick up some fan fungus on the way back. What else? Are the flashers good to eat? Could we transplant those shelled things?"

The Grad was catching fire. "Get them growing just above the tuft. It might work. Sure I'd like to go on. I want to see what it's like when there isn't any tidal force at all."

"We already know what Merril would say. Anyone else?"

Alfin grunted. Nobody else spoke.

"We go on," Clave said.

Chapter Five

Memories

IT WAS THERE AGAIN. THERE WAS A SPECIAL FREQUENCY OF LIGHT that Sharls Davis Kendy had sought for five hundred years. He had found it fifty-two years ago, and forty-eight, and twenty, and . . . six certain sightings and another ten probable. The locus moved about. This time it was west of his position, barely filtering through the soup of dust and gas and dirt and plant life: the light of hydrogen burning with oxygen.

Kendy held his attention on a wavering point within the Smoke Ring. Rarely did the CARM even acknowlege that his signal had penetrated the maelstrom; but he never considered not trying. "Kendy for the State. Kendy for the State."

The CARM's main motor would run for hours now. It would accelerate slowly, too slowly: pushing something massive. What were they doing in there?

Had they entirely forgotten *Discipline* and Sharls Davis Kendy?

Kendy had forgotten much, but what remained to him was as vivid as the moment it had happened. These futile attempts at contact needed little of his attention. Kendy took refuge in memory.

* * *

The target star was yellow-white, with a spectrum very like Sol's, circling an unseen companion. At 1.2 solar masses, T3 was minutely brighter and bluer than Sol: about G0 or G1. The companion, at half a solar mass, would be a star, not a planet. It should at least have been visible.

The State had telescopic data from earlier missions to other stars. There was at least a third, planet-sized body in this system. There *might* be a planet resembling the primordial Earth; in which case *Discipline* would fulfill its primary mission by seeding its atmosphere with oxygen-producing algaes. On a distant day the State would return to find a world ripe for colonization.

But someone would have come anyway, to probe the strangeness of this place.

Discipline was a seeder ramship, targeted for a ring of yellow stars that might host worlds like the primordial Earth. Its secondary mission was a secret known only to Kendy; but exploration was a definite third on the list; *Discipline* would not stop here. Kendy would skim past T3, take pictures and records, and vanish into the void. He might slow enough to drop a missile with a warhead of tailored algae, if a target world could be found.

Four of the crew were in the control module. They had the telescope array going and a watery picture of a yellow-white star on the big screen, with a pinpoint of fierce blue-white light at its edge. Sam Goldblatt had a spectrum of T3 displayed on a smaller screen.

Sharon Levoy was lecturing for the record; nobody else was listening. "That solves *that*. Levoy's Star is an old neutron star, half a billion to a billion years beyond its pulsar stage. It's still hotter than hell, but it's only twenty kilometers across. The radiating surface is almost negligible. It must have been losing its spin and its residual heat for all of that time. We didn't see it because it isn't putting out enough light.

"The yellow dwarf star might have planets, but we can expect that their atmospheres were boiled away by the supernova event of which Levoy's Star is the ashes—"

Goldblatt snarled, "We're supposed to be the first expedition here! *Prikazyvat Kendy!*"

The crew were not supposed to be aware that the ship's computer and its recorded personality could eavesdrop on them. Therefore Kendy said, "Hello, Sam. What's up?"

Sam Goldblatt was a large, round man with a bushy, carefully tended moustache. He'd been chewing it ever since Levoy found and named the neutron star. Now his frustration had a target. "Kendy, do you have records of a previous expedition?"

"No."

"Well, check me out. Those are absorption lines for oxygen and water, *here*, aren't they? Which means there's green life somewhere in that system, doesn't it? And that means the State sent a seeder here!"

"I noticed the spectrum. After all, Sam, why shouldn't plant life develop somewhere on its own? Earth's did. Besides, those lines can't represent an Earthlike world. They're too sharp. There's too much oxygen, too much water."

"Kendy, if it isn't a planet, what *is* it?"

"We'll learn that when we're closer."

"Hmph. Not at this speed. Kendy, I think we should slow down. Decelerate to the minimum at which the Bussard ramjet will work. We won't waste onboard fuel, we'll get a better look, and we can accelerate again when we've got the solar wind for fuel."

"Dangerous," said Kendy. "I recommend against it." And that should have been that.

For five hundred and twelve years Kendy had been editing clumps of experience from his memory wherever he decided they weren't needed. He didn't remember deciding to follow Goldblatt's suggestions. Goldblatt must have persuaded Captain Quinn and the rest of the crew, and Kendy had given in . . . to them? or to his own curiosity?

Kendy remembered:

Levoy's Star and T3 circled a common point in eccentric orbits, at a distance averaging 2.5×10^8 kilometers, with an orbital period of 2.77 Earth years. The neutron star had been behind the yellow dwarf while *Discipline* backed into the system. Now it emerged into view of *Discipline*'s telescope array.

He saw a ring of white cloud, touched with green, with a bright spark at its center. The spectral absorption lines of water and oxygen were coming from there. It was tiny by astronomical standards: the region of greatest density circled the neutron star at 26,000 kilometers—about four times the radius of the Earth.

"Like a Christmas wreath," Claire Dalton breathed. The sociologist's body was that of a pretty, leggy blonde, but her corpsicle memories reached far back . . . and what was she doing on the bridge? Captain Dennis Quinn might have invited her, the way they were standing together. It indicated a laxity in discipline that Kendy would have to watch.

The crew of *Discipline* continued to study the archaic Christmas wreath. Until Sam Goldblatt suddenly crowed, "Goldblatt's World! Prikazyvat Kendy, record that, Goldblatt's World! There's a planet in there."

"I'm not close enough to probe that closely, Sam."

"It has to be there. You know how a gas torus works?"

It was there in Kendy's memory. "Yes. I don't doubt you're right. I can bounce some radar off that storm complex when we pass."

"Pass, hell. We've got to stop and investigate this thing." Goldblatt looked about him for support. "Green means life! Life, and no planet! We've got to know all about it. Claire, Dennis, you see that, don't you?"

The crew included twelve citizens and eight corpsicles. The corpsicles might argue, but they had no civil rights; and the citizens had less than they thought. For reasons of morale, Kendy maintained the fiction that they were in charge.

Goldblatt's suggestion was not worth considering. Kendy said, "Think. We've got fuel to decelerate once and once only. We'll need it when we reach Earth."

"There's water in there," Dennis Quinn said thoughtfully. "We could refuel. I bet the water's rich in deuterium and tritium. Why not, it's circing the ashes of a supernova!"

Claire Dalton was gazing at the screen, at a perfect smoke ring with a tiny hot pinpoint in its center. "The neutron star has cooled off, lost most of its rotation and most of its heat and most of that ferocious magnetic field the pulsars have. It's bright, but it's too small to be giving off much real heat. We could probably live in there ourselves." She looked around her. "Isn't this what we came for? The strangeness of the universe. If we don't stop now, we might as well be back on Earth." The contempt in her voice was unmistakable.

Kendy's memory jumped at that point. Hardly surprising. That must have been the true beginning of mutiny.

He remembered reviewing and updating his files on gas torus mechanics.

Two planets circled wide around the twin stars: Jupiter-style gas giants with no moons. The old supernova must have blasted away anything smaller.

A body did circle the neutron star. One limb of the Smoke Ring was curdled, a distorted whirlpool of storm. Hidden within was a core of rock and metals at 2.5 Earth masses. There was some oxygen and some water vapor in its thick, hot atmosphere. Goldblatt's World was tidally locked, and uninhabitable. Strip away its atmosphere and it might have harbored Earthly life— but its atmosphere was tremendous, dwindling indefinitely into the Smoke Ring itself.

The strong oxygen-water lines were coming from the gas torus.

A gas torus is the result of a light mass in orbit around a heavy mass, as Titan orbits Saturn. It may be that the light mass is too weak to hold its atmosphere. The faster molecules of air escape—but they go into orbit about the heavy mass. Thus, Titan circles Saturn within a ring of escaped Titanian atmosphere, as Io orbits Jupiter within a ring of sulfur ionized by Jupiter's ferocious magnetic field.

A gas torus is thin. The gas must be so rarefied that each molecule can be considered to be in a separate orbit: it must reasonably expect to circle halfway round the primary mass without bumping another molecule. Under such circumstances, a gas torus is stable. The occasional stray photon will bump a molecule into interstellar space; but the molecules are continually reencountering the satellite body.

Titan—smaller than Mars, no larger than Ganymede—carries an atmosphere of refined smog at one and a half times Earth's sea level pressure. The atmosphere is continually being lost, of course, but some of it continually returns from the gas torus.

Levoy's Star was an extreme case, and a slightly different proposition too.

The Smoke Ring was the thickest part of the gas torus around Levoy's Star. At its median it was as dense as Earth's atmosphere a mile above sea level: too dense for stability. It must be continually leaking into the gas torus. But the gas torus *was* stable: dense, but held within a steep gravitational gradient. Molecules continually returned from the gas torus to the Smoke Ring, and from the Smoke Ring to the storm of atmosphere surrounding Goldblatt's World.

"Goldblatt's World must have started life as a gas giant planet like, say, Saturn. Probably it didn't fall into range until the pulsar had lost a good deal of its heat and spin." Sharon Levoy's crisp voice spoke within Kendy's memory. "Then it was captured by strong Roche tides. It may have dropped close enough to lose water and soil as well as gas. For something like a billion years Goldblatt's World has been leaking gas into the Smoke Ring, and the Smoke Ring has been leaking to interstellar space. It's not stable, exactly, but hell, *planets* aren't stable over the long run."

"It won't be stable that much longer," Dennis Quinn interrupted. "Most of Goldblatt's World is already gone. Ten million years, or a hundred million, and the Smoke Ring will be getting rarefied."

Kendy remembered these things. The records had been made while *Discipline's* instruments probed the Smoke Ring from close range. Already some of the crew were exploring the Smoke Ring via CARMs. Their reports were enthusiastic. There was life,

DNA-based; the air was not only breathable, but tasted fine...

Kendy didn't remember bringing *Discipline* into orbit around Levoy's Star. He must have expended his onboard fuel, postponing by several years his arrival at the target stars along his course. Why?

Claire Dalton's voice: "We've got to get out of this box. It's running down. A little of what we recycle is lost every time around. There's more than water in there; there's air, there's probably even fresh fertilizer for the hydroponics tanks!"

It was Sharls Davis Kendy who ruled *Discipline*. *Discipline*'s crew of twenty was hardly necessary to run a seeder ramship. The State had chosen them as a reservoir of humanity: a tiny chunk of the State, far removed from any local disaster. One planet, one solar system, were too fragile to ensure the survival of the State or humankind itself. Every ship in the sky had a crew large enough to begin the human race over again: their secondary mission, if it ever became necessary. The State expected no such disaster, ever; but the investment was trivial compared to the reward.

When had he lost control? Perhaps they had threatened to bypass the computer and go to manual control. They couldn't; but morale would disintegrate if they ever learned how little control they really had. Kendy might have surrendered on that basis.

Or he might have been curious.

He did not remember any part of what must have been a mutiny. He must have been played for a fool; he might not *want* to remember that. The crew had departed with eight of the ten CARMs and rifled the hydroponics to boot! It should never have been allowed.

He was reasonably sure that seven of the CARMs were inoperable. Some equipment might have been salvaged...and the last CARM had now ceased its spray of incandescent water vapor. Kendy ceased beaming his message. The Smoke Ring glowed white and featureless beneath him.

One day he would know. Would they remember him at all? Kendy waited.

Chapter Six

Middle Ground

THE PATCH OF OLD-MAN'S-HAIR SHOULD HAVE BEEN TENDED LONG since. It was fifty to sixty meters across and had eaten half a meter deep into live wood. Parasol plants had rooted in the resulting compost, and matured, and spread their brightly colored blossoms to attract passing insects.

Minya watched the fire spread in intersecting curves within the fungus patch. Breezes tossed the choking smoke in unpredictable directions. The smoke drove clouds of mites out of the fungus and into the open. She was wishing Thanya's triad would arrive with water.

There were three triads of the Triune Squad now on the trunk. Minya, Sal, and Smitta were nearing the median. Jeel's triad traversed up and down the trunk, ferrying provisions from the tuft, while Thanya's brought water from the lee.

Fire was usually no problem, but mistakes could happen.

"I love these climbs," Smitta said. She floated with her toes gripping an edge of bark. This close to the median, it was enough to hold her against the feeble tide. "I like floating... and where else can you see the *entire* Smoke Ring?"

Minya nodded. She didn't want to talk. When a problem

couldn't be solved and wouldn't go away, what could one do but run? She had run as far as a human being could go. It was working: she felt at peace here, halfway between infinities.

The tree seemed to run forever in both directions. The Dark Tuft, backlit by Voy and the sun, was a halo of green fluff with a black core. Outward, Dalton-Quinn Tuft was barely larger. A few drifting clouds, wisps of green forest, whorls of storm were all outward. Eastward was a point of bright light off-center in a dark rim: the same small pond that had been drifting tantalizingly closer for a score of days.

Maybe, maybe it would come. They didn't talk about it. Bad luck.

Between the drought and the recent political upsets, it had been too long since the Triune Squad had been free for tree-tending duty. They had been needed as police. One could hope that the executions had settled the troubles; but now the triads were finding parasites and patches of old-man's-hair everywhere on the trunk. Today they were burning virtually a *field* of the horrid stuff.

Motion caught Minya's eye, outward and windward. Blue-against-blue, hard to see, something big. The sun was nearly at nadir, glaring up. She held a hand beneath her eyes, and squinted, and presently said, "Triune."

Smitta snapped alert. "Interested in us? *Sal!*"

Sal sang out from behind the smoke cloud. "I see it."

Minya said, "They're interested. They're pretty close already."

Smitta had pulled herself against the trunk and was readying her weapons. "I fought a triune once. They're smarter than sword-birds. You can scare them off. Just remember, if we kill one, we'll have to kill all three."

The torpedo-shaped object was closer now. It was nearly the blue of the sky, slowly rotating. Six big eyes showed in turn around the circumference, and three great gauzy fins...one smaller than the other. That would be the juvenile. Minya whispered, "What do we need?"

"Bows and arrows ready? Tether your arrow and scoop up some

burning old-man's-hair on the point. Lucky we had a fire going. Know where your jet pods are, you may need them."

Minya could feel her heart pulsing in her throat. It was her second trip up the trunk... but Smitta and Sal had been up many times. They were tough and experienced. Sal was a burly, red-haired forty-year-old who had joined the Triune Squad at age twelve. Smitta had been born a man; she was a woman by courtesy.

Stay clear of Smitta, Minya told herself. Smitta was slow to anger, but under pressure something could snap in her mind. Then Smitta fought like a berserker, even among her own, and the only way to stop her was to pile on her.

Minya strung her hardwood bow and used an arrow point to dig out a gob of burning fungus. Ready—?

The torpedo split in three. Three slender torpedoes flapped lazily toward them, showing small lateral fins and violent-orange bellies. A male and a female, forever mated, plus a single juvenile who would put on body mass fast, then mature more slowly. They divided only to hunt or fight. The Triune Squad itself was named for the triune family's interdependence.

The juvenile would be the smallest, the one hanging back a little. Two adults swept forward.

"Aim for the male," Smitta said and loosed, the line trailing out behind the arrow. Which was male? Minya waited a moment to judge Smitta's target, then loosed her own weapon. She judged that they weren't in range yet... and she was right; the male's body rippled him free of the arrows' paths, while the female bored in. Sal had held back. Now she loosed, and the veering female caught an arrow in her fin.

She bellowed. She flapped once, and the arrow snapped free. Sal appeared from the smoke, yanked into the sky. It didn't seem to bother her as she reeled in, her ancient metal bow slung safe over her shoulder. The smoldering old-man's-hair had been left on the female's tail, and she was flapping madly.

Smitta sent a tethered arrow winging at the juvenile.

Both adults screamed. The female tried to block the arrow.

Too slow. The juvenile didn't seem to see the arrow coming. Smitta yanked at the line and stopped it a meter short.

The female gaped.

The women were reeling frantically, but it wasn't necessary. The adults moved in alongside the infant, infinitely graceful. Small hands reached out from their orange bellies to pull them together. They moved away like a single blurred blue ghost against the blue sky.

"See? They're smart. You can reason with them," Smitta said.

Sal pulled a teardrop-shaped jet pod from one of the cluster of pockets that ran down and across the front of her tunic. She twisted the tip. A cloud of seeds and mist spurted away from her, thrusting Sal back toward the bark.

She coiled line and stowed her weapons, including the valuable bow. Springy metal, it was, handed down from old to young within the Triune Squad for at least two hundred years. "Well done, troops, but I think the fire is getting to the wood. I wish Thanya would get here. She couldn't have missed us, could she?"

To Minya's eye, the fire might have reached wood by now, or not. Hard to tell where old-man's-hair shaded over into rotted wood. "It's not bad yet," she said.

"I hate to waste jet pods, but...treefodder. I want to look for them," Sal decided. She gathered her legs under her, hands gripping the bark to brace herself, and jumped. She waved her arms to flip herself around until she could see the trunk. They watched her drift along the trunk, out toward Dalton-Quinn Tuft.

"She worries too much," Smitta said.

Seventy days had passed since Clave's citizens had departed Quinn Tuft.

The tree fed a myriad parasites, and the parasites fed Clave's team. They had killed another nose-arm, easily, chopping through its nose, then jabbing harpoons into its den. There were patches of fan fungus everywhere. Merril had slept a full eight days after eating from the red fringe of a fan fungus. The subsequent throbbing headache didn't seem to affect her climbing, and presently it went away. So the fan fungus served them as food, and they had found more of the shelled burrowers and other edibles . . .

The Grad saw it all as evidence of the tree's decline.

They had found a jet pod bush, like a mass of bubbles on the bark. Clave had packed a dozen ripe pods in a pouch of scraped nose-arm hide.

They had taken to camping just outside the water-washed wood. Clave laughed and admitted that they should have been doing that all along. They'd slept three times more on the tree: last night in a nose-arm's den, twice before in deep wounds in the wood, cracks overgrown with "fuzz" that had to be burned out first. The char had turned their clothing black.

They had learned not to try to boil water. The bubbles just foamed it out in a hot, expanding mass.

Tidal gravity continued to decrease until they were almost floating up the trunk. Merril loved it. Recovering from the fan fungus hadn't changed that. You *couldn't* fall; you'd just yell for help, and someone would presently throw you a line. Glory loved it, and Alfin smiled sometimes.

But there were penalties. Now water had grown scarce too. There was no wind this high, and thus no leeward stream of water. Sometimes you found wet wood, wet enough to lick dry. There was water in fan fungus flesh.

Here was the DQ mark Jinny had found. Good: it looked nearly clean. And half a klomter farther up the trunk, a fan-shape showed like a white hand against the sky. It must be huge. The Grad pointed. "Dinner?"

Clave said, "We'll find smaller ones around it."

"But wouldn't it look grand," Merril asked, "coming into the Commons?"

The Grad was pulling himself toward the tribal mark when Clave said, "Hold it."

"What?"

"This mark isn't overgrown like the others were. Grad, doesn't it look funny to you? *Tended?*"

"There's some fuzz growing, but maybe not enough." Then

the Grad was close enough to see the *real* discrepancy. "There's
no takeout mark. Citizens, this isn't Quinn territory."

Gavving and Jiovan had been left behind to tend the smokefire.

Hard-learned lessons showed here. Bark torn from the rim of
a patch of fuzz served as fuel. Healthy bark resisted fire. A circle
of coals surrounded the meat, all open to the fitful breezes. A
sheltered fire wouldn't burn. The smoke wouldn't rise; it would
stay to smother the fire. Even here in the open, the smoke hovered
in a squirming cloud. The heat of burning stayed in the smoke,
so the fire didn't need to be large. Gavving and Jiovan stayed
well back. A shift in the breeze could smother an incautious
citizen.

The meat should be rotated soon. It was Gavving's turn, but
it didn't have to be done instantly.

"Jiovan?"

"What?"

Even Gavving wouldn't ask Jiovan how he lost his leg—
nobody would; but one thing about that tale had bothered him
for years. And he asked.

"Why were you hunting alone, that day? Nobody hunts alone."

"I did."

"Okay." Topic closed. Gavving drew his harpoon. He pulled
air into his lungs, then lunged into the smoke. Half-blind, he
reached over the coals with the harpoon butt to turn the nose-
arm legs—one, two, three. He yanked hard on his line to pull
himself into open air. Smoke came with him, and he took an
instant to fan it away before he drew breath.

Jiovan was looking in, past the small green tuft that had once
enclosed his life, into the bluish white spark that was Voy. His
head came up, and Gavving faced a murderous glare. "This *isn't*
something I'd want told around."

Gavving waited.

"All right. I've got . . . I had a real gift for sarcasm, they tell
me. When I was leading a hunt . . . well, the boys were there to
learn, of course, and I was there to teach. If someone made a
mistake, I left him in no doubt."

Gavving nodded.

"Pretty soon they were giving me nothing but the fumblers. I couldn't stand it, so I started hunting alone."

"I shouldn't have asked. It used to bother me."

"Forget it."

Gavving was trying to forget something else entirely. This last sleep period he had wakened to find three citizens missing. He'd followed a sound . . . and watched Clave and Jayan and Jinny moor lines to the bark, and leap outward, and make babies while they drifted.

What lived in his head now was lust and envy balanced by fear of Clave's wrath or Jinny's scorn (for he had fixed on Jinny as marginally lovelier.) He might as well dream. Any serious potential mate was back in Quinn Tuft, and Gavving couldn't offer anyway; he hadn't the wealth or the years.

That would change, of course. He would return (of course) as a hero (of course!). As for the Chairman's wrath . . . he hadn't been able to send Harp. Possibly Clave could have resisted him too. If they could end the famine, the Chairman could do nothing; they would be heroes.

Gavving could have his choice of mates—

"So I was hunting alone," Jiovan said, "the day Glory busted open the turkey pen."

For an instant Gavving couldn't imagine what Jiovan was talking about. Then he smiled. "Harp's told that tale."

"I've heard him. I was down under the branch that day, with one line to tether me and another loose, nibbling a little foliage with my head sticking down into the sky, you know, just waiting. It was full night at the New Year's occlusion. The sun was a wide bright patch shining up at me, and Voy drifting right across the center.

"Here came a turkey, flapping against the wind, still moving pretty fast, and backward. I put a net on my free line, quick, and threw it. The turkey's caught. Here comes another one. I've got more nets, and in two breaths I've got a turkey on each end. But here come two more, then four, and they're coming from above, and by now I can guess they're ours. I throw the end of the line I'm moored to, and I get a third turkey—"

"Good throwing," Gavving said.

"Oh, sure, there wasn't *anything* wrong with my throwing that day. But the sky was full of turkeys, and most of them were going to get away, and I *still* thought it was kind of hilarious."

"Yeah."

"That's why I never told this story before."

Gavving suddenly guessed what was coming. "I can live with it if you don't want to finish."

"No, that's okay. It *was* funny," Jiovan said seriously. "But the sky was full of turkeys, and a triune family came to do something about all that meat on the wing. They split up and went after the loose turkeys. There wasn't a thing I could do but pull in my three."

Jiovan certainly wasn't smiling now. "The male went after one of my turkeys. Swallowed it whole and tried to swim away. It got the wrong line... picture one end of a line spiked deep in the branch, and that *massive* beast pulling on the other, and me in a loop in the middle. I suddenly saw what was happening, and I pulled the loop open and tried to jump out, and the loop snicked shut and my leg was ripped almost off and I was falling into the sky."

"Treefodder."

"I thought I was treefodder, all right. Remember, I still had a line in my hands? But with a turkey on each end, flapping like crazy, and I was *falling*. I tried throwing a turkey, I really did, I thought it might get caught in the branchlets, but it didn't.

"Meanwhile the triune male's been caught by something, and it doesn't know what. It pulls back against the line and feels a tug in its belly and throws up. I think that's what must have happened. All I know is something smacks me in the face, and it's a dead turkey covered with goo, and I grab it—I hug it to me with all my heart and climb the line back into the tuft."

Gavving was afraid to laugh.

"Then I tie off what's left of my leg. What's hanging loose,

I had to cut off. Well, kid, did Harp ever tell you a story like that?"

"No. Treefodder, he'd *love* it! Oh."

"He'd make me famous. I don't want to be famous that way."

Gavving chewed it over. "Why tell me now?"

"I don't know. My turn," Jiovan said suddenly. He filled his lungs and disappeared into the smoke.

Gavving felt burdened. Always he asked too many questions. He grinned guiltily, picturing Jiovan trying to throw a line with a turkey flapping at each end. But what if Jiovan regretted telling it?

He saw Clave appear from behind the curve of the trunk.

Jiovan emerged, bringing smoke, and Gavving held his breath while it cleared. Jiovan coughed a little. "It's been so long," he said. "Maybe it doesn't hurt as much. Maybe I just wanted to tell it. Maybe I had to."

"They're coming back," Gavving said. "I wonder what's got them so excited?"

Clave bellowed, "I will not go home without learning something about them!"

"I know quite a lot about them," the Grad answered. "We all lived in the far tuft once. The Quinns left after some kind of disagreement. Before that, it was Dalton-Quinn Tribe."

"Then they're relatives."

The argument had grown a little less chaotic, but only because half the troop was trailing back. It was no less vehement. Alfin shouted, "You're not listening. They kicked us out! For all we know, they think they're still at war with us!"

The Grad said, "Clave, the tribemarks are tended, and we aren't finding as many fan fungi lately, or the shelled things either. I'm thinking they keep this stretch of trunk clean. They must be still around. Our move is to get out of here!"

"You want to run from something you haven't even seen!"

"We saw the tribal insignia," the Grad said. "DQ. No takeout mark across the Q. Maybe they still call themselves Dalton-Quinn. What does that make us? Intruders on *their* tree? We've passed the median anyway, we're in their space. Clave, let's go home. Kill another nose-arm, pick some fan fungus and one of the shells, and go home with plenty of food." Clave was shaking his head. "The tribe won't have to go thirsty any more either! We bring water from the trunk—"

Clave waved it away. "That water would get to the tuft anyway. No. I want to meet the Daltons. It's been hundreds of years, we don't know *what* they're like . . . maybe they know better tending methods for the earthlife, or ways to get water. Maybe they grow food we never heard of. *Something.* 'Day, Jiovan."

"'Day. What's going on?"

"We found a tribemark and it isn't ours. The question before the citizenry is, do we say hello before going home? Or do we just run?"

The Grad jumped in. "Don't you see, we can't fight and we can't negotiate! We've got one good fighter, and two cripples and a boy and four women and a treemouth tender, and all of us thrown out of Quinn Tuft, we can't even make promises—"

Clave broke in. "Alfin, you're for leaving too?"

"Yes."

"Jiovan?"

"What are we running from?"

"Maybe nothing. That mark wasn't tended for a long time. Treefodder, the drought could have killed them off! We could *settle* the far tuft—"

Merril broke in, though she was puffing from the climb. "Oh no. If everyone died there . . . we won't want to . . . go anywhere near it. Sickness."

"Are you for going back or going on?"

"I don't . . . back, I guess, but . . . let's get that . . . big fan fungus first. Wouldn't that impress the citizens! And smoke another nose-arm . . . if we can. Far as that goes . . . we know there's meat to be hunted on the trunk. We should tell the Chairman that."

"Jayan? Jinny?"

"She makes sense," Jinny said, and Jayan nodded.

"Gavving?"

"No opinion."

"Treefodder. Glory?"

"Go back," Glory said. "I haven't tasted foliage in days and days."

Clave sighed. "If I was sure I was right, we'd go on. Aaall right." His voice became fuller, more resonant. "We'll have enough to carry anyway, what with the giant fan and whatever meat we find. Citizens, we've done very well for ourselves and Quinn Tuft. We go home as heroes. Now, I *don't* want to lose anyone on the way down, so *don't* take the tide for granted! It'll get stronger with every klomter. Most of the way down we'll need lines for the meat and the fan fungus—"

Their goals had become Clave's own. Gavving noticed, and remembered.

The flashers had come back. Minya watched them at their mating dance. Two males strutted before the same female with their wing-cloaks spread wide, and the female's head snapped back and forth almost too fast to see. *Decisions, decisions—*

"Something's been worrying you, woman."

—Decisions. Was it any of Smitta's business? Minya made a swift decision: she *had* to talk to someone, or burst. "I've started wondering if—if I'm right for the Triune Squad."

Smitta showed shock. "Really? You were eager enough to join eight years ago. What's changed?"

"I don't know."

But she did, and suddenly Smitta did too. "Don't talk to Sal about this. She wouldn't understand."

"I was only fourteen."

"You looked older...more mature. And maybe the loveliest recruit we ever got."

Minya grimaced. "Every man in the tuft wanted to make babies with me. I must have heard every *possible* way of saying that. I just didn't want to *do* that with anyone. Smitta, that's what the Triune Squad is for!"

"I know. What would I be without the Triune Squad? A woman born as a man, a man who wants to be a woman..."

"Do you ever want—" What was the right word? Not *make babies*, not for Smitta.

"I used to," Smitta said. "With Risher—he was a lot prettier once—and lately with Mik, the Huntmaster's boy." Minya flinched. Maybe Smitta noticed. "We give all that up when we join. You just have to hold it inside. You know that."

"Does anyone ever..."

"What? Quit? Cheat? Alse jumped into the sky, a little after I joined, but nobody really knows why. That's the only way to quit. If you get caught cheating, I can name some would tear you apart. Sal's one."

Tight lips and clenched teeth held back Minya's secret. Now Smitta did notice. "Don't get caught cheating," she repeated. "Maybe you don't know how citizens feel about us. They tolerate us. We won't give the tribe babies, so we do the most dangerous jobs anyone can think of, and pay the debt that way. But you don't ask any ordinary man to, you know, help you be in both worlds."

Minya nodded. Lips pressed together, teeth clenched: if only she had kept them that way when she was with Mik! Mik had been impossible to get rid of, eight years ago. How had he changed so much? *Would he tell?*

"Smitta—"

"Drop it, Sal's coming."

Minya looked. There were *four* figures down there, four women rising on jets of sprayed gas and seeds; and they carried no water. Sal shouted something the wind snatched away.

"They're wasting jet pods," Smitta observed.

They were closer now and in range to snag the bark. This time Minya heard Sal's joyful bellow.

"Invaderrrsss!"

Chapter Seven

The Checker's Hand

THE TWO TRIADS MOVED INWARD, STAYING IN CRACKS IN THE bark where they could. Every minute or so Denisse, a tall, dark woman of Thanya's triad, would pop up, look around fast, and drop back into the bark.

"We counted six of them around the tribemark," Thanya said. "Dark clothes. Maybe they're from the Dark Tuft."

"Intruders on the tree." Sal's voice was eager, joyful. "We've never fought invaders! There were some citizens thrown out for mutiny, long ago... some of them killed the Chairman, and the rest went with them. Maybe they settled in the Dark Tuft. Mutineers... Thanya, what kind of weapons were they carrying?"

"We couldn't go ask them, could we? Denisse says she saw things like giant arrows. I couldn't even tell their sexes, but one had no legs."

They veered to avoid a crack clogged with old-man's-hair. Smitta said, "Six of them, six of us, you may have missed a few... shall we send someone back for Jeel's triad?"

Sal grinned wolfishly. "No."

"And no," said Thanya for her triad.

Minya said nothing—her triad leader spoke for her—but she

felt a fierce joy. Right now there was nothing she needed more than a fight.

Denisse dropped back from her next survey. Her voice was deadly calm. "Intruders. We have intruders, three hundred meters in and a hundred to port, moving outward. At least six."

"Let's go slow," Thanya said suddenly. "I'd like to question one. We don't know what they want here."

"Do we care? What they want isn't theirs."

Thanya grinned back. "We're not a debating team. We're the Triune Squad. Let's go look."

They worked their way along the bark. Presently Denisse poked her head up, dropped back. "Intruders have reached the Checker's Hand."

Clearing the trunk of parasites was one of the Triune Squad's duties. Fan fungi were dangerous to the tree and edible besides; but one large and perfect fan had special privileges. Found twenty-odd years ago, it had been left to grow even larger. Minya had only heard of the squad's unusual pet. She eased her head above the bark...

They were there: men, women, looking entirely human. "More than six. Eight, nine, dressed like dirty civilians. Sooty red clothes, no pockets...they're chopping at the stalk! They're killing it, the Checker's Hand—"

Smitta screamed and launched herself across the bark.

No help for it now. Sal cried, "Go for Gold!" and the Triune Squad leapt toward the intruders.

The fan fungus reached out from the trunk like a tremendous hand, white with red nails. Its stalk, disproportionately narrow and fragile-looking from a distance, was still thicker than Gavving's torso. He set to chopping at it with his dagger. Jiovan worked the other side.

"We'll get it down the trunk," Jiovan puffed, "but how will we ever get it through the tuft to the Commons?"

"Maybe we don't," said Clave. "Bring the tribe to the fungus. Let them carve off pieces to suit themselves."

"Tear the fringe off first," Merril said.

The Grad objected. "The Scientist will want some of the red part."

"And try it on who? Oh, all right, save some fringe for the Scientist. Not a lot, though."

The stalk was tough. They'd made some progress, but Gavving's arms were used up. He backed away, and Clave took over. Gavving watched the cut deepen.

Maybe they'd weakened it enough?

He pounded a stake into the bark and tethered his line to it. Then he leapt at the fungus with the full strength of his legs.

The great hand bent to his weight, then sprang back, flipping him playfully into the sky. Floundering, gathering in his line, he saw what the others had missed through being too close to the trunk.

"Fire!"

"What? Where?"

"Outward, half a klomter, maybe. Doesn't look big." The sun was behind the out tuft, leaving the trunk somewhat shadowed; he could see an orange glow within a cloud of smoke.

A flicker at the corner of his eye. He pulled hard at the line before his forebrain had reigstered anything at all...and a miniature harpoon zipped past his hip.

He yelled, "Treefodder!" Not specific enough. "Harpoons!"

Jiovan was stumbling, indecisive; a sharp point showed behind his shoulder blade. Clave was slapping shouders and buttocks to send his citizens to cover. Something sailed past at a distance: a woman, a burly red-haired woman garbed in purple, with pockets clustered from breasts to hips, giving her a look of lumpy pregnancy. She flew loose through the sky while she pulled something apart with both hands. Something that glittered, a line of light.

Their eyes met, and Gavving knew it was a weapon even before she let it snap shut. He clutched the bark and rolled. Something came as a tiny blur, thudded into the bark alongside his spine: a mini-harpoon with gray and yellow flasher feathers at the butt end. He rolled again to put the fan fungus between them.

Clave was nowhere in sight. Purple-clad enemies sailed along the wall of bark, yelling gibberish and throwing death. The red-haired woman had a harpoon through her leg. She tore it loose, cast it away, and sought a target. She picked the easiest: Jiovan, who wasn't even trying to seek cover. He took a second mini-harpoon through his chest.

They were using jet pods. A lean purple-clad man spotted Gavving; he pulled his weapon apart and a string snapped. He screamed in rage and opened a jet pod to hurl him down at Gavving. His other hand waved a meter's-length of knife.

Gavving leapt out of his way, drew his knife, yanked at the line to pull himself back. The man smacked into the bark. Gavving was on his back before he could recover. He slashed at the man's throat. Inhumanly strong fingers sank into his arm like a swordbird's teeth. Gavving shifted his own grip and jabbed his knife into the man's side. *Hurry!* The grip relaxed.

The tree shuddered.

Gavving didn't notice at once. He was shuddering with re-action. He saw the great wall of bark shuddering too, decided it was the least of his problems, and looked for enemies.

The red-haired woman was coasting treeward not far out, ignoring the blood spreading across her pants; her eye was on the shuddering tree. Out of range? Gavving tried a harpoon cast and instantly dived behind the great fan.

Not necessary. He'd skewered her. She stared at him, horrified, and died.

Purple-clad enemies screamed to each other, voices drowned by a rising background roar. Jiovan was dead with two feathered shafts in him. Jinny held a smaller fan fungus in front of her, harpoon in her other hand. The Grad rolled out of a crevice in the bark, saw what Jinny was doing, and imitated her. A mini-harpoon thudded into Jinny's shield, and she bared her teeth and launched herself in that direction, followed by Jayan and the Grad.

Gavving reeled in his harpoon. The dead woman came with it, her arms and legs jerking. A wave of nausea clawed at his throat. He worked his harpoon loose, and was minded to examine the peculiar gleaming weapon still clutched in the woman's hand. He wasn't given time.

The tree shuddered again. The bass background roar continued, a sound like worlds ripping apart. Bark slid past Gavving; the red-haired corpse tumbled, flailing. He was scrambling for a foothold when someone came at him from the side.

Dark hair, lovely pale heart-shaped face—purple clothing. Gavving thrust a harpoon at her eyes.

"The fire!" Thanya screamed. "It'll block us from the tuft! We've got to get past it!" She blew jet pods and was skimming outward across the bark.

Minya heard, but she didn't pause. Smitta was dead, and Sal was dead, and a single invader boy had killed them both. Minya stalked him.

The boy wore scarlet clothing, citizen's garb; his blond hair curled tightly as a skullcap; his beard was barely visible. His face was set in a rictus of fear or killing-rage. He thrust at her, threw himself back from her sword's counterthrust, lost his toe-grip on the bark. For an instant Minya was minded to go after him. Pierce him, kill him for the honor of Sal's triad, then go!

There wasn't time. Thanya was right. The fire could block them all, maroon them away from Dalton-Quinn Tuft... and there was Sal's bow to be recovered. Minya whirled and leapt away, and fired a jet pod for extra speed.

Sal's corpse floated free, her dead hand clutching the tribal treasure. Behind Minya the blond youth gripped bark to set himself and hurled his hand-arrow. Minya kicked to alter her course and watched the weapon whisper past her. She turned back as a shape popped up directly in front of her.

The shape was wrong, not human. It froze her for an instant. Minya hadn't quite grasped what was happening when a fist exploded in her face.

Gavving had ignored the yells from the purple-clad women. Now two were fleeing, firing jet pods to carry them outward along the trunk. Another leapt in a zigzag pattern along the bark. But the dark-haired woman who had tried to kill him was now moving crosswise, back to where Gavving had left . . . left a burly red-haired corpse clutching a curve of silver metal.

Merril popped out of a crack just in front of her. Merril's fist smacked into the stranger's jaw with a sound Gavving heard even above the—

—bass ripping sound he'd been ignoring while he fought for his life: a sound like the sky tearing apart. Now he heard the Grad shrilling like a cricket, a sound of panic, the words drowned in the roar.

But Gavving didn't need to hear. He *knew*.

"Clave! Claaave!"

Clave popped out of a deep crack and shouted, "Ready. What do you need?"

"We have to jump!" the Grad screamed. "All of us!"

"What are you talking about?"

"The tree's coming apart! That's how they survive!"

"What?"

"Get everyone to jump clear!"

Clave looked around. Jiovan was dead, floating tethered, but dead. The Grad was already loose in the sky, with line coiled! Gavving . . . Gavving moved across the shuddering bark, ripped something loose from a purple-clad corpse, continued in along the trunk. Jayan and Jinny weren't visible. Alfin snarled as he watched his enemies disappear into the outward smoke cloud. Glory and Merril watched too, not believing it.

Make a decision. Now. You don't know enough, but you've got to decide. It has to be you, it's always you.

Gavving. Gavving and the Grad were old friends. Did Gavving know something? He'd captured an invader weapon, and now he was far in along the trunk . . . headed for the meat they'd left when they went after the mushroom. Of course, they'd need food if they were to cast loose from the tree.

The Grad's mind could have snapped. But Gavving trusted him . . . and everything was happening at once: fire blazing on the tree, the trunk shuddering and moaning, strangers killing and then fleeing . . . There were jet pods in Clave's pack. He could get his citizens back once things settled down. He bellowed, "Grad! Lines to the tree?"

"Nooo! Treefodder, *no!*"

"All right." He bellowed above the end-of-the-world roar. *"Jayan! Jinny! Glory, Alfin, Merril, everybody jump! Jump away from the tree! Do not moor yourselves!"*

Reactions were various. Merril stared at him, thought it over, pushed herself free. Glory only stared. Jayan and Jinny emerged from hiding like a pair of birds taking wing. Alfin clutched the bark in a deathgrip. Gavving? Gavving was working to free one thick leg of nose-arm meat.

The bark still shuddered, the sound filled tree and sky, the purple-clad killers were nowhere to be seen, and . . . nobody had gone after the fan fungus. Clave hurled himself at the stalk.

The fan bent under his weight, then tore loose and was turning end for end. Clave's fingers were sunk into white fungus. The tumbling thing seemed to be picking up speed. Faster, the bark raced beneath the tumbling fan fungus, faster . . . a fiery wind rushed past him and was gone before he could draw breath.

It wasn't possible. Bewildered, Clave saw tufts of flame receding in both directions. No tree. Citizens floundered in the sky. Even Alfin had jumped at last. But the tree, where was the tree? There wasn't any tree. Fistfuls of fungus turned to mush in Clave's closing fists, and he screamed and wrapped his arms around the stalk. They were lost in the sky.

Chapter Eight

Quinn Tribe

WOOD SNAPPED EXPLOSIVELY, SPATTERING GAVVING WITH SPLIN-ters as he leapt across the bucking, tearing bark. A million insects poured from a sudden black gap that must have reached a klomter into the heartwood. Gavving cried out and waved his arms through the buzzing cloud, trying to clear enough air to breathe.

The tree was everything that was, and the tree was ending. If he'd stopped to think, his fear would have frozen him fast. He held to the one thought: *Get the meat and get out!*

The nose-arm legs tumbled loose within a cloud of burning coals. One haunch was in reach. Gavving caught a line to pull it free of the coals, then jumped to catch it against his shoulder. Hot grease burned his neck. He yelled and thrust himself away.

Now what? He couldn't *think* in this end-of-the-world roar. He doffed his backpack, tied it against the nose-arm leg, braced against the pack, and pushed himself into the sky.

Clouds of insects and pulverized wood half hid the shuddering, thundering tree. Dagger-sized splinters flew past.

Gavving braced one of his jet pods against the pack and twisted the tip. Seeds and cold gas blasted past him. The pod ripped itself free of his hands, spat seeds into the flesh of his face, and was gone.

His hands shook. Beads of blood were pooling on his cheek and his neck. He dug out his remaining jet pod and tried again, his tongue between his teeth. This time the pod held steady until it had gone quiet.

The world came apart.

He watched it all while his terror changed to awe. Fiery wind swept past him and left him in the open sky. Two fireballs receded in and out, until the home tree had become two bits of fluff linked by an infinite line of smoke.

Awesome! Nobody could hope to live through a bigger disaster. All of Quinn Tribe must be dead...the idea was really too big to grasp...all but Clave's citizens, and they'd lost Jiovan too, and who was left? He looked about him.

Nobody?

A cluster of specks, far out.

He'd used both his jet pods, and now he was lost in the sky. At least he wouldn't starve...

Thrashing his arms didn't stop the Grad's spin. He wasn't willing to use his jet pods for only that. He settled for spreading his arms and legs like a limpet star, which slowed him enough to search for survivors.

The left side of his face was wet. His fingertips traced a bloody gash that ran from temple to chin. It didn't hurt. Shock? But he had worse to worry him.

Three human shapes tumbled slowly nearby: purple marked with scarlet. His stomach lurched. It was their own doing; he hadn't come here to kill.

The giant fan fungus floated free, turning, turning to reveal Clave clutching the stalk. Good. Clave still wore his backpack: *very* good. That was their store of fresh jet pods. Then why wasn't Clave doing something about rescue?

Feet outward, Jayan and Jinny rotated slowly around their two pairs of clasped hands. It looked almost like a dance. Spreading out like that greatly reduced their spin. Good thinking, and no sign of panic.

Merril was a fair distance in. Her arms hadn't pushed her far, and the tree's wind-wake had caught her.

The world's-end roar had dwindled, allowing lesser sounds. The Grad heard a thin wail. Alfin had leapt free after all. He was thrashing and spinning and crying, but he was safe.

The Grad couldn't find Gavving, nor Glory, nor Jiovan. Jiovan's corpse must have gone with the tree, but where were the others? And why wasn't Clave doing something? He and the fan were drifting away.

The Grad sighed. He shrugged out of his backpack and searched out his jet pods. Old jet pods, from Quinn Tuft stores. Were they still active?

He'd never fired a jet pod. He knew nobody who had. Hunters carried them in case they fell into the sky; but no hunter lost in the sky had ever returned in the Grad's lifetime. He did it carefully: he donned his pack again, then clutched a jet pod in both hands over his navel. When Clave was approximately behind him, he twisted the tip, smartly.

The pod drove into his belly. He grunted. He maneuvered the point, hoping to kill his spin. The push died; he released the pod, and it jumped away on the last of its stored gas.

Looking over his shoulder, he found the fan fungus drifting toward him. Clave still wasn't doing anything constructive, and he hadn't noticed the Grad.

The smoke of the disaster split the sky from end to end. Dense, flickering black clouds were pulling free of the paler smoke. The same insects that had eaten the tree apart were now casting loose to find other prey.

Other debris floated in the smoke trail. The Grad made out great fragments of torn wood and bark; a cloud of flashers whirling in panic; a flapping mote, perhaps a nose-arm fled from its burrow. In that confusion he could still see that the cloud of citizens and corpses was slowly drifting apart.

Far in toward Voy, Gavving maneuvered half his own weight

in smoked meat. He'd be hard to reach. He'd gone far to save that meat, and the wind-wake must have pulled him further. Save Gavving for last, and hope.

The fan brushed against the Grad and he clutched it, fungus springy under his hands. Clave watched as if bemused. He asked, "What happened?"

Safe now. "The tree came apart. Clave, I'm going to dig in your pack. We've got to start rescuing citizens."

Clave neither helped nor resisted as the Grad searched through his pack. They could use the big fan as a base of operations... rescue Alfin first, because he was nearest... He took half a dozen pods. He slid to somewhere near the fan's center of mass and fired a jet pod, then another.

"The *tree* came apart?"

"You saw it."

"How? Why?"

The Grad was judging distances. He cast a line in a wide circle. It brushed Alfin's back, and Alfin convulsed and snatched the line in a deathgrip. He didn't try to reel it in. The Grad had to do that, while Alfin watched in near mindless terror. Alfin lunged across the last meter or so and wrapped himself around the stalk and buried his fingers in white fungus to the last knuckle.

A hand closed around the Grad's neck. Long, strong fingers overlapped the thumb, tightening like a steel collar. Clave's voice was a hot snarl in his ear. "You'll tell me now!"

The Grad froze. Clave had gone crazy.

"Tell me what happened!"

"The tree came apart."

"Why?"

"Maybe the fire set it off, but it was ready. Clave, everything in the Smoke Ring has some way of getting around. Some way to stay near the median... middle, where there's water and air. Where do you think jet pods come from?" The hand relaxed a little, and the Grad kept talking. "It's a plant's way of getting around. If a plant wanders out of the median, too far into the gas torus region—"

"The what?"

Alfin asked, "What on Earth is going on?"

"Clave wants to know what happened. Alfin, can you steer this thing and pick up some more of us? Here—" He passed across his store of jet pods.

Alfin took them. He took his time deciding what to do with them, and the Grad ignored him while he lectured. "The Smoke Ring runs down the median of a much bigger region. That's the gas torus, where the molecules . . . the bits of air have long mean-free-paths. The air is very thin in the gas torus, but there's some. It gets thicker along the median. That's where you find all the water and the soil and the plants. That's what the Smoke Ring is, just the thickest part of the gas torus, and that's where every living thing wants to stay."

"Where it can breathe. All right, go on."

"Everything in the Smoke Ring can maneuver somehow. Animals mostly have wings. Plants, well, some plants grow jet pods. They spit seeds back toward the median where they can grow and breed, or they spit sterile seeds farther into the gas torus, and the reaction pushes the plant back toward the median. Then there are plants that send out a long root to grab anything that's passing. There are kites—"

"What about the jungles?"

"I . . . I don't know. The Scientist never—"

"Skip it. What about the trees?"

"Now, that's really interesting. The Scientist came up with this, but he couldn't prove it—"

The hand tightened. The Grad babbled, "If an integral tree falls too far out of the median, it starts to die. It dies in the center. The insects eat it out. They're symbiotes, not parasites. When the center rots, the tree comes apart. See, half of it falls further away, and half of it drops back toward the median. Half lives, half dies, and it's better than nothing."

Clave mulled that. He said, "Which half?"

"East takes you out, out takes you west, west—"

"What are you doing?"

"I'm trying to remember. We were too far in toward Voy, so our end—" It only hit him then. The revelation blocked his throat.

A moment later, so did Clave's fingers. "Keep talking, you copsik. I've had it up to here with you telling half a secret!"

Thickly the Grad said, "Mister Chairman, you may call me the Scientist."

The hand relaxed in shock.

"Quinn Tribe is dead. We are Quinn Tribe."

Alfin broke the long silence that followed that terrible declaration. "Are you happy, Grad? You were right. The tree was dying."

"Shut up," said Clave. He released the Grad's neck. Maybe that had been a mistake, maybe not; he'd have to apologize presently. For now, he clambered around to the edge of the fan. Jayan and Jinny were coming near, watching his approach alternately as they spun.

He'd never felt like this, so helpless, so fearful of making decisions. It bothered him that Alfin and the Grad had seen him like that. He tried his voice and found it normal:

"They're almost here. Good work, Alfin. Go for Merril next. I don't see Glory."

The Grad said, "I haven't seen her since...since." He rubbed his throat.

"She may not have jumped. Seven of us. Seven." He flung a line. Jinny snagged it in her toes, and Clave pulled them both in together. He said, "Welcome to what's left of Quinn Tribe."

They clung to Clave more in desperation than affection. Jinny pulled back to look into his face. "They're dead? All the rest?" As if she'd already guessed.

Alfin demanded, "Why didn't the Scientist see *that* coming?"

"He did," said the Grad.

"Treefodder. Why did he stay, then?"

"He was an old man. He couldn't climb fifty klomters of tree."

Alfin gaped. "But . . . but that's the same as murdering every-one who *could* climb!"

There wasn't time for this. Clave said, "Alfin, pay attention to what you're doing."

Alfin set off two jet pods, then another. The fan drifted toward Merril, who waited in what might have been stoic calm. He murmured, "The children!"

Somewhere off to the side, there was motion.

What Clave had taken for a purple-clad corpse was floundering in air. Clave pointed. "One killer left."

They watched. She wasn't floundering now. She'd tied a line to her long knife, and now she cast it out. She snagged a dead companion and reeled it in. She searched the corpse, then pushed off from it in the direction of the next.

She hadn't found much, but it must have been what she wanted. Now she fired two jet pods in turn. The thrust carried her in toward Voy. Alfin said, "She's not coming here. Or going home. What does she think she's doing?"

"Not our problem."

Merril caught a line thrown by Alfin and pulled herself close. By now there was no room to clutch the fan itself. Clave asked her, "Did you see any sign of Glory?"

"Hanging on to the bark for dear life, last I saw her. She was in the out section. Gavving's a good distance in."

"We'll go after him. I hope we get there in time."

By then it was obvious. The woman in purple had passed them and was heading toward Gavving.

Gavving watched her coming. There was little else he could do. When he could see her face he watched her watching him. The rictus of hate he'd seen earlier wasn't there. He saw close-cut dark hair, a triangular face with an oddly narrow chin, an expression that was thoughtful, judging.

She was going to go past.

He didn't know how to feel about that. He didn't want to die alone; but he surely didn't want to die with those mini-harpoons through him. She was close now. She reached behind her back for a tethered mini-harpoon. He could only try to put the meat between them as she pulled her odd weapon apart, looking him in the eye, and released it.

The feathered thing buried itself in warm meat.

Then Gavving moved in frantic haste, pulling his knife, reaching for her line—

Her words were strangely twisted, but he understood her. "No, no, no, let me live! I have water! I have jet pods! I beg you!"

It might be so. He shouted, "Freeze! Don't reel yourself in! I have to think."

"I obey."

She hung, tethered, motionless.

"You've got water and I've got food. What if you kill me and keep both?"

"My sword," she answered and produced the long knife and threw it. Startled, Gavving reached out and managed to catch it by the handle. "My bow," she said, and he had time to bed the knife in the meat before she threw him the pull-it-apart weapon. He caught that too.

Now what? She was just waiting.

"What do you want?"

"I want to join you, your people. There's nobody else."

He could festoon himself with his weapons and hers, and so what? With nothing between them but forty kilograms of smoked meat, either could snatch a weapon and kill the other at any time. He'd have to sleep sometime . . . and still she waited.

He thought suddenly, *Why not? I'm dead anyway.* He called, "Come on."

She coiled the line as she came. Gavving had been hanging onto his pack, but she hugged herself up against the meat with no thought for what it would do to her purple clothing. She worked a jet pod out of one of the dozen pockets that gave her body its shapeless, lumpy look. She set it and twisted the end. When it had expended itself there was some change in their velocity. She used another. Then another.

"Why were you carrying so many?" he asked.

"I took them from my friends."

From their corpses. Gavving turned away. Quinn Tribe now formed a single clump around—

"The Checker's Hand," said his enemy. He had trouble understanding her odd pronunciation. "They're all moored to the Checker's Hand. Good enough. Fans are edible. So is dumbo meat."

"I know that word. *Checker*: the Grad's used it, but he never tells anyone what it means."

"You should not have attacked the Checker's Hand. We tend it . . . tended it."

"Is that why you killed Jiovan? For a *fan fungus*?"

"For that, and for returning from exile. You were cast out for assassinating a Chairman."

"That's news to me. We've been in Quinn Tuft for over a hundred years."

She nodded as if it didn't matter. She was strange . . . she was a stranger. Gavving knew every man, woman, and child in Quinn Tuft. This citizen had dropped on him out of the sky, complete and unknown. He wasn't even sure he should hate her.

"I'm thirsty," he said.

She passed him a squeezegourd pod half-full of water. He drank.

The clump that was Quinn Tribe seemed minutely closer. Gavving might have been imagining it. He said, "What do we do now? The way you use a jet pod, maybe you handle yourself better in the sky than we do. Can you tell us what to do next? Dalton Tuft—"

"Dalton-Quinn Tuft," she corrected him.

"Your half of the tree is probably safe, but it's being pulled out by the tide. I can't think of any way to reach it. We're lost." Then his curiosity suddenly became unbearable. "Who *are* you?"

"Minya Dalton-Quinn."

"I'm Gavving Quinn," he said for the second time in his life. The first had been at his rite of passage into adulthood. He tried again. "Who are you all? Why did you want to kill us?"

"Smitta was . . . excitable. Some of us are like that in the Triune Squad, and you were killing the Hand."

"Triune Squad. Mostly women?"

"All women. Even Smitta, by courtesy. We serve the tuft as fighters."

"Why did you want to be a fighter?"

She shook her head, violently. "I don't want to talk about it. Will your citizens accept me or kill me?"

"We're not—" killers? He'd killed two himself. It came to him that if the Grad had taught him rightly, those times when the Scientist would have whipped them both for such talk, then . . . then Minya's half of the tree, falling out from Voy, was also falling out of a drought. So. "Can I tell them this? If we can get you back to the far tuft, you'll see to it that we're made members of your tribe. It looks better if I can say that. Well?"

She didn't speak at once, and then she said, "I have to think."

The meat and the fan were passing at fair speed when Clave cast out a weighted line. He'd reserved their last pod. Another mistake, maybe. Now they'd have only one chance . . . but the dark stranger caught the line neatly and made it fast. They braced against their mutual spin.

Gavving shouted across the gap. "This is Minya of Dalton-Quinn Tribe. She wants to join us."

"Don't pull in yet. Is she armed?"

"She was."

"I want her weapons." Clave cast another line. An impressively thick bundle came back. Clave studied the haul: a knife the length of his own arm, a smaller knife, a bundle of mini-harpoons, and two of the pull-it-apart weapons, one of wood and one of metal. He preferred the look of the wooden one. The metal thing looked like it had been made from something else. By now he'd guessed how they must work, and he liked the idea.

Alfin said, "She tried to kill us all."

"True." Clave handed the Grad his last jet pod, not without reluctance. "Stop our spin. Wait. See that sheet of bark, out from us and not moving very fast? See if you can stop our spin and move us that way too."

Alfin persisted. "What are you going to do?"

"Recruit her, if she'll stand for it," Clave answered. "Seven citizens in a tribe is ridiculous."

"There isn't room to guard her."

"Where do you want to spend the rest of your life?"

The jet pod sprayed gas and seeds. The Grad said, "We won't reach the bark this way. Not enough push."

Alfin still hadn't answered. Clave told him, "Unless you've learned to like falling, I'd guess you want to live in an integral tree tuft. We now have a prisoner who lives in a tuft. We have the chance to earn her gratitude."

"Bring her in."

Chapter Nine

The Raft

THE POND WAS A SMALL, PERFECT SPHERE, TWENTY KLOMTERS out from the Checker's Hand: a giant water droplet trailing a tail of mist in the direction away from the sun. When the sun shone through from behind, as it did now, Minya glimpsed shadows wriggling within it.

It was going to drift past.

The ends of the tree were far away and still separating: Dalton-Quinn Tuft drifting out and west, the Dark Tuft in and east. The smoke trail that joined them was growing faint, save for dark streamers that were indecisive clouds of insects.

Something surged from the pond, and the pond rippled and convulsed in its wake. The creature was big even at this distance. Hard to judge its size, but it seemed little more than a mouth with fins. Minya watched it uneasily. It didn't seem to be coming toward them. It was flapping toward the smoke trail.

A loose cluster of citizens floated about the Checker's Hand. They couldn't all cling. There wasn't room, and the fungus wasn't holding together that well, either. They used spikes and tethers and showed a reluctance to approach Minya too closely.

The old one, Alfin, clung to the stalk. His look of terror had smoothed out, but he wouldn't talk and he wouldn't move.

The Grad studied her. He said, "Meen Ya. Have I got that right?"

"Close enough. *Minya.*"

"Ah. Mineeya—if we could reach your end of the tree, could you help us join your tribe?"

Their eyes were on her. The old one's seemed desperate. Well, it had had to come. She said, "We have a drought. Too many mouths to feed already."

The Grad said, "Your drought's probably ending about now. There'll be water."

"You're the Quinn Tribe Scientist's apprentice?"

"That's right."

"I accept what you say. How long before that new water grows new food? In any—"

"There'll be meatbirds in the wind now—"

"I don't want to go back!" There, it was said.

Clave asked, "Did you commit a crime?"

"I was thinking about committing a crime. I would have *had* to. Please!"

"Leave it then. But if we spend our lives here, they're likely to be short. Any passing triune family would think we're some kind of mushroom tidbit. Or that flying mouth that came out of the pond a minute ago—"

"Can't we get to another tree, one with nobody in it? I know we can't go anywhere now, but if we *could* get to Dalton-Quinn Tuft, we could get to another tree, don't you think?" They weren't buying it. Distract them? "Anyway, we can do better than we're doing now. We should be eating the Hand, not clinging to it. It won't last long now that it's been picked. We need a place to moor ourselves."

She pointed. "That."

That was a ragged sheet of bark, ten meters long and half that wide, a couple of hundred meters away. Most of its spin had by now been lost to air friction. Clave—the Chairman?—said, "I've been watching it for the past day. It isn't getting any closer. Treefodder, if we could move ourselves, I'd go for the pond!"

The Grad said, "Maybe the tree left a partial vacuum. That might pull it in. We can hope."

"We can do more than that. The bark may be close enough." Minya reached for the weapons.

A hand clamped on her wrist, the fingers circling almost twice around. "What do you think you're doing?"

Long, strong fingers, and no qualms about touching another citizen. There were men like this Clave in Dalton-Quinn Tuft. They had driven Minya into the Triune Squad... Minya shook her head, violently. She was his prisoner, and she had come as a killer. She spoke slowly, carefully.

"I think I can put a tethered arrow into that wood."

He hesitated, then released her. "Go ahead and try."

She used Sal's metal bow. The arrow slowed as it flew, and presently drifted. She tried another. Now two arrows floated at the ends of slack lines. There were murmurs of disgust as the boy Gavving reeled the lines in.

"I'd like to try that," Clave said and took the bow. When he released it, the string brushed his forearm, and he cursed. The arrow stopped short.

Minya never dithered. She made decisions fast, important or no: that too had helped to put her in the Triune Squad. Now she said, "Hold your left arm straight and rigid. Pull as hard as you can. Swing the string a little right and you won't hit your arm. Look along the arrow. Now don't move."

She picked up the loop of line and hurled it as hard as she could in the direction of the sheet of bark. Now the arrow wouldn't pull so much weight. "Whenever you feel ready."

The arrow sped away. It ticked a corner of the bark and stayed. Clave put pressure on the line, slowly, slowly... it was coming... the arrow worked itself free.

Clave repeated the exercise with no sign of impatience. The bark was meters closer now. He reached it again and pulled line in as if he were fighting some huge meatbird.

The bark came to them. Clave fired another arrow deep into the wood. They crossed on the line. Minya noticed Alfin's shuddering breath once he was safely moored to the bark.

And she noticed Clave's, "Well done, Minya." But he kept the bow.

"We'll used the other side of the bark for privacy," Clave instructed. "Now, the bark is all we've got, so there's no point in getting it dirty. When you feed the tree, the fertilizer should go outward."

"It'll float around us," Alfin said, his first words in hours. He must have seen how they looked at him. "Yes, I *do* have a better idea. Be at the rim when you feed the tree. The spin will throw it away from us. Won't it, Grad?"

"Yes. Good thinking."

Minya chewed on fan fungus. It was fibrous and nearly tasteless, but there was damp in it, and the damp was delicious. Minya looked longingly toward the pond, which was no closer. So near, so far...

They had eaten the smoked dumbo meat down to the bone, to prevent its spoiling. Maybe that had been a mistake. Their bellies were full, even overfull, but they were left thirstier yet. They could die of thirst here.

Aside from that, things were going well.

The golden-haired boy, Gavving: she had made a good choice there. Perhaps he thought he owed her his life. Perhaps it was true. Harmless as he looked, she had seen him kill twice. He'd make a better ally than enemy.

Alfin she couldn't judge. If he was *that* terrified of falling, he'd be dead soon anyway.

Merril was something else again. Legless, but she swung a fist like another woman's kick! After all she'd lived through, she must be tough. More: handicapped as she was, she'd be dead without friends. She must be well thought of, then. Minya intended to make Merril her friend.

The Grad was a dreamer. He'd never notice whether Minya was dead or alive.

Clave was the dominant male. Perhaps he still considered her an enemy. But she had brought them to this raft and let Clave take the credit. It couldn't hurt. If Clave thought he needed her, she didn't care if he trusted her.

But what else might he want of her?

Jayan and Jinny: they *both* acted as if Clave belonged to them, or vice versa. Two women sharing a man was not unheard of. They seemed to accept Clave's decisions. But would they resent a potential third? Best stay clear of Clave, if she could.

She could solve that problem, perhaps—

Merril spoke around a prodigious yawn. "Does it feel like sleeptime? I personally feel like I've been hit on the head."

Clave said, "I want someone awake at all times on each side of the tree. Is there anyone who *isn't* sleepy?"

"I'm not," said Alfin.

So Alfin and Jayan took the first day's watch. Gavving and Merril would be next, then—Minya ignored the rest. Physically and emotionally, she was exhausted. She settled for sleep, floating next to the bark, curled half into fetal position.

The sun was just passing north of Voy. She half noticed activity as citizens took their turns behind the bark, feeding the tree. Clave and Jinny slapped bugs off each other. Jayan presently disappeared around the edge. Alfin . . . Alfin was hovering next to her. He said, "Mineeya?"

She straightened. "Alfin. What do you want?"

"I want you for my wife."

Suddenly she was utterly awake. She *could not* afford enemies now. She said carefully, "I had not considered marriage." *He hadn't recognized her uniform!*

"You'd be a fool to turn me down. What better way to become one of us?"

"I will consider what you say," she said and closed her eyes.

"I'm a respected man. In Clave Tuft I supervised the tending of the treemouth."

Her arms hugged her knees and tightened her into a ball, without her volition.

Alfin's hand shook her shoulder. "Mineeya, your choices aren't wide, here on this sheet of bark. You came as a killer. Some of us may still see you that way."

He wouldn't leave her alone. Well. She tried to keep her voice cool, but she couldn't make herself uncoil, and it came out muffled. "Your argument is good. I should marry one of you. Clave is spoken for, isn't he?"

Alfin laughed. "Thrice."

"Amazing. And the Grad?"

"You're playing games with me. Consider my offer." Then he saw that she was sobbing.

Minya was horrified, but she couldn't stop. The sobs racked her like convulsions. She couldn't even muffle the sounds of distress. She wanted a man, yes, but not this man! Did she have a choice? She might find herself forced to mate this ugly, abrasive old man, only to prevent Quinn Tribe from killing her. Or she could speak of her oath to the Triune Squad and never be mated at all. It was just too much.

"I—I'll come back when you're feeling better." She heard Alfin's distress and guilt, then quiet. When she forced herself to look, she saw him weaving among the sleepers—stealthily?—to reach the far edge of the bark.

She had lost her home, her family, her friends; she was lost in the sky, cast among strangers. *Copsik!* How could he inflict such a decision on her now? *Filthy treefeeding copsik!*

The tears were drying on her face. At least no Triune Squad companion had seen her so shamed. It came to her that her tears had driven Alfin away...just as they had been her primary defense when she was fourteen.

But what could she *do*? She hadn't been quite fair to the old man. He had spoken a partial truth, one she'd already considered: marriage was the way into Quinn Tribe.

—And she found that she had made her decision after all.

Dared she sleep now? She must. The sun was a hand's breadth past Voy; and she curled up and slept.

* * *

When the sun neared Voy again, Minya woke. Some had the knack. Minya could tell herself when to sleep and when to wake, and she would.

She flexed muscles without moving much. She was thirsty. There was restless motion around her. The Grad seemed to be having a nightmare. She watched until he was quiet.

Alfin shook Gavving awake, then Merril. He settled down while Gavving disappeared to his post on the far side. Minya waited a little longer, for Jayan and Alfin to fall asleep.

Alfin clutched the bark with all his fingers and toes and, for all Minya could tell, his teeth. His face was pressed to the bark, denying the sky. He'd never sleep that way; but he wouldn't see her either.

She uncurled and made her way to the edge of the bark. Merril watched her go. Minya waved and pulled herself around to the smooth side of the bark sheet.

Gavving saw her coming. He started moving away from her— to give her privacy? She called, "Wait! Gavving!"

He paused.

"Gavving, I want to talk to you."

"All right." But he was wary.

She didn't want that. "I don't have any weapons," she said, and then, "Oh. I'll prove it."

"You don't have to—"

She pulled her blouse over her head and moored it to the bark. She came closer, wishing for toeholds to let her walk upright. This crawling lacked the dignity she wanted. At least she'd shed the lumpy-pregnant look of the Triune Squad.

She said, "There are no pockets in my pants. You can see that. I want to tell you why I can't go back to Dalton-Quinn Tuft."

"Why?" He was trying to keep his eyes off her breasts, on her face. "I mean, I'm willing to listen. I've got a name for asking embarrassing questions." He tried to laugh; it stuck in his throat. "But shouldn't everyone hear this?"

She shook her head. "They might have killed me, without you. Gavving, let me tell you about the Triune Squad."

"You told me. You're fighters, and you're all women, even the men."

"That's right. If a man wants to be a woman, or a woman doesn't ever want to be pregnant, she joins the Triune Squad. She can serve the tribe without making babies."

Gavving digested that. "If you don't want to make babies, they make you fight?"

"That's right. And it isn't just fighting. It's anything dangerous. This—" She pulled the rim of her pants down, and he shied, perhaps flinching at the scar. It ran half a meter from her short ribs past her hip. "Tip of a swordbird's tail. If my jet pod hadn't fired I would have been all over the sky."

She suddenly wondered if he might see it as a flaw, rather than a matter of pride. Too late . . . and better that he see it now than later.

He said, "Three of us fought a swordbird a few waketimes ago. Two came back."

"They're dangerous."

"So. You don't like men?"

"I didn't. Gavving, I was only fourteen."

He stared. "Why would a man bother a fourteen-year-old girl?"

She hadn't thought she could still laugh, but she did. "Maybe it was the way I looked. But they all . . . bothered me, and the only way out was the Triunes."

He waited.

"And now I'm twenty-two and I want to change my mind and I *can't*. Nobody changes her mind once she's in the Triune Squad. I could be killed for even asking, and I *did* ask—" She caught her voice rising. This wasn't going as planned. She whispered, "He told me I should be ashamed of myself. Maybe he'll tell. I don't care. I'm not going back."

He reached as if to pat her shoulder and changed his mind. "Don't worry about it. We can't move anyway. If we could, well, an empty tree would still be a better bet."

"And I want to make babies," she said and waited.

He *must* have understood. He didn't move. "With me? Why me?"

"Oh, treefodder, why can't you just...all right, who else? The Grad lives all in his head. Alfin's afraid of falling. Clave? I'm *glad* he's here, he's a good leader. But Clave's...type pushed me into the Triunes in the first place! He scares me, Gavving. I saw you kill Sal and Smitta, but you still don't *scare* me. I think you had to do that." She knew instantly that she'd said the wrong thing.

He started to tremble. "I didn't hate them. Minya, they were killing us! Without a word. They were your friends, weren't they?"

She nodded. "It's been a bad, bad waketime. But I'm not going back."

"All for a fan fungus."

"Gravving, don't turn me down. I...couldn't stand it."

"I'm not turning you down. I've just never done this before."

"Neither have I." She pulled her pants off, then didn't have a spike to tether them. Gavving saw the problem and grinned. He pounded a spike into the bark and added two tethers. One he tied to Minya's pants, then to his own pants and tunic. The other he tied around his waist.

"I've watched," he confided.

"That's a relief. I never did." She reached to touch what his pants had covered. A man had put his male member into her hand once, against her will, and it hadn't looked like this...except that it was changing before her eyes. Yes.

She had thought she could just let it happen. It wasn't like that. But she was used to using her feet as auxiliary hands, and thus she pulled him against her. She'd been warned against the pain; some of the Triunes had not joined while they were still virgins. She had known far worse.

Then Gavving seemed to go mad, as if he were trying to make two people one. She held him and let it happen...but now it was happening to her! She'd made this decision in the cool aftermath of disaster, but now it was changing her, *yes* she wanted them joined forever, she could pull them closer yet with her heels and her hands...no, they were coming apart...it was ending...ending.

When she had her breath back she said, "They never told me *that*."

Gavving heaved a vast sigh. "They told me. They were *right*. Hey, didn't you hurt?" He pulled away from her, a little, and looked down. "There's blood. Not a lot."

"It hurt. I'm tough. Gavving, I was so afraid. I didn't want to die a virgin."

"Me too," he said soberly.

A hand shook the Grad's ankle and pulled him out of a nightmare. "Uh! What... ?"

"Grad. Can you think of any reason Gavving shouldn't make a baby with a woman?"

"What then, a musrum?" His head felt muzzy. He looked around. "Who is it, the prisoner?"

Merril said, "Yes. Now, I don't see any reason to stop it, unless she's got something else in mind. I just want to keep an eye on them. But someone has to be on watch."

"Why me?"

"You were closest."

The Grad stretched. "Okay. You're on watch. I'll keep track of the prisoner."

Merril's glare lost out to a smile. "All right, that's fair."

The Grad heard voices as he poked his head around the edge of the bark. Gavving and Minya floated at the end of a tether, quite naked, talking. "A hundred and seventy-two of us," Minya was saying. "Twice as many as you?"

"About that."

"Enough to crowd the tuft, anyway. The Triune Squad isn't a punishment. It's a refuge. We *shouldn't* be having children any faster than we are. And I was good, you know. I fight like a demon."

"You need a refuge from... uh, this?"

A laugh. "This, and being pregnant. My mother died of her fourth pregnancy, and that was me."

"Aren't you afraid now?"

"Sure. Are you volunteering to carry it for me?"

"Sure."

"Good enough." They moved together. The Grad was intrigued and embarrassed. His eyes shifted... and the sky had opened a mouth.

The shock only lasted a moment. A great empty mouth closed and opened again. It was rotating slowly. An eye bulged above one jaw; something like a skeletal hand was folded below the other. It was a klomter away and *still* big.

The beast turned, ponderously, still maintaining its axial rotation. Its body was short, its wings wide and gauzy. No illusion: it really was mostly mouth and fins, and big enough to swallow their entire bark raft. Sunlight showed through its cheeks.

It was cruising the clouds of bugs left in the wake of the disaster. *Not* a hunting carnivore. Good. But wasn't there such a beast in the Scientist's records? With a funny name—

Merril touched the Grad's shoulder, and he jumped. "I'm a little worried about the bug-eater," she said. "We're embedded in bugs, have you noticed?"

"Noticed! How could I not?" But in fact he had learned to ignore them. The bugs weren't stinging creatures, but they were all around the bark raft, millions and millions of winged creatures varying from the size of a finger down to dots barely big enough to see. "We're a little big to be eaten up by accident."

"Maybe. What's happening with—?"

"I would say Gavving is in no danger. I'll keep an eye open, though."

"Good of you."

"We're being watched."

Minya's whole body convulsed in reflex terror. Gavving said, "Easy! Easy! It's only the Grad."

She relaxed. "Will they think we're doing wrong?"

"Not really. Anyway, I could marry you."

He heard an incipient stutter when she said, "Are you sure you want to do that?"

For a fact, he was not. His mind lurched and spun. The destruction of the tree had been no more disorienting than this first act of love. He loved Minya now, and feared her, for the pleasure she could give or withhold. Would she think she owned him? The lesson of Clave's marriage, what he knew of it, was not lost on him. Like Mayrin, she would be older than her mate . . .

And none of that mattered. There were four women in Quinn Tribe. Jayan and Jinny were with Clave; that left Merril and Minya. Gavving said, "I'm sure. Shall we go make an announcement?"

"Let them sleep," she said and snuggled close. Her eyes tracked a moving mouth sweeping through the clouds of bugs. It was closer now. It didn't have teeth, just lips, and a tongue like a restlessly questing snake. It rotated slowly: a way of watching the entire sky for danger.

"I wonder if it's edible," Gavving said.

"Me, I'm thirsty."

"There has to be a way to reach that pond."

"Gavving . . . dear . . . we need sleep too. Isn't your watch about over?"

His face cracked in a great yawn, closed in a grin. "I've got to tell someone."

The Grad was curled half into the fetal position, snoring softly. Gavving jerked twice on his tether and said, "We're getting married."

The Grad's eyes popped open. "Good thinking. Now?"

"No, we'll wait till sleeptime's over. It's your watch."

"Okay."

Chapter Ten

The Moby

VOICES WOKE HER. SHE CAME AWAKE FULLY ALERT, THIRSTY AND nervous.

He was young. She had given him what he wanted, had virtually forced it on him. He would lose interest. He would remember that she'd tried to kill him. He'd had hours to change his mind—

The voices were some distance away, but she heard them clearly. "—Ten years older than you, and you don't have the bride-price . . . but that's trivia. Six or seven days ago she was trying to kill us all!"

"She could have her pick of us." Clave speaking, and he was amused. "All but me, of course. You wouldn't like that, would you, loves?"

"I think it's wonderful," said Jayan or Jinny. The other twin said, "It's—hopeful."

"Gavving, you are not old enough to know what you're doing!"

"Feed it to the tree, Alfin."

Gavving noticed Minya when she stirred and pulled herself back to the bark. "Hello," he called. "Ready?"

"Yes!" Too eager? It was a little late to be coy! "What kind

100

of ceremony will it be? We can't use mine. I left our Scientist in the Tuft." *And he'd have me killed.*

"There's that too," said Alfin. "The Scientist—"

The Grad said, "I'm the Scientist now."

Ignoring Alfin's contemptuous snort, he opened his pack and spread the contents. Packed in spare clothing were four small flat boxes of starstuff—plastic—and a flat, polished surface that was glassy, like the Chairman's mirror, but didn't reflect.

Quinn Tribe seemed as surprised as Minya. Gavving asked, "Have you been carrying that all along?"

"No, I materialized it from thin air. We Scientists have our ways, you know."

"Oh, sure."

They grinned at each other. The Grad picked up the mirror and one of the boxes. He fitted the box into the thick rim of the mirror. "Prikazyvat Menu."

The Grad's pronunciation had shifted; it was odd, archaic. Minya had heard the Dalton-Quinn Scientist speak like that. The mirror responded: it glowed like the diffuse nighttime sun, then bloomed with tiny black print.

Minya couldn't read it. The Grad apparently could. He pulled the box loose and substituted another. "Prikazyvat Menu...Okay. Prikazyvat Record," he said briskly. "First day since sleeptime, the first sleep following the breakup of the tree, year three hundred and seventy. Jeffer speaking as Scientist. Quinn Tribe consists of eight individuals...Prikazyvat Pause."

Then nothing happened, until Minya couldn't stand it anymore. "What's wrong?"

The Grad looked up. His face was a mask of pain. A keening moan tore through his throat. Crystal lenses trembled over his eyes. Tears didn't run here, without tide to pull them.

Clave put his hand on the Grad's shoulder. "Take a minute. Take as long as you need."

"I've been trying not to...think about it. The Scientist. He knew. He sent these with me. What good does it do if we're dying too?"

"We're not dying. We're a little thirsty," Clave said firmly.

"We're all dead except us! I feel like recording it makes it real."

Clave glared around him. The tears were about to become contagious. Jayan and Jinny were sniffling already. Minya had to remind herself that Dalton-Quinn Tuft still lived, invisibly far, somewhere.

Clave snapped, "Come on, Scientist. You've got a marriage to perform."

The Grad gulped and nodded. Teardrops broke loose and floated away, the size of tuftberries. He cleared his throat and said in a creditably crisp voice, "Prikazyvat Record. The tree has been torn in half. Seven of us survive, plus a refugee from the outer tuft. Marriage between Minya Dalton-Quinn and Gavving Quinn exists as of now. No children are yet born. Terminate." He pulled the box from the mirror and said, "You're married."

Minya was stunned. "That's it?"

"That's it. My first act as Scientist. Tradition says you should consummate the marriage the first chance you—"

"Just what have you got there?" Alfin demanded.

"Everything I need," the Grad said. "This cassette is recent records. It used to be medicine, but the Scientist ran out of room and erased it. We couldn't use that stuff anyway. Starmen got sick in ways nobody ever heard of and used medicines nobody ever heard of either... This cassette is life forms, this one is cosmology, this one is old records. They're all classified, of course."

"Classified?"

"Secret." The Grad started rolling the gear in clothing again.

Clave said, "Hold it."

The Grad looked at him.

"Is there anything in your classified knowledge that we might need to know, to go on living?" Clave paused, not long enough for the Grad to answer. "If not, why should we guard that stuff, or let you carry it to slow you down?" Pause. "If so, you're hiding knowlege we need. Why should we protect you?"

The Grad gaped.

"Grad, you're valuable. We're down to eight, we can't spare

even one. But if you know why we need a Scientist more than an apprentice hunter, you'd better show us now."

It was as if the Grad had been frozen with his mouth open. Then...he gave a jerky nod. He chose a cassette and fitted it into the rim of the nonmirror. He said, "Prikazyvat Find *moby*: em, oh, bee, wye."

The screen lit, filled with print. The Grad read, "'*Moby* is a whale-sized creature with a vast mouth and vertical cheek slots that are porous, used as filters. It feeds by flying through clouds of insects. Length: seventy meters. Mass: approx eight hundred metric tons. One major eye. Two smaller eyes, better protected and probably near-sighted for close work, on either side of a single arm. It stays near ponds or cotton-candy jungles. It prefers to be spinning, for stability and to watch for predators, since there is no safe direction in the free-fall environment. Moby avoids large creatures and also shies from our CARMs. When attacked it fights like Captain Ahab: its single arm is tipped with four fingers, and the fingers are tipped with harpoons grown like fingernails.'"

Clave glanced over his shoulder. They had a side view of the flying mouth. Despite the swarm of insects near the raft, it was going around them. "That?"

"I'd think so."

"Carms? Captain Ahab? Whale-sized?"

"I don't know what any of that means."

"Doesn't matter, I guess. So. It's timid, and it eats bugs, not citizens. Doesn't sound like a threat."

"And *that* is why you need a Scientist. Without the cassettes you wouldn't know anything about it."

"Maybe," said Gavving, "we don't want it to go around us."

He explained, stumbling a little. Nobody laughed. Maybe they were too thirsty. Clave studied the massive bug-eater, pursed his lips, nodded...

Clave stood as Minya posed him, gripping the steel bow in his left hand, drawing the bowstring halfway back toward his cheek. It felt awkward. Instead of one of Minya's mini-harpoons, a meter and a half of his own harpoon protruded before him.

The moby was watching him. He waited until the creature's spin put the major eye on its far side. "Throw the line," he said.

Gavving hurled the coiled line toward the moby. Clave let it unroll for a moment, then sent the harpoon after it.

The harpoon wobbled in flight, until the trailing line dragged it straight again. With the steel bow and Clave's muscles to propel it, the massive harpoon might have flown as far as the moby. It didn't. It didn't even come close.

"Reel it in and coil the line," he told Alfin. To the others he said, "Arrows. Put some arrows in the beast. Get it mad. Get its attention."

The Grad's arrow went wide, and Clave stopped him from wasting another. Gavving's and Minya's were flying true, and each had fired another when Clave said, "Stop. We want it mad, not scared, not injured. Grad, how timid is that thing likely to be?"

"I read you everything I know."

Classified! The first chance he got, Clave was going through all of the information on all of those "cassettes." He'd make the Grad read them to him.

The moby's gauzy tail was in motion. It had spotted the harpoon's motion and was edging away. Then the first arrows reached it. One struck the fin, one a cheek, neither with any great force.

The moby convulsed. Its fins thrashed and it turned. A third arrow struck near its major eye. It turned to face them.

"Alfin, have you got that line coiled?"

"Not yet."

"Then hurry, you copsik! Are we all tethered?"

The sky had opened a mouth; it gaped and grew huge. A skeletal arm folded forward, presenting four harpoons. Alfin asked, "Do we want to hurt it now?"

Clave discarded the metal bow and took up the harpoon. "Treefodder. I want this in its *tail*."

The moby obliged. Its tail flicked forward—and they felt the wind—as it circled to examine the situation. As the tail came into sight, Clave cast. The harpoon struck solidly in the meaty part, ahead of the spreading translucent fin. The moby shuddered and continued to advance.

The "hand" lashed forward. Gavving whooped and leapt from between closing horn harpoons, away into the sky, until his tether went taut and pulled him around the edge of the bark. Minya yelled and slashed at the "hand." "Feels like bone," she reported and swung again.

Clave snatched up another harpoon and jumped toward the tremendous face. He pricked the creature's lip before his line pulled him back. The great skeletal fingers curled around behind him. Minya's sword slashed at a joint, and one of the harpoon-fingers was flying loose.

The moby snatched its hand back fast. Its mouth closed and stayed that way. The creature backpedaled with side fins.

Gavving reeled himself back to the bark. They watched the moby turning, retreating.

The bark raft surged. The moby stopped, turned to look back. The raft was following it. It began swimming strongly against the air.

A point of sunlight blazed near the edge of the pond. Vagrant breezes rippled the surface. Shadows moved within. A distant seed pod sent a tendril growing across a klomter of space toward the water. Gavving licked his lips and yearned.

Tens of thousands of metric tons of water dwindled in their wake.

Clave was cursing steadily. He stopped, then said, "Sorry. The moby was supposed to dive into the water and try to lose us."

Gavving opened his mouth, reconsidered . . . and spoke anyway. "My idea. Why aren't you blaming me?"

"I'd still get the blame. I'm the Chairman. Anyway, it was worth a try! I just wish I knew where the beast was taking us."

They waited to learn.

Gavving's eyes traced the line of the Smoke Ring, congealing out of the background of sky into the pale blue of water vapor and distance. Toothpick splinters, all aligned, might have been a grove of integral trees. Tens of thousands of klomters beyond, a clot of white storm marked Gold. A thickening halfway down the arch toward Voy would be the far Clump.

Here were all the celestial objects a child had once wondered about. Harp had told him that he might see them someday. More practical heads had denied this. The tree moved at the whim of natural forces, and nobody left the tree.

He had left the tree, and was married, and marooned, and thirsty.

Quinn Tribe clung along the forward edge of the bark raft. At Clave's insistence they had donned their packs. Anything could happen... but nothing had, except that the pond continued to dwindle.

"So near and yet so far," the Grad said. "Don't we still have a few jet pods?"

"Not enough." Clave looked around him. "At least we haven't lost anyone. Okay. We're moving, and we're moving *out*; that's good, isn't it, Scientist? Thicker air?"

"Thicker anything," said the Grad. "Air, water, plants, meat, meat-eaters."

The moby was turning, swinging gradually east, and slowing. Tiring. Its fins folded against its side, presenting a streamlined egg-shape to the wind; it continued to fall outward, towing the bark raft. The pond had become a tiny jewel, glowing with refracted blue Voylight.

Clave said, "We'll cut loose as soon as we get near anything interesting. Integral tree, pond, forest, anything with water in it. I don't want anyone cutting the line too soon."

"Cloud ahead," Merril said.

A distant, clotted streamer of white fading into blue. Clave barked laughter. "How far ahead? Sixty, seventy klomters? Anyway, it isn't ahead, it's straight out from us. We're aimed almost east."

"Maybe not," said the Grad. "We're aimed out from east and moving pretty fast. Gavving, remember? 'East takes you out, out takes you west, west takes you in, in takes you east, port and starboard bring you back.'"

"What the treefodder is *that?*" Clave demanded. Gavving remembered, but he said nothing. It was 'classified'... and the
Grad had never told him what it meant.

But Minya was saying, "Every child learns that. It's supposed
to be the way to move, if you're lost in the sky but you've got
jet pods."

The Grad nodded happily. "We're being pulled east. We're
moving too fast for our orbit, so we'll fall outward and slow
down. I'll bet the moby is making for that cloud bank."

The moby's fins were spread and flapping slowly. There was
nothing at all ahead of them, out to where the arch of the Smoke
Ring formed from infinity. Minya moved her tether to bring
herself alongside Gavving. They clung to the rim of the bark and
watched the wisp of cloud out from them, and hoarded their
thirst.

The sun circled behind Voy.

Again. Already they had moved many klomters outward; the
day-night cycle had grown longer.

The cloud bank was growing. It was!

"It'll try to lose us in the fog," the Grad said with more hope
than conviction.

The moby hadn't moved for some time. The spike that tethered
the harpoon was working itself loose. Clave pounded another into
the wood and wrapped the slack line around it. But the cloud
bank was spreading itself across the sky.

Details emerged: streamlines, knots of stormy darkness. Lightning flashed deep within.

Jayan and Jinny took off their shirts. Alfin, enjoying the sight
without questions, suddenly said, "They're right. Get our shirts
off. Try to catch some of that wet."

Darkness brightened as the sun emerged below the edge of
the cloud. It continued to sink. They watched the first tenuous
edge of mist envelope them and began flapping their shirts.
Gavving asked, "Do you feel damp?"

Merril snarled, "I feel it, I smell it, I can't drink it! But it's
coming!"

Lightning flashed, off to the west. Gavving felt the mist now.

He tried to sqeeze water out of his shirt. No? Keep swinging it. Now? He wrung the shirt tight and tried to suck it, and got sweaty water.

They were all doing it now. They could barely see each other. Gavving had never in his life seen such darkness. The moby was invisibly far, but they felt the tugging of the tether. They swung their shirts and sucked the water and laughed.

There were big fat drops around them. It was getting hard to breathe. Gavving breathed through his shirt and swallowed the water that came through.

Light was gaining. Were they emerging from the cloud? "Clave? Maybe you want to cut that tether. Do we want to stay in here?"

"Anybody still thirsty?" Silence. "Drink your fill, but we can't live in here, breathing through our shirts. Let's trust the moby a while longer."

The pale green light was getting stronger. Through thinning fog Gavving thought he could see sky . . . green-tinged sky, with a texture to it. Green? Was this some effect in his eyes, due to the long, abnormal darkness?

Clave bellowed, "Treefodder!" and swung his knife. The harpoon tether sang a deep note, cut short as Clave slashed again. The line whipped free; the bark sheet shuddered.

Then they were out of the mist, in a layer of clear air. Gavving glimpsed the moby flapping away, free at last, and spared it only a glance. He was looking at square klomters of textured green, expanding, growing solid. It was a jungle, and they were going to ram.

Chapter Eleven

The Cotton-Candy Jungle

THE CARM WAS LIKE NOTHING ELSE IN THE UNIVERSE. IT WAS all right angles, inside and out; all plastic and metals, unliving starstuff. The white light that glowed from the dorsal wall was neither Voylight nor sunlight. Weirder lights crawled across the control panel and the bow window itself. The carm was mobile, where London Tree moved only with the help of the carm. If London Tree was a living thing inhabited by other living things, then Lawri saw the carm as a different form of life.

The carm was a mighty servant. It served Klance the Scientist, and Lawri. Sometimes it went away into the sky with Navy men as its masters. This time it carried Lawri too.

It grated on her nerves that she was not the carm's master here.

Seen through the picture-window bow, the jungle was green, dotted with every color of the rainbow—including overlaid scarlet dots that were heat sources. The Navy pilot pushed the talk button and said, "Let go."

Several breaths went by before Lawri heard, "We're loose."

The pilot touched attitude jet keys. A tide pulled Lawri for-

ward against her straps. Warriors had been clinging to nets outside the hull. Now they swept into view of the bow window as
the carm decelerated. A cloud of sky-blue men fell toward un-
dulating clouds of green.

The pilot released the keys after (by Lawri's count) twelve
breaths. She'd watched numbers flickering on a small display in
front of him. He'd released at zero. And the jungle was no longer
moving toward the carm's bow window.

"The savages haven't moved yet," he reported. He was ignoring
Lawri, or trying to; his eyes kept flicking to her and away. He'd
made it clear enough: a nineteen-year-old girl had no place here,
no matter what the First said. "They're just under the greenery.
Are you sure you want to do this?"

"We don't know who they are." The ancient microphone
put a squawk in the Squad Leader's voice. "If it's just fighters,
we'll retreat. We don't need fighters. If it's noncombatants, hiding—"

"Right."

"Have you found any other heat sources?"

"Not yet. That greenery is a pretty good reflector unless you're
looking right into it. We can pick up some meat. Flocks of
salmon birds... Squad Leader, I see something off to the side.
Something's falling toward the jungle."

"Something like what?"

"Something flat with people clinging to it."

"I see it. Could they be animals?"

"No. I'm using science," the pilot said.

The display superimposed on the bow window showed scarlet
dots clustered close. Warmer objects—salmon birds, for in-
stance—showed more orange in that display. Ribbon birds showed
as cooler: wavy lines of a darker, bloodier red... The pilot turned
and caught Lawri looking.

"Learned anything, darling?"

"Don't call me *darling*," Lawri said primly/evasively.

"Pardon me, Scientist's Apprentice. Have you learned enough
to fly this ship, do you think?"

"I wouldn't like to try it," Lawri lied. "Unless you'd like to teach me?" It was something she wanted very much to try.

"Classified," the pilot said without regret. He returned to his microphone. "That thing hit pretty hard. I'd say it's not a vehicle at all. Those people may be refugees from some disaster, just what we need for copsiks. Might even be glad to see us."

"We'll get to you when we . . . can." The Squad Leader sounded distracted, and with reason. Spindly savages taller than a man ought to be were boiling out of the green cloud, riding yellow-green pods bigger than themselves. They were clothed in green, hard to see.

There was a quick exchange of arrows as the armies neared each other. London Tree's warriors used long footbows: the bow grasped by the toes of one or both feet, the string by the hands. The cloud of arrows loosed by the savages moved more slowly, and the arrows were shorter.

"Crossbows," the pilot murmured. He played the jets, kicking the carm away from the fight. Lawri felt relief, until he started his turn.

"You'll endanger the carm! Those savages could snatch at the nets!"

"Calm down, Scientist's Apprentice. We're moving too fast for them." The carm curved back toward the melee. "We don't want them close enough for swordplay, not in free-fall."

If the Scientist had his wish, the carm would never be used for war at all. Putting his Apprentice aboard had been a major strategic victory. He'd told her, "Your sole concern is for the carm, not the soldiers. If the carm is threatened, it *must* be moved out of danger. If the pilot won't, you must."

He had not told her how to subdue a trained fighter, nor how to fly the ancient machine. The Scientist had never flown it himself.

Savages flew toward the bow window. Lawri saw their terrified eyes before the pilot spun the carm about. Masses thumped against the carm's belly. Lawri shuddered. She would do nothing, this time. She would more likely wreck the carm than save it . . . and there would be hell to pay even if she got home to London Tree.

The savages were grouping to attack again. The pilot ignored them. He eased the carm into the midst of his own warriors.

"Nice going. Thanks," said the radio voice. Lawri watched the cloud of savages advancing.

"We're all aboard," said the Squad Leader.

The carm turned and coasted across the green cotton, south-west. Savages screamed or jeered in its wake. They hadn't a hope of catching up.

There was time to look, and time to feel rising fear. Gavving tried to take it all in before the end.

It was curves and billows of green wall spotted with blossoms: yellow, blue, scarlet, a thousand shades and tones. Insects swarmed in clouds. Birds were there in various shapes, dipping into the blossoms or the insect clouds. Some looked like ribbons and moved with a fluttering motion. Some had membranous triangular tails; some were themselves triangles, with whiplike tails sprouting from the apex.

Far to the east was a dimple in the green, funnel-shaped, perhaps half a klomter across; distances were hard to judge. Would a jungle have a treemouth? Why would it be rimmed with gigantic silver petals? The biggest flower in the universe set behind the jungle's horizon as they fell.

The storm had hidden a jungle. He'd never seen one close, but what else could it be? The moby had planned this well, Gavving thought.

Birds were starting to notice the falling mass. Motionless wings and tails blurred into invisibility. Ribbons fluttered away, as if in a strong wind. Larger torpedo-shapes emerged from the greenery to study the falling bark sheet.

Clave was snapping orders. "Check your tethers! Arm yourselves! Some of those things look hungry. We'll be shaken up when we hit. Has anybody noticed anything I might miss?"

Gavving thought he saw where they'd strike. Green cloud. Could it be as soft as it looked? East and north, far away, more darting swarms of...dots at this distance...men?

"Men, Clave. It's inhabited."

"I see them. Treefodder, they're fighting! Just what we need, another war. Now what's *that*? Grad, do you see something like a moving box?"

"Yes."

"Well?"

Gavving located a brick-shape with rounded corners and edges. It was turning in sentient fashion, moving away from the battle. A vehicle, then...big...and glittering as if made of metal or glass. Men clung to its flanks.

The Grad said, "I never saw anything like it. Starstuff."

The aft end of the box was spiky with bell-shaped structures: four at each corner and one much larger in the middle. Nearly invisible flames, not flame-colored but the blue-white color of Voy, puffed from some of the small—nostrils? The vehicle stopped its turn and surged back into the battle.

"That should do it," Clave said. Gavving turned and saw what he had been doing: setting his last jet pods to orient the turning raft, so that the underside would strike first. It seemed to be working, but the jungle was hidden now. Gavving clutched the bark, waiting...

His head was ringing, his right arm was banged up somehow, his stomach was trying to find something to reject, and he couldn't remember where he was. Gavving opened his eyes and saw the bird.

It was torpedo-shaped, about the mass of a man. It hung over him, long wings stretched out and motionless while it studied him with two forward-facing eyes in deep sockets. The other side of its head bore a saw-toothed crest. Its tail was a ribbed fan; the four ribs ended each in a hooked claw.

Gavving looked around for his harpoon. The crash had bounced it free of his hand. It was meters away, slowly turning. He reached for his knife instead and eased himself out of the greenery in which he was half-buried. He whispered, "I'm meat. Are you?" intending it as a threat.

The bird hung back. Two companions had joined it. Their

mouths were long and blunt, and closed. *They don't bluff*, Gavving thought.

A fourth bird skimmed across the green cloud, moving fast, right at his head. He scrambled for cover as the bird dipped its tail hooks into the foliage and stopped dead. Gavving stayed where he was, half under the raft. The birds watched him mockingly.

A tethered harpoon thudded into a bird's side.

It screamed. The open mouth had no teeth, just a scissors-action serrated edge. The bird set itself whirling as it tried to snap at its belly. A third eye was behind the crest, facing backward.

The rest made their decision. They fled.

With his toes locked in branchlets, Alfin reeled the bird into knife range. By then Gavving had retrieved his own harpoon. He used it to pin the bird's tail while Alfin finished the kill, a performance that left Alfin's sleeves soaked in pink blood. A wide grin stretched his wrinkles into uncustomary patterns.

"Dinner," he said and shook his head as if he'd drunk too much beer. "I can't believe it. We made it. We're alive!"

During all the years in Quinn Tuft, Gavving couldn't remember seeing Alfin grin. How could Alfin be consistently morose in Quinn Tuft, and happy while lost in the sky? He said, "If we'd hit something solid at that speed we'd all be dead. Let's hope the luck holds."

Missing citizens emerged from the green depths. Merrill, Jayan, Jinny, Grad... Minya. Gavving whooped and gathered her in his arms.

Alfin asked, "Where's Clave?"

The others looked around. The Grad tethered himself to the bark and jumped toward the storm, with a turning motion. "I don't see him anywhere," he shouted back.

Jayan and Jinny burrowed into the foliage. Minya called, "Wait, you'll get lost!" and prepared to follow.

"He's here."

Clave was under the bark sheet. They moved it to expose him.

He was half-conscious and moaning softly. His thigh bent in the middle, and white bone protruded through skin and blood.

The Grad hung back, squeamishly; but everyone was looking at him, and it was clearly the Scientist's job. He set Alfin and Jayan to holding Clave's shoulders, Gavving to pulling on the ankle, while the Grad moved the bones into place. It took too long. Clave revived and fainted again before it was finished.

"That flying box," Alfin said. "It's coming here."

"We're not finished here," said the Grad.

The starstuff box fell toward them through the clear air between foliage and storm cloud. Men garbed in sky-blue clung to all four sides. The glassy end faced them like a great eye.

Clave's eyes had opened, but it didn't seem he understood. *Somebody* had to do something. Gavving said, "Alfin, Minya, Jinny, let's get the bark sheet out of sight, at least."

They turned it edgewise and pushed it down into the greenery. Gavving moved after it, and Minya after him, forcing their way through the thicket into dark green gloom. The foliage was dense at the surface. Underneath were open spaces and masses of springy branchlets.

"Grad?"

The Grad looked up. "Scientist."

"All right, Scientist. I need a Scientist," Alfin said. "Can you leave him for a moment?"

Clave was half-conscious and whimpering. He should be all right with two women watching him. "Call me if he starts thrashing around," he told them. He moved away, and Alfin followed.

"What's the problem?"

"I can't sleep."

The Grad laughed. "It's been a busy time. Which of us do you accuse of sleeping well?"

"I haven't slept since we reached the midpoint. We're in a jungle, we've got food and water, but Grad—Scientist, we're still falling!" Alfin's laugh surprised the Grad; it had a touch of hysteria in it.

Alfin didn't look good. His eyes were puffy, his breathing was irregular, he was as jumpy as tonight's dinner turkey. The Grad said, "You know as much about free-fall as I do. You learned it the same way. Are you about to run amok?"

"Feels that way. I'm not helpless. I killed a bird that was after Gavving." And for that moment his pride was showing.

The Grad mulled the problem. "I've got a bit of that scarlet fringe from the fans. You know how dangerous it is. Anyway, you don't want to sleep now."

Alfin glanced at the sky. The starstuff box was taking its sweet time, but... "No."

"When it's safe. And I haven't got much."

Alfin nodded and turned away. The Grad stayed where he was. He wanted solitude to nurse his jumpy stomach. He'd never set a broken bone before, and he'd had to do it without the Scientist's help...

Alfin made his way back toward Jayan and Merril and Clave. He looked back once, and the Grad was looking at the sky.

He looked back again, and the Grad was gone. Jayan screamed.

The darkness and the strange, dappled shadows made them almost invisible, even to each other. "We can hide in here," Gavving said.

Minya was nodding. "Burrow deep. Stick together. What about Clave?"

"We'll have to pull him through. What looks like a good spot?"

"None of it," Jinny said. "It would hurt him."

Gavving tracked a dense cluster of branchlets back to a single spine branch. "Cut here," he told Minya.

She didn't have room to swing. She used the sword as a saw, and it took her a hundred breaths or thereabouts. Then Gavving pushed against the freed end and found that the entire cluster moved outward as a plug. He pulled himself into open air and looked about him. "Merril! Here!"

"Good," Merril called. She and Alfin towed Clave toward the

opening, moving with frantic haste. The one-eyed box was too close. The occupants must be watching them by now.

They'd have to dig in fast, get lost in the deep branchlets. But—"Where's Jayan? Where's the Grad?"

"Gone," Merril puffed. "He's gone. Something pulled him down... into the thicket."

"*What?*"

"Move it, Gavving!"

They got Clave inside and pulled the plug-bush closed. Gavving saw that Clave's leg had been splinted with strips of a blanket and two of Minya's arrows.

"The men on the box," Minya said, "they'll follow us."

"I know. Merril, what got the Grad? An animal?"

"I didn't see. He yelled and disappeared. Jayan snatched up a harpoon and ducked through and saw people disappearing deeper in. She's trailing a line. Gavving, should we stop her? They'll trap her too."

Why did it all have to happen at once? Clave's leg, the kidnappers, the moving box—"Okay. The soldiers on the box would be fools to come in here. It's the natives' territory—"

"We're here."

"We're more desperate... never mind, you're right. We go after Jayan right *now*, because it gets us away from that starstuff relic. Merril—" Would Merril slow them down? Probably not, in free-fall. Okay. "Merril, me, Minya. We'll follow Jayan and see what's going on. Maybe we *can* bust the Grad loose. Jinny, you and Alfin follow as fast as you can, with Clave. Merril, where's Jayan's line?"

"Somewhere over there. Treefodder, why does it all have to happen at once?"

"Yeah."

Chapter Twelve

The Copsik Runners

BIRDS WERE RAISING AN INCREDIBLE RUCKUS. UNSEEN HANDS pulled the Grad headfirst through darkness and the rich smell of alien foliage. Branchlets no longer scratched his face; there must be open space around him.

He'd had no warning at all. Hands had grasped his ankles and pulled him down into another world. His yell was strangled by something stuffed into his mouth, something that wasn't clean, and a rag was tied to hold it in. A blow on the head convinced him not to struggle.

His eyes were beginning to adjust to the gloom.

A tunnel wound through the foliage. It was narrow: big enough for two to crawl side by side, not big enough to walk in. No need, the Grad thought. You couldn't walk with no tide.

His captors were human, roughly speaking.

They were all women, though this needed a second glance. They wore leather vests and trousers, dyed green. The looseness of the vests was their only concession to breasts. Three of the five wore their hair very short, and they all had a gaunt, stretched-out look: two and a half to three meters, taller than any of Quinn Tribe's men.

They held implements: small wooden bows on wooden platforms, the bowstrings pulled back, ready to fire.

They were making good time. The tunnel turned and twisted until the Grad was entirely disoriented. His directional senses wouldn't give him an *up*. It presently opened into a bulb-shape four or five meters across, with three other tunnels leading off. Here the women stopped. One pulled the rag out of his mouth. He spit to the side and said, "Treefodder!"

A woman spoke. Her skin was dark, her hair a compact black storm cloud threaded with white lightning. Her pronunciation was strange, worse than Minya's. "Why did you attack us?"

The Grad shouted in her face. "Stupid! We saw your attackers. They've got a traveling box made of starstuff. That's science! *We* got here on a sheet of bark!"

She nodded as if she'd expected that. "An eccentric way to travel. Who are you? How many are you?"

Should he be hiding that? But Quinn Tribe must find friends somewhere. Go for Gold—"Eight of us. All of Quinn Tribe, now, plus Minya, from the opposite tuft. Our tree came apart and left us marooned."

She frowned. "Tree dwellers? The copsik runners are tree dwellers."

"Why not? You don't get a tide anywhere else. Who're you?"

She studied him dispassionately. "For a captured invader, you are most impertinent."

"I've got nothing to lose." A moment after he said it, the Grad realized how true it was. Eight survivors had done their best to reach safety, and this was the end of it. Nothing left.

She had spoken. He said, "What?"

"We are Carther States," the black-haired woman repeated impatiently. "I am Kara, the Sharman." She pointed. "Lizeth. Hild." They looked like twins to the Grad's untrained eye: spectrally tall, pale of skin, red hair cropped two centimeters from the skull. "Ilsa." Ilsa's pants were as loose as her vest. That discrete abdominal bulge: Ilsa was pregnant. Her hair was blond fuzz; her scalp showed through. Long hair must be a problem among the branchlets. "Debby." Debby's hair was clean and straight and soft brown, and half a meter long, tied in back. How did she keep it that neat?

Sharman could mean *Shaman*, an old world for *Scientist*. Could mean *Chairman*, except that she was a woman...but strangers wouldn't do everything the way Quinn Tribe did. Since when did the Chairman take a name?

"You haven't given us your name," Kara said pointedly.

There was something left to him after all. He said it with some pride: "I'm the Quinn Tribe Scientist."

"Name?"

"The Scientist doesn't take one. Once I was called *Jeffer*."

"What are you doing in Carther States?"

"You'd have to ask a moby."

Lizeth snapped her knuckles across the back of his skull, hard enough to sting. He snarled, "I meant it! We were dying of thirst. We hooked a moby. Clave was hoping he'd try to lose us in a pond. He brought us here instead."

The Sharman's face didn't reveal what she thought of that. She said, "Well, it all seems innocent enough. We should discuss your situation after we eat."

The Grad's humiliation kept him silent...until he saw their meal and recognized the harpoon. "That's Alfin's bird."

"It belongs to Carther States," Lizeth informed him.

He found he didn't care. His belly was stridently empty. "That wood looks too green to make a cookfire—"

"Salmon bird is eaten raw, with falling onion when we can get it."

Raw. Yuk. "Falling onion?"

They showed him. Falling onion was a plant parasite that grew at the forks of the branchlets. It grew as a green tube with a spray of pink blossoms at the tip. The pretty brown-haired woman named Debby assembled a handful and cut the blossom-ends off. Ilsa's sword carved the scarlet meat in translucently thin slices.

Meanwhile Kara bound the Grad's right wrist to his ankles,

then freed his left. "Don't untie anything else," she warned him.

Raw meat, he thought and shuddered; but his mouth watered. Hild wrapped sheets of pink meat around the stalks and passed one to the Grad. He bit into it.

His mind went blank. You learned to put hunger out of your mind during a famine . . . but he had definitely been hungry. The meat had an odd, rubbery texture. The flavor was rich; the onion taste was fiery, mouth-filling.

They watched him eat. *I have to talk to them*, he thought hazily. *It's our last chance. We have to join them. Otherwise, what is there? Stay here and be hunted, or let the invaders catch us, or jump into the sky* . . . The man-sized bird was dwindling. Lizeth seemed content to carve slices until they stopped disappearing; Debby was now cutting the falling onions to stretch them. The women had long since finished eating. They watched with irritating smiles. The Grad wondered if they would consider a belch bad manners, and belched anyway, and had to swallow again. He'd learned while climbing the tree: a belch was bad news in free-fall, without tide to bring gas to the top of the stomach.

He asked for water. Lizeth gave it to him in a squeezegourd. He drank a good deal. The falling onion had run out. Feeling pleasantly full, the Grad topped off his meal with a handful of foliage.

Nothing could be entirely bad when he felt this good.

Kara the Sharman said, "One thing is clear. You are certainly a refugee. I never saw a starving copsik runner."

A test? The Grad took his time swallowing. "Cute," he said. "Now that that's established, shall we talk?"

"Talk."

"Where are we?"

"Nowhere in particular. I wouldn't lead you to the rest of the tribe until I knew who you were. Even here, the copsik runners might find us."

"Who are they, these . . . runners?"

"Copsik runners. Don't you use the word *copsik*?" It sounded more like *corpsik* when she said it.

He answered, "It's just an insult-word."

"Not to us or them. They take us for corpsiks, to work for them the rest of our lives. *Boy, what are you doing?"*

The Grad had reached for his pack with his free hand. "I am the Quinn Tribe Scientist," he said in freezing tones. "I thought I might find some background on that word."

"Go ahead."

The Grad unwrapped his reader. He had Carther States' undivided attention. The women were awed and wary; Lizeth held her spear at the ready. He chose the records cassette, inserted it into the reader, and said, "Prikazyvat Find copsik."

NOT FOUND

"Prikazyvat Find—" the Grad said and held the reader to Kara's face. The Sharman shied, then spoke to the machinery. "Corpsik."

CORPSICLE?

The Grad said, "Prikazyvat Expound."

The screen filled with print. The Grad asked, "Can you read it?"

"No," Kara said for them all.

"'*Corpsicle* is an insult-term first used to describe people frozen for medical purposes. In the century preceding the founding of the State, some tens of thousands were frozen immediately after death in the hope of someday being revived and cured. This was found to be impossible. The State later made use of the stored personalities. Memory patterns could be recorded from a frozen brain, and RNA extracted from the central nervous system. A brainwiped criminal could thus be fitted with a new personality. No citizenship was conferred upon these corpsicles. The treatment was later refined and used by passengers and crew on long interstellar voyages.

"'The seeder ramship *Discipline*'s crew included eight corpsicles. The memory sets were those of respected citizens of advanced age, with skills appropriate to an interstellar venture. It was hoped that the corpsicles would be grateful to find themselves in healthy, youthful bodies. This assumption proved—' I can't make sense of all that. One thing seems clear enough. A copsik isn't a citizen. He has no rights. He's property."

"That's right," said Debby, to the Sharman's evident annoyance.

So the Sharman doesn't trust me. So? "How do they find you in here? There must be cubic klomters of it, and you know it and they don't. I don't see why you fight at all."

"They find us. Twice now they have found us hidden in the jungle," Kara said bitterly. "Their Sharman is better than I am. It may be that their science enhances their senses. Grad, we would be glad to have your knowledge."

"Would you make us citizens?"

The pause lasted only seconds. "If you fight," said Kara.

"Clave broke his leg coming down."

"We make citizens only of those who will fight. Our warriors are fighting now, and who knows if they will repell the corpsik runners? If we can hurt a few, perhaps they will not seek out the children and old men and women who host guests."

Guests? Oh, the *pregnant* ones. "What about Clave and the women? What happens to them?"

The Sharman shrugged. "They may live with us, but not as citizens."

Not good, but it might be the best they could get. "I can't say yes or no. We'll have to talk. Kara...ah!"

"What is it?"

"I just remembered something. Kara, there are kinds of light you can't see. There used to be machines that could see the warmth of a body. That's how they find you."

The women looked at each other in dread. Debby whispered, "But only a corpse is cold."

"So light little fires all through the forest. Make them check each one."

"Very dangerous. The fire might..." she trailed off. "Never mind. Fires go out unless fanned. The smoke smothers them. It might be possible after all, near the jungle surface."

The Grad nodded and reached for more foliage. Things were looking better. If some could become citizens, they could protect the rest. Perhaps Quinn Tribe had found a home...

* * *

"Three groups, and they're all going deeper. The traces are getting blurred," said the pilot's blurred voice. The carm hung behind Squad Leader Patry's shoulder, bow aimed at the jungle. "Are you going after them?"

"Groups how big?"

"Three and three and a bigger group. The big group started first. You probably won't catch them."

In the hands of Patry's men a mass of greenery rose from the rest and floated free. Patry reported, "We've found where they dug in. Okay, we're going after them." He joined the waiting men. "Mark, take the point. The rest of you follow me. Go wide of that yellow stuff, it's poison fern."

Mark was a dwarf, the only man in London Tree who could wear the ancient armor, and thus the only possible custodian of the spitgun. Ten years ago he had tended to shy back from an attack, until he gained confidence in his invulnerability. The men had called him Tiny until Patry himself raised hell about it. Mark was born to wear the armor. He'd learned to wear it well.

He climbed past the severed bush and into the dark with London Tree's infantry behind him.

The agony was real, centered above Clave's knee, but spreading in flashes throughout his body. The rest faded in and out. He was being towed through a tunnel. Soon the Scientist's plant extracts would erase the pain. But hadn't the plants died in the drought? And... the tree was gone. There wasn't any Scientist, and the Grad had no drugs, and the Grad was gone too. Too few survivors followed the Grad through green gloom. Clave's pitiful remnant of a tribe was split, and there was no medicine for an injured man.

Jinny and Minya stopped abruptly, jarring his leg. The pain shouted in his brain. Then they had plunged into the tunnel's branchlet walls, and Clave tumbled in free-fall, abandoned.

His tumble turned him and the dream turned nightmare. He faced a bulky, faceless silver thing. The apparition raised something...metal? A splinter stabbed into Clave's ribs. He plucked it out. His mind was muzzy...was it a thorn? The metal-and-glass creature forced itself through the tunnel wall, ignoring Clave. Acolytes followed it in, blue men carrying huge, unwieldy bows.

The pain had gone and reality was fading. Here was medicine after all.

"I see you've caught up with the first group," the pilot said. "The forward group has stopped. The middle group has joined them. Maybe you should quit."

"I sent Toby back with two copsiks. The third had a broken leg, so we left him. We're almost at full strength. Let's just see what happens."

"Patry, is there something unusual about your mission?"

Classified...oh, what did it matter? "Catch some copsiks. Shoot some meatbirds. Collect some spices. Pick up anything scientific." That last wasn't usual. Maybe the First Officer wanted the Scientist to owe him a favor. Patry didn't comment, not with the Scientist's Apprentice listening.

"Fine. You've got copsiks. How many do you need? You don't really expect to find science here, do you?"

"There's a big group ahead. I'm going to at least look at the situation." Patry turned the volume down. Pilots tended to argue a point to death, and Patry wanted silence.

Gavving hadn't burrowed far before Jayan's line led them to a tunnel carved through the foliage. They moved faster then.

Despite its alien smell, Gavving was hungry enough to try the foliage. The taste was alien too; but it was sweet and went down well. He ate more.

In fact, he felt almost at home here. His toes thrust into branchlets and pushed him down the tunnel in remembered rhythm. Cheeping and croaking rose from thousands of unseen throats. They wouldn't be birds, this deep in the thicket; but they chirped, and if need came they could probably fly. The sound was the sound of Gavving's childhood, before the drought killed the small life throughout the tuft.

It was an effort to remember that this wasn't Quinn Tuft; that he followed enemies who knew this thicket as Gavving knew his tree.

Minya, it seemed, didn't have that problem. She was snatching handfuls of foliage, but the hand she used clutched an arrow, and her bow was in the other.

They were moving faster than the line that slithered ahead of them. Merril wound it up as they went. The coil trailed from a thumb; she used both hands to move herself. When Gavving noticed, he said, "Let me do that for a while. Eat."

"Keep your hands free!" A little later, perhaps regretting her sharpness, she said, "I need my hands to move. You can fight with your hands. Where's your harpoon?"

"On my back. We're all right as long as Jayan is still pulling on the line," he said and immediately noticed that the line had gone slack. Gavving reached for his harpoon before he moved again.

A disembodied white arm thrust out of the tunnel wall and beckoned.

Jayan looked out through a screen of branchlets. Her voice was a hoarse and frightened whisper. "They're ahead of us."

"Where?"

"Not far. Don't take the tunnel. There's a long, straight part, then it swells out. They'd see you. Go where I go, or they'll hear branchlets breaking."

They followed her into the thicket.

Jayan had broken a trail. Twice she'd had to cut thicker spine branches. In the end they watched from behind a screen of branchlets as the Grad spoke with the weird women.

They were lean and elongated, like exaggerated cartoons of the ideal woman, or like a further stage in human evolution. They looked relaxed. So did the Grad. His feet and one hand were bound, but he was casually eating foliage while they talked. The carcass of a bird was mostly bones.

Minya's breath was warm on his shoulder. She whispered, "It looks like the Grad may have talked them around. I can't hear, can you?"

"No." There was too much birdsong...and an occasional crackling as someone moved, making Gavving glad for the birdsong. Still, someone was making too much noise...

Minya leapt through the branchlets in a hideous crackling, straight into the midst of the wierd women, screaming, "Monster made of starstuff! There!"

Gavving leapt after her, ready to do battle. He'd have appreciated some warning—

The weird women didn't hesitate an instant. Five of them jumped toward other tunnels and were gone in three directions. The sixth jumped clumsily. She struck the edge of the opening and tumbled away unconscious. Had she struck *that* hard?

The Grad was struggling to free his hands. Gavving felt something sting his leg. He turned to fight.

To fight *what?* A thing of glass and metal! There were men behind it—ordinary men who floated free, sighting over their toes as they pulled huge bows taut with their hands—but they didn't fire. The thing of science pointed a metal tube at Minya, then at the Grad. Gavving's harpoon bounced off its mirror-glass face. It pointed at Gavving and stung him again.

You can't fight science, Gavving thought, and he drew his long knife and leapt at the monster. Then everything went dreamy.

"You're too deep," the pilot said. "I can't get individual readings on you. I've got a hot spot, a cluster of a dozen or so. You and the copsiks together?"

"Sounds right. We've got six copsiks here, one already tied up for us. We'll leave the one with no legs. That gives us seven total. A bunch went off through the tunnels. Can you locate them?"

"Yes. It looks like they're together again. There's you, and there's a tighter, brighter spot east of you. I'd say quit now. Kill some meatbirds on the way out."

"There's something here...I've got something scientific here, something I don't understand. Too scientific by half." Squad Leader Patry picked up a rectangular mirror that didn't reflect, a mirror that shone by its own light. With some trepidation he flipped an obvious switch. The light went out, to his relief. "You're right, we've got enough. We're coming out."

Chapter Thirteen

The Scientist's Apprentice

LASSITUDE... AN ODD, PLEASANT SENSATION LIKE FIZZING IN the blood... constriction and resistance at his wrists and ankles... memories drifting into place, sorting themselves. The Grad waited until his mind was straight before he opened his eyes.

He was bound again, tension at wrists and ankles holding his body straight. *Getting to be a habit.* His bonds gave as he tugged at them. He was tied to netting, face down to a wall that was hard and cold and smooth, and translucent to a millimeter's depth, over a gray substrate.

He'd never seen the like before; but from a distance this stuff might look like metal.

It was the flying box. He was tied to the flying box. He twisted his head left and saw others: Minya, Gavving, Jayan (already awake and trying to hide it), Jinny. To his right, a row of dead salmon birds and ribbon birds, Alfin smiling in his sleep, and one of the Carther Tribe women, the pregnant one, Ilsa. Her eyes were open and empty of hope.

A jovial voice boomed at them. "Some of you are awake by

now—" The Grad arched his back to see over his head. The copsik runner was big, burly, cheerful. He clung to the net near the windowed end. "Don't try to wriggle loose. You'll just get lost in the sky, and we won't come back for you. We don't want fools for copsiks."

Minya called to him. "May we talk among ourselves?"

"Sure, if you don't interrupt *me*. Now, you're wondering what's going to happen to you. You're going to join London Tree. There's tide when you're in a tree. You'll have to get used to the pull on things, and balancing on your feet without falling, and so forth. You'll get to like it. You can heat water till it boils without it spewing all over the place, and that lets you cook things you never tasted. You always know where you are, by what a thing does if you let go of it. You can drop garbage—" From below their feet came an unnerving whistling roar. The copsik runner's voice rose "—and know it won't float back at you." He stopped talking because some of his prisoners were screaming.

A tide pulled toward the Grad's feet. He was not surprised to see sky wheeling past: green forest, a strip of blue, billowing white. The textured green below his feet began to contract.

A wet wind blew past. Mist thickened around them. The panicky screams thinned to whimpers, and the Grad heard Alfin's, "Treefodder! We're going back into the treefeeding storm cloud! Whose bright idea—" and he must have silenced himself, because nobody else could have reached him.

Their guard waited for quiet. He said, "It's *very* impolite for a copsik to interrupt a citizen. I am a citizen. I'll forget it for the duration of this voyage, but you will learn. Questions?"

Minya screamed, "What gives you the *right*?"

"Don't ever say that again," the copsik runner said. "Anything else?"

Minya seemed to calm herself in an instant. "What about our children? Will they be copsiks too?"

"They'll have the chance to be citizens. There's an initiation. Some won't want to take it. Some won't pass."

Mist enclosed them completely. The copsik runner himself

was half-invisible. A wave of droplets each the size of a thumb swept across them, leaving them soaked.

Nobody else seemed inclined to, so the Grad spoke. "Is London Tree stuck in this storm cloud?"

The copsik runner laughed. "We're not stuck anywhere! We moved into the cloud because we need water. After we get you home we'll move out, I expect."

"How?"

"Classified."

Gavving was just waking up. He looked left and right and found the Grad. "What's happening?"

"The good news is we're going to live in a tree."

Gavving tested his bonds while he absorbed that. "As what?"

"Copsiks. Property. Servants."

"Huh. Better than dying of thirst. Where are we? The flying box?"

"Right."

"I don't see Clave. Or Merril."

"Right again."

"I feel wonderful," Gavving said. "Why do I feel so good? Something was on those thorns, maybe, like the red fringe on a fan fungus."

"Could be."

"You're not saying much."

The Grad said, "I don't want to miss anything. If I know how we get to London Tree, maybe I could get us back. I had some Carther Tribe citizens convinced that we should join them."

Gavving turned to Minya. They spoke together at length. The Grad didn't try to hear. It was too noisy anyway. The whistling roar had faded, but the windsong was nearly as loud.

"Too many changes," Minya said.

"I know."

"I can't seem to *feel* anything. I want to get angry, but I can't."

"We're drugged."

"It's not that. I was Minya of the Triune Squad of Dalton-Quinn Tuft. Then I was lost in the sky and dying of thirst. I found you and married you and joined the Dark Tuft People. We hitched a ride with a moby and got slung into a jungle. Now we're what? Copsiks? It's too many changes. Too much."

"All right, I'm a little numb myself. We'll get over it. They can't keep us drugged forever. You're still Minya, the berserker warrior. Just...forget it till you need it."

"What will they do with us?"

"I don't know. The Grad's talking escape. I think we'd better wait. We don't know enough."

She found a laugh, somewhere. "At least we don't die virgins."

"We met each other. We were dying, and now we're not dying at all. We're going to a tree, and it can move itself. We'll never see another drought. It could be worse. It's *been* worse....I wish I could see Clave, though."

It was dark and wet around them. Lightning marched a meandering path across the bow. The vehicle swung around. Now the wind blew up from their feet. In that direction a bushy shadow was forming.

"There," said Minya.

The roar of motors resumed.

Gavving watched for a time before he convinced himself that it was one tuft of an integral tree. He'd never seen any tree from such a vantage. They were coming up on the in branch. The tuft was greener and healthier-looking than Quinn Tuft had been, and foliage reached farther to cover the branch. The bare wooden tail sported a horizontal platform of hewn wood, clearly a work of tremendous labor.

The roar of science-in-action wavered, rose and fell, as the flying box settled toward the platform. A great arching gap had been chopped through the branch itself, linking this platform to one on the other side. At its west end, where foliage began to sprout, a large hut had been woven.

The whistling roar died.

Then things happened fast. People left the hut on the jump. More appeared from underneath, perhaps from inside the flying box. London Tree's citizens didn't have the incredible height of the forest denizens. Some wore gaudy colors, but most wore tuftberry red, and the men had smooth faces scraped clean of hair. They swarmed to what was now the roof of the flying box and began pulling prisoners loose.

Jinny, Jayan, Minya, and the tall Carther Tribe woman were freed in turn and escorted off the roof of the vehicle. Then nothing happened for a time.

They took the women first. The drug on the needles still held him calm, but that bothered Gavving nonetheless. He couldn't see what was happening on the ledge. Presently he was pulled free of the net, lifted, and walked off the roof.

Somehow he had expected normal tides. Here was no more than a third of the tidal force at Quinn Tuft. He drifted down.

Alfin's eyes popped open when the copsik runners turned him loose. They were closing again when he hit the platform. He grunted in protest, then went back to sleep. Two men in tuftberry red picked him up and carried him away.

A copsik runner, a golden-haired woman of twenty or so with a pretty, triangular face, held up the Grad's reader and tapes. "Which of you belongs to these?" she demanded.

The Grad called from above Gavving's head; he was still falling. "They're mine."

"Stay with me," she commanded. "Do you know how to walk? You're short enough to be a tree dweller."

The Grad staggered when he touched down, but stayed upright. "I can walk."

"Wait with me. We'll use the carm to reach the Citadel."

Strangers were among them, leading Gavving and Alfin toward the big hut. The Grad's eyes followed them, and Gavving would have waved, but his wrists were still tied. A smallish, fussy-looking man in red pushed a bird's carcass into his hampered arms—it was nearly his own mass—and said, "Take this along. Can you cook?"

"No."

"Come." The copsik's hand shoved against the small of his back. He moved in that direction, toward where the fin flowered into tuft. But where were the women?

The flying box had blocked his view. Now he saw the women

through the arch, on the other ledge. Minya began struggling, crying, "Wait! That's my husband!"

The drug slowed him down, but Gavving threw the bird into the copsik's arms, sending him tumbling backward under its mass, and tried to jump toward Minya. He never completed the first step. Two men stepped in from either side and caught his arms. They must have been waiting for just such a move. One clouted him across the head hard enough to set the world spinning. They hustled him into the hut.

The copsik was studying Lawri as she studied him. He was thin, with stringy muscles; three or four ce'meters taller than Lawri herself, and not much older. His blond hair and beard were raggedly cut. He was dirty from head to foot. A line of dried blood ran from his right eyebrow to the corner of his jaw. He was very much the kind of copsik who might come spinning from the sky on a sheet of bark, and hardly a convincing man of science.

But his eyes inquired; they judged her. He asked, "Citizen, what will happen to them?"

"Call me Scientist's Apprentice," Lawri said. "Who are you?"

"I'm the Quinn Tribe Scientist," he said.

That made her laugh. "I can hardly call you *Scientist*! Don't you have a name?"

He bristled, but he answered. "I did. Jeffer."

"Jeffer, the other copsiks don't concern you now. Get aboard the carm and stay out of the pilot's way."

He stood stupidly. "Carm?"

She slapped its metal flank and pronounced the syllables as she had been taught. "Cargo And Repair Module. CARM. In!"

He got through both doors and a few paces beyond, and there he stopped, gaping, trying to see in every direction at once. For the moment she left him to it. She didn't blame him. Few copsiks ever saw the interior of the carm.

Ten chairs faced into a tremendous curved window of thick glass. Images were there that couldn't be outside the glass, nor could they be reflections. They must be in the glass itself: numbers and letters and line drawings in blue and yellow and green.

Behind the chairs was thirty or forty cubic meters of empty space. There were bars set to swivel out of the walls and floor and ceiling, and numerous loops of metal: anchorage for stored goods against the jerky pull of the motors. Even so, the cabin was only a fifth the size of the...carm. What was the rest?

When the carm moved, flame had spurted from nostrils at the rear. It seemed that something must burn to move the carm...a good deal of it, if it occupied most of the carm's bulk...and pumps to move the fuel, and mysteries whose names he'd glimpsed in the cassettes: *attitude jet, life support system, computer, mass sensor, echo laser*...

The calm left by the needle had almost left his blood. He was starting to be afraid. Could he learn to read those numbers in the glass? Would he have the chance?

A man in blue lounged before the box window. A big-boned man of average height, he was still too tall for the chair; what would have been a curved head rest poked him between the shoulder blades. The Scientist's Apprentice spoke briskly. "Please take us to the Citadel."

"I don't have orders to do that."

"Just what are your orders?" Her voice was casual, peremptory.

"I don't have orders yet. The Navy may be interested in these...scientific items."

"Confiscate them, if you're sure enough. And I'll tell the Scientist what happened to them, as soon as I'm allowed to contact him. Will you confiscate the copsik too? He says he knows how to work them. Maybe you'd better confiscate me, to talk to him."

The pilot was looking nervous. His glance at the Grad was venomous. A witness to his discomfiture...He decided. "Citadel, right." His hands moved.

The girl, forewarned, was clutching the back of a chair. The Grad wasn't. The lurch threw him off balance. He grabbed at something to stop his fall. A handle on the back wall: it twisted in his hand, and dirty water spilled from a nozzle. He turned it off quick and met the girl's look of disgust.

After perhaps twenty heartbeats the pilot lifted his fingers. The familiar whistling roar—barely audible through the metal walls, but still fearfully strange—went quiet. The Grad immediately made his way to one of the chairs.

The carm was moving away from the tuft, east and out. Were they leaving London Tree? Why? He didn't ask. He was uncharacteristically leery of playing the fool. He watched the pilot's hands. Symbols and numbers glowed in the bow window and in the panel below it, but the pilot touched only the panel, and only the blue. He could feel the response in shifting sound and shifting tide. *Blue moves the carm?*

"Jeffer. How did you get those wounds?" The blond girl spoke as if she didn't care very much.

Wounds? Oh, his *face*. "The tree came apart," he said. "They do that if they fall too far out of the Smoke Ring. We had a close encounter with Gold some years ago."

That touched her curiosity nerve. "What happens to the people?"

"Quinn Tuft must be dead except for us. Five of us now." He'd accepted that Clave and Merril were gone too.

"You'll have to tell me about it sometime." She tapped what she was carrying. "What are these?"

"Cassettes and a reader. Records."

She thought it over, longer than seemed necessary. Then she reached to plug one of the Grad's cassettes into a slot in front of the pilot. The pilot said, "Hey—"

"Science. My perogative," she said. She tapped two buttons. (*Buttons*, permanent fixtures in a row of five: yellow, blue, green, white, red. The panel was otherwise blank, save for the transitory glowing lights within. A tap of the yellow button made all the yellow lights disappear; the white button raised new symbols in white.) "Prikazyvat Menu."

The familiar table of contents appeared within the glass: white print flowing upward. She'd chosen the cassette for cosmology. The Grad felt his hands curling to strangle her. *Classified, classified! Mine!*

"Prikazyvat Gold." The print shifted. The pilot was gripped by terrified fascination, unable to look away. The Scientist's Apprentice asked the Grad, "Can you read?"

"Certainly."

"Read."

"'Goldblatt's World probably originated as a Neptune-like body, a gas giant world in the cometary halo that circles Levoy's Star and Tee-Three, hundreds of billions of kilometers... klomters out. A supernova can spew its outer envelope asymmetrically due to its trapped magnetic field, leaving the remaining neutron star with an altered velocity. The planetary orbits go all to hell. In Levoy's s-scenario Goldblatt's World would have dropped very close to Levoy's Star, with its per... perihelion actually inside the neutron star's Roche Limit. Strong Roche tides would quickly warp the orbit into a circle. The planet would have continued to leak atmosphere to the present day, replacing gasses lost from the Smoke Ring and the gas torus to interstellar space.

"'Goldblatt estimates that Levoy's Star went supernova a billion years ago. The planet must have been losing atmosphere for all of that time. In its present state Goldblatt's World defies description: a world-sized core of rock and metals—'"

"Enough. Very good, you can read. Can you understand what you read?"

"Not that. I can guess that Levoy's Star is Voy and Goldblatt's World is Gold. The rest of it—" The Grad shrugged. His eye caught the pilot's, and the pilot flinched. He seemed shrunken into himself.

Dominance games. The Scientist's Apprentice had assaulted the pilot's mind with the wonders and the cryptic language of science. Now she was saying, "We have that data on our own cassettes, word for word, as far as I can remember. I hope you brought us something new."

A shadow was congealing in the silver fog around them. They were drifting back toward London Tree.

The carm's free-falling path had curved back toward the tree's midpoint. *East takes you out. Out takes you west*—He had a great deal to learn about flying the carm. Because he *must* learn. He would learn to fly this thing, or end his days as a copsik.

There were structures here. Huge wooden beams formed a square. Inward, four huts in a column, not of woven foliage, but of cut wood. Cables and tubes ran down the trunk in both directions, further than the Grad could follow. A pond had touched the trunk: a silvery globule clung to the bark, and that seemed strange. A single pond in this region of mist? Men in red moved around it, feeding it water carried in seed pods. It too must be artificial.

With all these artificial structures, London Tree made Quinn Tuft look barbaric! But was it wise to—"Scientist's Apprentice, do you cut the wood for these structures from the tree itself?"

She answered without looking at him. "No. We bring it from other integral trees."

"Good."

Now she turned, startled and annoyed. He wasn't expected to judge London Tree. The Grad was developing a dislike for the Scientist's Apprentice . . . which he would try to keep in check. If she was behaving as a typical citizen toward a copsik, it augured badly for Quinn Tribe.

The trunk was coming at them, too fast. The Grad was relieved when he heard the motors start and felt the carm slowing. Those wooden beams would just about fit against the carm's windowed end . . . and that was what the pilot was doing, tapping at blue lights, fitting the window into that wooden frame. *Watch his hands!*

Chapter Fourteen

Treemouth
and Citadel

IN THE LARGE HUT THE WOMEN WERE STRIPPED NAKED AND examined by two women taller than humans, like Ilsa of Carther Tribe. Their long hair was white and thin enough to expose scalp. The skin seemed to have withered on their bones. Forty to fifty years old, Minya thought, though that was hard to judge; they looked so strange. They wore ponchos in tuftberry-juice scarlet, closed between the legs. Their walk was easy, practiced. Minya judged that they had spent many years in the tide of London Tree.

"It looks like people live a long time here," she whispered to Jayan, and Jayan nodded.

The supervisors would not answer questions, though they asked many.

They found dirt and wounds in plenty, but no disease. They treated Minya's bruises, and brusquely advised her to avoid offending citizens in future. Minya smiled. Offended? She was sure she had broken a man's arm before they clubbed her unconscious.

Ilsa was clearly pregnant. Jayan was also declared pregnant, to her obvious surprise, and sent off with Ilsa. Minya gripped

Jinny's arm, afraid that she would attempt a futile battle for her twin.

One of the supervisors noticed Jinny's distress. "They'll be all right," she said. "They carry guests. One of the Scientist's apprentices will have to look them over. Also, the men won't be allowed near them."

The *what* would *what*? But she would say no more, and Minya had to wait.

The Grad watched through the small windows; the big bow window now gave on to rugged bark four ce'meters distant. Things were happening outside.

A man in a white tunic was talking to men in blue or red ponchos that fit like oversized sacks. Presently the others all launched themselves along the bark toward the lowest of the column of huts.

"Who's that?" the Grad asked.

The Scientist's Apprentice disdained to answer. The pilot said, "That's Klance the Scientist. Your new owner. No surprise there, he thinks he owns the whole tree."

Klance the Scientist was arguing with himself as he approached the carm. His white smock reached just below his hips; the ends of a citizen's loose poncho showed below. He was tall for a tree dweller, and lean but for a developing pot belly. Not a fighter, the Grad thought—forty-odd, with slack muscles. His hair was thick and white, his nose narrow and convexly curved. In a moment the Grad heard his voice speaking out of the air.

"Lawri." Sharp, with a peremptory snap in it.

The pilot tapped the yellow button and spread two fingertips apart over the resulting pattern of yellow lines (*remember*), beating Lawri to it. The carm's two doors swung out and in.

The Scientist was already in conversation as he entered. "They want to know when I can move the tree. Damn fools. They only just finished topping off the reservoir. If I moved it now the water would just float away. First we have to—" He stopped. His eyes flicked to the pilot's back (the pilot hadn't bothered to turn around), then to the Grad, then to Lawri. "Well?"

"He's the Scientist of a ruined tribe. He carried these." Lawri held up plastic boxes.

"Old science." His eyes turned greedy. "Tell me later," he said. "Pilot."

The Navy man's head turned.

"Was the carm damaged in any way? Was anything lost?"

"Certainly not. If you need a detailed report—"

"No, that will do. The rest of the Navy party is waiting for the elevator. I think you can still catch it."

The pilot nodded stiffly. He rose and launched himself toward the twin doors. He nearly brushed the Scientist, who held his ground; pulled himself through the doors and was gone.

The Scientist tapped at yellow lights. The window sprouted a display. "Fuel tanks are damn near dry. We'll be filling them for weeks. Otherwise...looks all right. Lawri, from you I do want a detailed report, but tell me now if anything happened."

"He seemed to know what he was doing. I don't love the treefeeder, but he didn't bump any rocks. The foray team brought back these, and him."

The Scientist took the plastic objects Lawri handed him. "A reader!" he breathed. "You bring me treasure. What's your name?"

The Grad hesitated; then, "Jeffer."

"Jeffer, I'll wait for your story. We'll get you cleaned up first. All these years I've been waiting for the Navy to lose my carm, reader and all. I can't tell you what it means to have a spare."

The tide was lighter. Otherwise Minya couldn't tell London Tree from her own tuft. Here was the same green gloom, the same vegetable smells. Branching tunnels ran through foliage stripped bare by passersby. The tall women led them in silence. Jinny and Minya followed. They passed nobody.

They were still naked. Jinny walked hunched over, as if that would cover her. She hadn't spoken since Jayan was taken away.

They had traveled some distance before Minya felt the wind. Minutes later the tunnel swelled out into a great cavity, lit by harsh daylight at the far end.

"Jinny. Was the Commons this big in Quinn Tuft?"

Jinny looked about her, dutifully, and showed no reaction. "No."

"Neither was ours." The cavity ran round the trunk and all the way to the treemouth itself. She could see the empty sky beyond. The shadows were strange, with the blue tinge of Voylight glaring from below. In Dalton-Quinn Tuft Voy had been always overhead.

All that foliage had had to be torn out. Weren't the copsik runners afraid of killing the tree? Or would they only move to another?

Thirty or forty women had formed a line for food. Many were attended by children: three years old and younger. They ignored Minya and Jinny as they were marched past, toward the treemouth.

"Tell me what bothers you most," Minya said.

Jinny didn't answer for several breaths. Then, "Clave."

"He wasn't on the box. He must be still in the jungle. Jinny, his leg has to heal before he can do anything."

"I'll lose him," Jinny said. "He'll come, but I'll lose him. Jayan's got his child. I won't be his anymore."

"Clave loves you both," Minya said, though she hadn't the remotest idea how Clave actually thought.

Jinny shook her head. "We belong to the copsik runners, the men. Look, they're already here."

Minya frowned and looked about her. Was Jinny imagining...? Her eye picked up something in the green curve that roofed the Commons, a dark shape hidden in shadow and foliage. She found two more...four, five...men. She said nothing.

They were led to the edge of the treemouth, almost beneath the great reservoir mounted where branch merged into trunk. Minya looked downslope. Offal, garbage...two bodies on platforms, completely covered in cloth. When she turned away, their escorts had stepped out of their ponchos.

They took their charges by the arms and led them beneath the huge basin. One of the supervisors heaved on a cord, and water poured forth like a flood in miniature. Minya shuddered with the shock. The women produced lumps of something, and one began rubbing it over Minya's body, then handed it to her.

Minya had never experienced soap before. It wasn't frightening, but it was strange. The supervisors soaped themselves too, then let the flood pour forth again. Afterward they dried themselves with their garments, then donned them. They handed scarlet ponchos to Jinny and Minya.

The suds left her skin feeling strange, tingly. Minya had little trouble stepping into the poncho despite its being sealed between the legs; but it did seem uncomfortably loose. Was it made for the elongated jungle people? It bothered her more that she wore tuftberry-red. Copsik-red here, citizen-red at home. She had worn purple too long.

Their escorts abandoned them at the serving table. Four cooks— more of the elongated women—ladeled a stew of earthlife vegetables and turkey meat into bowls whose rims curved inward. Minya and Jinny settled themselves into a resilient arm of foliage and ate. The fare was blander than what she was used to in Dalton-Quinn Tuft.

Another copsik settled beside them: two and a half meters tall, middle-aged, walking easily in London Tree's tide. She spoke to Jinny. "You look like you know how to walk. You from a tree?"

Jinny didn't answer. Minya said, "A tree that came apart. I'm Minya Dalton-Quinn. This is Jinny Quinn."

The stranger said, "Heln. No last name, now."

"How long have you been here?"

"Ten years, or something like. I used to be Carther. I keep expecting . . . well."

"Rescue?"

Heln shrugged. "I keep thinking they'll try *something*. Of course they couldn't, then. Anyway, I've got kids now."

"Married?"

Heln looked at her. "They didn't tell you. Okay, they didn't tell me either. The citizens *own* us. Any man who wants you owns you."

"I . . . thought it was something like that." She moved her eyes only, toward the shadows at the outskirts. And they'd watched her naked—"What are they doing, making their selections?"

"That's right." Heln looked up. "Eat faster if you want to finish." Two shadowy men were coming toward them, drifting at leisure along the interlocked branchlets that formed the ground.

Minya watched them while she continued eating. They paused several meters away, waiting. Their ponchos fit more closely than hers and were a riot of colors. They watched the women and talked. Minya heard "—one with the bruises broke Karal's—"

Heln ignored them. Minya tried to do the same. When her bowl was empty, she asked, "What do we do with these?"

"Leave them," Heln said. "If no man takes you, take it back to the cooks. But I think you'll have company. You look like citizens; the men like that." She grimaced. "They call us 'jungle giants.'"

Too many changes. Three sleeptimes ago, no man in her local universe would have dared to touch her. What would they do to her if she resisted? What would Gavving think of her? Even if they could escape later—

If she strolled toward the treemouth now, Minya thought, would anyone stop her? She'd be "feeding the tree." A short sprint past the treemouth would put her into the sky before anyone could react. She'd been lost in the sky and survived . . .

But how could she alert Gavving to jump too? He might not have the chance. He might think it was a mad idea.

It *was* mad. Minya dropped it. And the men strolled over to join them.

The Grad's first meal at the Citadel was simple but strange. He was given a gourd with a fair-sized slot cut in it, and a squeezegourd for liquids, and a two-pronged wooden fork. Thick stew, shipped from the out tuft, had cooled by the time it reached the Citadel. He could recognize two or three of the ingredients. He wanted to ask what he was eating, but it was Klance who asked the questions.

One of the first was, "Were you taught medicine?"

"Certainly." The word was out of his mouth before his mind quite caught up.

Lawri looked dubious. Klance the Scientist laughed. "You're too young to be so sure. Have you worked with children? Injured hunters? Sick women? Women carrying guests?"

"Not with children. Women with guests, yes. Injured hunters, yes. I've treated malnutrition sicknesses. Always with the Scientist supervising." His racing mind told him what to tell Klance. In fact he had worked with children; he had inspected a pregnant woman, once; he had set the bone in Clave's leg. *The old copsik runner won't let me practice on citizens, will he? He'll try me out on copsiks first! My own people . . .*

Klance was saying, "We don't get malnutrition here, thank the Checker. How did you come to be found in a jungle?"

"Inadvertently." Eating strange food with strange implements in free-fall took concentration. Not letting it make him sick took a distraction; the Grad was glad for the chance to talk. He ate what he was given and told the tale of Quinn Tribe's destruction.

The Scientist interrupted with questions about Quinn Tuft, treemouth tending, musrums, flashers, the dumbo, the moby, the insects at the tree median. Lawri seemed fascinated. She burst in only once, demanding to know how one fought swordbirds and triunes. The Grad referred her to Minya and Gavving. Maybe she'd let them know where he was.

The meal ended with a bitter black brew which the Grad refused; and he continued to talk. He was hoarse when he finished.

Klance the Scientist puffed at his pipe—shorter than the one the Quinn Chairman had used—and clouds of smoke drifted sluggishly about the room and out. The room was more a cage of timber than a hut; there were narrow windows everywhere, and boards would swing to cover them. Klance said, "This giant mushroom had hallucinogenic properties, did it?"

"I don't know the word, Klance."

"The red fringe made you feel strange but nice. Maybe that was the reason they were protecting it?"

"I don't think so. There were too many of those fan fungi. This one was big and nicely formed and had a special name."

"The Checker's Hand. Jeffer, have you ever heard that word *Checker* before?"

"My grandmother used to say, 'Treefeeder must think he's the Checker himself,' when she was mad at the Chairman. I never heard anyone else—"

The Scientist reached for the Grad's reader and one of his own cassettes. "I think I remember..."

CHECKER. Officer entrusted with seeing to it that one or a group of citizens remains loyal to the State. The Checker's responsibility includes the actions, attitudes, and well-being of his charges. The Checker aboard *Discipline* was the recording of Sharls Davis Kendy in the ship's master computer.

"This is strictly starman stuff. Hmp. The State...it took me four days to read the insert on the State. Have you seen it?"

"Yes. Strange people. I did get the feeling that they lived longer than we do."

Klance snorted. "Your Scientist never tumbled to that? They had shorter years. They used one whole circle of their sun for their year. We only use half a circle, but it's still about seven-fifths of a State year. The truth is, we live a little longer than they do, and grow up more slowly too."

To hear his teacher so slighted set the Grad's ears burning. He barely heard Klance add, "All right, Jeffer, from now on you must think of me as your Checker."

"Yes, Scientist."

"Call me Klance. How do you feel?"

The Grad answered with careful half-truth. "I'm clean, fed, rested, and safe. I'd feel even better if I knew the rest of Quinn Tribe was all right."

"They'll get showers and food and drink and clothing. Their children may become citizens. The same goes for you, Jeffer, whether or not I keep you here; but I think you'd be bored in the tuft."

"So do I, Klance."

"Fine. For the time being I have two apprentices."

Lawri exploded. "It's unheard of for a freshly claimed copsik to be at the Citadel at all! Won't the Navy—"

"The Navy can feed the tree. The Citadel is mine."

Chapter Fifteen

London Tree

GAVVING WAS ON THE BICYCLE WITH THREE OTHER COPSIKS.

There wasn't tide enough to pull him against the pedals. Straps ran from the belt around his waist to the bicycle frame. Forcing his legs down against the pedals pushed him up against the belt. After the first session he'd thought he was crippled for life. The endless passage of days had toughened him; his legs no longer hurt, and the muscles were hard to the touch.

The bicycle gears were of old metal. They squealed as they moved and gave forth a scent of old animal grease. The frame was massive, of cut wood. There had been six sets of gears once; Gavving could see where two had been ripped out.

The frame was anchored to the trunk where the tuft grew thin. Foliage grew around the copsiks. Surrounded by sky, with most of the tuft below them, they could still snatch and eat a handful while pedaling. They worked naked, with sweat pooling on their faces and in their armpits.

High up along the trunk, a wooden box descended slowly. A similar box had risen almost out of sight.

Gavving let his legs run on while he watched the elevator

descend. The mindless labor let his eyes and ears and mind run free.

There were other structures around the trunk. This level was used for industry, and here were all the men. Man's work and woman's work never seemed to intersect in London Tree, at least not for copsiks. Sometimes children swarmed through or watched them with bright, curious eyes. Today there were none.

The citizens of London Tree must have kept copsiks for generations. They were skilled at it. They had chopped Quinn Tribe apart. Even if opportunity came to run, how would he find Minya?

Gavving, pumping steadily, watched storms move sluggishly around a tight knot on the eastern arm of the Smoke Ring. Gold was nearer than he had ever seen it, save for that eerie time when he was a child, when Gold had passed so near and everything had changed.

The jungle hovered hundreds of klomters beyond the out tuft: a harmless-looking green puffball. *How are you doing, Clave? Did that broken leg save your freedom? Merril, were those shrunken legs finally good for something? Or have you become copsiks among the jungle people, or are you dead?*

Over the past eighty-five days or so, twenty sleeps, the tree had drifted to the eastern fringes of the cloud bank. He'd been told, during the trip across the sky to London Tree, that the tree could move by itself. He had seen no evidence of it. Rain swept across them from time to time...surely the tree had collected enough water by now...

The elevator had settled into its slot and was releasing passengers. Gavving and the others stopped pedaling. "Navy men," Horse puffed. "Come for the women."

Gavving said, "What?"

"Citizens live in the out tuft. When you see a boxful come down and it's all men, they're come for the women."

Gavving looked away.

"Nine sleeps," said Horse. He was in his fifties, three ce'meters shorter than Gavving, with a bald, freckled head and tremendously strong legs. He had driven the bicycles for two decades. "Forty days till we meet the women. You wouldn't believe how rancy I get thinking about it." By now Gavving was strangling the handbar. Horse saw the muscles standing out along his arms and said, "Boy, I forgot. I was never married, myself. I was born here. Failed the test when I was ten."

Gavving forced himself to speak. "Born here?"

Horse nodded. "My father was a citizen; at least mother always said so. Who ever knows?"

"Seems likely. You'd be taller if—"

"Na, na, the jungle giants' kids aren't any taller than the citizens."

So: children raised in the jungle grew taller, without tide to compress them. "What are the tests like?"

"We're na supposed to say."

"Okay."

The supervisor called, "Pedal, you copsiks!" and they did. More passengers were coming down. Over the squeal of the gears Horse said, "I flunked the obedience test. Sometimes I'm glad I didn't go."

Huh? "Go?"

"To another tree. That's where you go if you pass the tests. Heh, you are green, aren't you? Did you think your kids would stay as citizens if they passed the tests?"

"That's...yes." He hadn't been told that; he'd been allowed to assume it. "There are other trees? How many? Who lives in them?"

Horse chuckled. "You want to know everything at once? I think it's four bud trees now, settled by any copsik woman's kid who passes the tests. London Tree goes between them, trading for what they need. Any man's kid has the same chance as a citizen's, because nobody ever knows, see? I thought I wanted to go, once. But it's been thirty-five years.

"I did think I'd be picked for service in the out tuft. I should've been. I'm second-generation...and when they turned me down for that, I damn near lost my testes for swatting a supervisor. Jorg, there"—Horse indicated the man pedaling in front of him—"he did. Poor copsik. I don't know what the gentled ones do when the Holidays come."

Gavving still hadn't learned to shave without cutting himself. It was not his choice. All copsiks shaved. He had seen no man wearing a beard in London Tree, save one; and that one was Patry, a Navy officer. "Horse, is that why they make us shave? So the gentled ones won't be quite so obvious?"

"I never thought of that. Maybe."

"Horse . . . you must actually have seen the tree move."

Horse's laughter brought a supervisor's head around. He lowered his voice. "Did you think it was just a story? We move the tree about once a year! I've been on water details too, to feed the carm."

"What's it like?"

"It's like the tide goes slantwise. Going to the treemouth is like climbing a hill. You don't want any hunting parties out when it happens, and you have to tilt the cookpot. The whole trunk of the tree bends a little . . ."

"Lawri," said the Grad, "trouble."

Lawri glanced back. The pond clung to the bark, a flattened hemisphere. The Grad had run the hose into the water. Now the water was flowing up the outside of the hose, forming a collar.

"Don't worry about it. Just get to the bicycle and pedal," Lawri told him. "And don't call me that."

The Grad strapped himself to the saddle and started the pedals turning. The gears moved a pump. It was all starstuff, metal, discolored with age. The collar of water shrank as water was sucked into the hose.

It was strange work for the Quinn Tuft Scientist, or for the London Tree Scientist's Apprentice, for that matter. Hadn't Klance suggested that he would be better off than the standard run of copsiks? He wondered what Gavving was doing now. Probably worrying about his new and alien wife . . . and with reason.

Water spurted from the hose as Lawri carried it into the carm. The Grad couldn't see what she was doing in there. He pedaled.

In Klance's presence the Grad was Lawri's equal. Otherwise Lawri treated him as a copsik, a spy, or both. He was clean, fed, and clothed. Of the rest of Quinn Tribe he had not even rumors.

He and Lawri and the Scientist explored the cassettes together for old knowledge, and that was fascinating enough. But he was learning nothing that would rescue Quinn Tribe.

It was night. Both Voy and the sun were hidden behind the in tuft. In the peculiar light that remained, two faint streamers of blue light fanned out from the tuft. If he stared at them they went away. He could catch them by looking near them. He could almost imagine human shapes pouring as smoke from a squeeze-gourd. To starboard, the Blue Ghost. To port, even fainter, the Ghost Child.

The Scientist (*the* Scientist) had told him that they were discharges of peculiar energies from the poles of Voy itself. The Scientist had seen them when he was younger, but the Grad had never been able to see them, not even from the midpoint of Dalton-Quinn Tree.

He was sweating. He watched the elevator climb the tree to its housing. A Navy man and two copsiks emerged. None were jungle giants; he had never seen a first-generation copsik at the Citadel, barring himself. They entered the Scientist's laboratory complex and presently left carrying the dishes from brunch.

Lawri called from the carm. "The tank's full."

The Grad moved with a briskness he didn't feel, unfastening the belt, jerking the hose free of the pond. There were lineholds, wooden hoops, set in the bark to crisscross the citadel region. The Grad used them to make his way toward the carm, calling ahead of him, "Can I help?"

"Just coil the hose," Lawri answered.

She hadn't yet let him into the carm during this operation. The hose must lead, somehow, into a water tank in the carm. They filled it repeatedly, and a couple of days later they would fill it again.

The Grad coiled the hose as he moved toward the carm. He heard cursing from within. Then Lawri called, "I can't move this damn fitting."

The Grad joined her at the doors. "Show me." That easy?

She showed him. The hose attached to a thing on the back

wall, with a collar. "It has to be turned. That way." She rotated her hands.

He set his feet, grasped the metal thing, put his back into it. The collar lurched. Again. He turned it until it was loose in his hands, and kept turning. The hose came loose. A mouthful of water spilled out. Lawri nodded and turned away.

"Scientist's Apprentice? Where does the water *go?*"

"It's taken apart," she said. "The skin of the carm picks up sunlight and pumps the energy into the water. The water comes apart. Oxygen goes in one tank and hydrogen goes in the other. When they come together in the motors, the energy comes back and you get a flame."

He was trying to imagine water coming apart, when Lawri asked, "Why did you want to know?"

"I was a Scientist. Why did you tell me?"

She sent herself skimming across the seats and settled herself at the controls. The Grad moored the coiled hose to fixtures in the cargo area.

The tank must be behind the wall. The carm had been nearly out of fuel . . . which came in two "flavors"? There must be fuel by now; the artificial pond was visibly shrunken.

Lawri tapped the blue button as he came up behind her. The display she'd been studying disappeared before he could see it. The Grad had half forgotten his question when she turned to him and said, "The Scientist quizzes me like that. Since I was ten. If I can't answer I get some dirty job. But I don't like having my buttons pushed, Jeffer, and that information is classified!"

"Scientist's Apprentice, who is it that calls you Lawri?"

"Not you, copsik."

"I know that."

"The Scientist. My parents."

"I don't know anything about marriage customs here."

"Copsiks don't get married."

"You're not a copsik. Would your husband call you Lawri?"

The airlock thumped, and Lawri turned in some relief. "Klance?"

"Yes. Put that display on again, will you, Lawri?"

She looked at the Grad, then back at Klance.

"Now," said the Scientist. Lawri obeyed. She'd made her point: she'd show scientific secrets to a copsik, but only under protest. Dominance games again. If she really cared, she would have removed the hose herself.

The blue lights and numbers had to do with what moved the carm, as green governed the carm's sensing instruments and yellow moved the doors and white read the cassettes . . . and more. He was sure that they all did more than he knew. And red? He'd never seen red.

Every time he saw this display, certain numbers were larger. Now they read O_2: 1,664. H_2: 3,181. Klance was nodding in approval. "Ready to go any time. Still, I think we'll feed in the rest of the reservoir. Jeffer, come here." He cut the blue display and activated the yellow. "This number tells you if there's a storm coming, if you watch it."

"What is it?"

"It's the external air pressure."

"Can't you *see* a storm coming?"

"Coming, yes. Forming, no. If the pressure goes up or down fast, over a day or so, there's a storm forming. Lets you impress hell out of the citizens. This is classified, of course."

The Grad asked, "Where does the tree go from here?"

"Out of this rain. Then on to Brighton Tree; they haven't seen us in a while. Grad, you'll get a good chance to look the bud colonies over and pick and choose among them."

"For what, Klance?"

"For your children, of course."

The Grad laughed. "Klance, how am I going to have children if I spend my life at the Citadel?"

"Don't you know about the Holidays?"

"I never heard of them."

"Well, every year's-end, when Voy crosses in front of the sun, the copsiks all get together at the treemouth. It's holiday for six days while the copsiks mate and gossip and play games. Even the food comes from the out tuft. The Holidays start in thirty-five days."

"No exceptions? Not even for a Scientist's Apprentice?"

"Don't worry, you'll go," Klance chuckled.

Lawri had turned away, showing her bowed back, the wealth of blonde hair floating around her. He wondered then: *How would Lawri have children?* The Scientist didn't seem to be her lover; the Grad knew that he imported copsik women from the in tuft. If she never left the Citadel—How would Lawri ever find a man? *Me?*

A copsik could have children, but Lawri could not. It couldn't be helped. He dared not think of Lawri as other than an enemy.

There was flesh against her as she woke. It happened often. Minya shifted position and refrained from wrapping her arms around the citizen who slept beside her. She might hurt him.

Her motion wakened him. He turned carefully—his arm was bound with cloth against his torso—and said, "Good morning."

"Good morning. How's your arm?" She searched her memory for his name.

"You did a good job on it, but it'll heal."

"I wondered why you came looking for me, given that I broke it."

He scowled. "You stuck in my head. While Lawri was setting the bone I kept seeing your face, two ce'meters away with your teeth bared like you were going for my throat next...yeah. So I'm here." The scowl relaxed. "Under, eh, different circumstances."

"Better now?"

"Yes."

His name surfaced. "Karal. I don't remember a Lawri."

"Lawri's not a copsik. She's the Scientist's Apprentice—one of his apprentices, now—and she treats Navy men if we get hurt."

One of his apprentices? Minya gambled. "I hear the new one is a copsik."

"Yes. I saw him from a distance, and he's not a jungle giant. One of yours?"

"Maybe." She stood, donned her poncho. "Will we meet again?"

He hesitated—"Maybe"—and added, "The Holidays are eight sleeps away."

She let her smile show through. *Gavving!* "How long do they last?"

"Six days. And all work stops."

"Well, I have to get to work now."

Karal disappeared into the foliage while Minya strolled into the Commons. She missed Dalton-Quinn Tuft. She'd grown almost used to the obtrusive differences: the huge Commons, the omnipresent supervisors, her own servility. But little things bothered her. She missed cupvines, and copter plants. Nothing grew here but the foliage and the carefully cultivated earthlife, beans and melons and corn and tobacco, as thoroughly regimented as herself.

A dozen copsiks were up and stirring. Minya looked for Jinny and spotted her at the treemouth, just her head showing above the foliage as she fed the tree.

The schedules were loose. If you arrived late, you would work late. Beyond that, the supervisors didn't care much . . . but Minya cared! She would do nothing badly. She would be an exemplary copsik, until the time came to be something else.

She tried to remember nuances of Karal's speech. A citizen's accent was odd, and she had been practicing it.

It had been strange for Minya. Her instincts were at war: a conditioned reflex that resisted sexual assault as blasphemy incarnate, versus the will to live.

Survival won. She would do nothing badly!

Jinny stood up, set her poncho in order, then sprinted west.

Minya screamed. She was too far to do anything but shout and point as she ran. A pair of supervisors, much closer, saw what was happening and ran too.

Jinny plunged through a last screen of foliage, into the sky.

Minya kept running. The supervisors (Haryet and Dloris, hard-faced jungle giants of indeterminate age) had reached the edge.

Dloris swung a weighted line round her head, twice and out. Haryet waited her turn, then swung her own line while Dloris pulled. The line resisted as she pulled it in, then gave abruptly. Dloris reeled back, off balance.

Minya reached the edge in time to see the stone at the end of Haryet's line spin round Jinny. Dloris threw her line while Jinny was still fighting Haryet's. Jinny thrashed, then went limp.

Haryet pulled her in.

Jinny huddled on her side, face buried in her arms and knees. By now they were surrounded by copsiks. While Dloris gestured them away, Haryet rolled Jinny on her back, groped for her chin, and pulled her face out of the protection of her arms. Jinny's eyes stayed clenched like fists.

Minya said, "Madam Supervisor, a moment of your attention."

Dloris looked around, surprised at the snap in Minya's voice. "Later," she said.

Jinny began to sob. The sobs shook her like Dalton-Quinn Tree had shaken the day it came apart. Haryet watched for a time, impassively. Then she spread a second poncho over the girl and sat down to watch her.

Dloris turned to Minya. "What is it?"

"If Jinny tries this again and succeeds, would it reflect badly on you?"

"It might. Well?"

"Jinny's twin sister is with the women who carry guests. Jinny has to see her."

"That's forbidden," the jungle giantess said wearily.

When citizens talked like that, Minya had learned to ignore them. "These girls are twins. They've been together all their lives. They should be given some hours to talk."

"I told you, it's forbidden."

"That would be your problem."

Dloris glared in exasperation. "Go join the garbage detail. No, wait. First talk to this Jinny, if she'll talk."

"Yes, Supervisor. And I'd like to be checked for pregnancy, at your convenience."

"Later."

Minya bent to speak directly into Jinny's ear. "Jinny, it's Minya. I've talked to Dloris. She'll try to get you together with Jayan."

Jinny was clenched like a knot.

"Jinny. The Grad made it. He's at the Citadel, where the Scientist lives."

Nothing.

"Just hang on, will you? Hang on. Something will happen. Talk to Jayan. See if she's learned anything." Treefodder, there must be something she could say . . . "Find out where the pregnant women are kept. See if the Grad ever comes down to examine them. He might. Tell him we're hanging on. Waiting."

Jinny didn't move. Her voice was muffled. "All right, I'm listening. But I can't stand it. I can't."

"You're tougher than you think."

"If another man picks me, I'll kill *him*."

Some of them like women who fight, Minya thought. She said instead, "Wait. Wait till we can kill them all."

After a long time, Jinny uncurled and stood up.

Chapter Sixteen

Rumblings of Mutiny

GAVVING WOKE TO A TOUCH ON HIS SHOULDER. HE LOOKED about him without moving.

There were three tiers of hammocks, and Gavving's was in the top layer. The daylit doorway made a black silhouette of a supervisor. He seemed to have fallen asleep standing up: easy enough in London Tree's gentle tide. In the dimness of the barracks, Alfin clung to Gavving's hammock-post. He spoke in a whisper that wanted to shout in jubilation.

"They've put me to work at the treemouth!"

"I thought only women did that," Gavving said without moving at all. Jorg snored directly below him—a "gentled" man, pudgy and sad, and too stupid to spy on anyone. But the hammocks were close-packed.

"I saw the farm when they took us for showers. There's a lot they're doing wrong. I talked to a supervisor about it. He let me talk to the women who runs the farm. Kor's her name, and she listens. I'm a consultant."

"Good."

159

"Give me a couple of hundred days and I might get you in on it too. I want to show what I can do first."

"Did you get a chance to speak to Minya? Or Jinny?"

"Don't even think it. They'd go berserk if we tried to talk to the women."

To be a treemouth tender again...seeing Minya, but not allowed to speak to her. Meanwhile, maybe Alfin could carry messages, if he could be talked into taking the risk. Gavving put it out of his mind. "I learned something today. The tree does move, and it's the carm, the flying box, that moves it. They've settled other trees—"

"What does that do for us?"

"I don't know yet."

Alfin moved away to his hammock.

Patience came hard to Gavving. In the beginning he had thought of nothing but escape. At night he could drive himself mad with worry over Minya...or he could sleep, and work, and wait, and learn.

The supervisors wouldn't answer questions. What *did* he know, what *had* he learned? The women farmed the treemouth and cooked; pregnant women lived elsewhere. Men tended machinery and worked with wood, here in the upper reaches of the tuft. The copsiks talked of rescue, but never of revolt.

They wouldn't revolt now anyway, with the Holidays eight sleeps away. Afterward, maybe; but wouldn't the Navy know that from experience? They'd be ready. The supervisors were never without their truncheons, sticks of hardwood half a meter long. Horse said the women supervisors carried them too. During an insurrection the Navy might be given those instead of swords...or not.

What else? Bicycle works wore out. Damaging them—damaging anything made of starstuff—would hurt London Tree, but not soon. Here was where the elevators could be sabotaged; but the Navy could still put down a revolt by using the carm.

The carm did everything. It lived at the tree's midpoint, where the Scientist kept his laboratory. Was the Grad there? Was he planning something? He'd seemed determined to escape, even before they reached London Tree.

Was any of that worth anything? *If we were together! We could plan something—*

He had learned that he might spend the rest of his life moving an elevator or pumping water up the trunk. He had not had an allergy attack since his capture. It was not a bad life, and he was dangerously close to becoming used to it. In eight sleeps he would be allowed to see his own wife.

Carther States was setting fires halfway around the biggest flower in the universe.

Clave flapped his blanket at the coals. His arms were plunged elbow-deep in the foliage to anchor him. His toes clutched the edge of the blanket. He undulated his legs and torso to move the blanket in waves, exerting himself just enough to keep the coals red.

Eighty meters away, a huge silver petal gradually shifted position, turning to catch the sun at a sharper angle.

A fire would die in its own smoke, without a breeze, and breezes were rare in the jungle. The day was calm and bright. Clave took it as a chance to exercise his legs.

There was a knot as big as a boy's fist where the break had been on his thighbone. His fingers could feel the hard lump beneath the muscles; his body felt it when he moved. Merril had told him it couldn't be seen. Would she lie to spare him? He was disinclined to ask anyone else.

He was disfigured. But the bone was healing; it hurt less every day. The scar was an impressive pink ridge. He exercised, and waited for war.

There had been tens of days of sleep merging into pain. He'd seen spindly, impossibly tall near-human forms flitting about him at all angles, green shapes fading like ghosts into a dark green background, quiet voices blurred in the eternal whisper of the foliage. He had thought he was still dreaming.

But Merril was real. Homely, legless Merril was entirely familiar, entirely real, and mad as hell. The copsik runners had taken everyone. "Everyone but us. They left us. I'll make them sorry for that!"

He had taken little notice, in the pain of a healing bone and the sharper ache of his failure. A hunt leader who had lost his team, a Chairman who had lost his tribe. Quinn Tribe was dead. He told himself that depression always followed a serious wound. He stayed where he was, deep in the dark interior of the jungle, for fear that fluff might grow in the wound; and he slept. He slept a great deal. He didn't have the will to do more.

Merril tried to talk to him. Things weren't that bad. The Grad had impressed the Carthers. Merril and Clave were welcome in the tribe...though as copsiks.

Once he woke to find Merril jubilant. "They'll let me fight!" she said, and Clave learned that the Carthers were planning war against London Tree.

Over the following days he grew to know the jungle people. Of around two hundred Carthers, half were copsiks. It didn't seem to carry any onus. Copsiks here lacked for nothing save a voice in the council.

He saw many children and many pregnancies and no starvation. The jungle people were healthy and happy...and better armed than Quinn Tribe had been.

He was questioned at a gathering of the tribe. Carther States' Commons was a mere widening in a tunnel, perhaps twelve meters across and twice that long. Surprisingly, the space held everyone. Men and women and children, copsiks and citizens, all clung to the cylinder wall, covering it with an inner layer of heads, while Comlink or the Sharman spoke from one end.

"How can you even *reach* London Tree?" he had asked, but only once. That information was "classified"; spies would not be tolerated. But he could watch the preparations. He was sure these fires were part of it.

He had been flapping wind at the coals for half a day now. His leg was holding up. Soon he would have to shift position.

Kara the Sharman came skimming toward him. She dipped

her grapnel into the foliage and stopped herself next to Clave. "How are you doing?"

"You tell me. Does the fire look right?"

She looked. "Keep it that way. Feed it another branch a few hundred breaths from now. How's the leg?"

"Fine. Can we talk?"

"I've other fires to check."

The Sharman was Carther States' equivalent to the Scientist. Maybe the world had meant *Chairman* once. She seemed to have more power than the political boss, the Comlink, who spent most of his time finding out what everybody else wanted. Getting her attention was worth a try. Clave said, "Sharman, I'm a tree dweller. We're going to attack a tree. Shouldn't you be using what I know?"

She considered that. "What can you tell me?"

"Tides. You're not used to tides. I am, and so are these copsik runners. If you—"

Her smile was twisted. "Put you in charge of our own warriors?"

"Not what I meant. Attack the *middle* of the tree. Make them come to us there. I saw them fighting in free-fall, and you're better."

"We thought of that—" She saw his grimace. "No, don't stop. I'm glad you agree. We've watched London Tree for decades now, and two of us did escape once. We know that the copsiks live in the inner tuft, but the carrier is kept at the center of the tree. Should we go after that first?"

Science at the level of the carrier, the flying box, made Clave uneasy. He tried to set the feeling aside . . . "I saw how they use that thing. They put their own warriors where they want them and leave yours floundering in air. Yes. Get the carrier first, even if you can't fly it."

"All right."

"Sharman, I don't know how you plan to attack. If you'll tell me more, I can give you better answers." He'd said it before. It was like talking to the tree.

Kara freed her grapnel with a snap of the snag line. She was moving on. *Treefodder!* Clave added, "One thing. If I know the Grad, he knows how to fly the carrier by now, if he's had any kind of a chance at it. Or Gavving might have seen something and told the Grad."

"There's no way we'll learn that."

Clave shrugged.

"We'll go for the carrier and try for the Grad."

Clave pushed a dead spine branch into the coals and resumed flapping his blanket.

Kara said, "You call yourself Sharman... *Chairman* of a destroyed people. I trust you know how to be a leader. If you learn things that should not be known to our enemies... if you ride to war in the first gust of warriors... what would you tell my citizens, if you were me?"

That was clear enough. "'Clave must not live to be captured and questioned.' Sharman, I have little to lose. If I can't rescue my people, I'll kill copsik runners!"

"Merril?"

"She'll fight with me. Not under tides, though. And... don't tell her anything. *I* won't kill Merril if she's captured."

"Fair enough. You called the funnel a 'treemouth'—"

"I was wrong, wasn't I? The jungle can't feed itself that way. There's not enough wind. What is it?"

"It's what makes the jungle move. The petals are part of it too. Whatever side of the jungle is most dry, there the funnel wants to face. The petals reflect sunlight to swing the jungle round in that direction."

"You talk like the jungle is a whole creature, that thinks."

She smiled. "It's not very smart. We're fooling it now. The fires are to make the jungle dry on one side."

"Oh."

"There are tens of life forms in the jungle. One of them is a kind of... spine for the whole thing. Its life is deep down, and it lives off the dead stuff that drifts toward the center. Everything in the jungle contributes something. The foliage is various plants that root in what the jungle-heart collects, but they rot and feed the jungle-heart and shield the jungle-heart if something big hits

the jungle. We do our part too. We transport fertilizer down—
dead leaves and garbage and our own dead—and we kill bur-
rowing parasites."

"How does a jungle move? The Grad didn't know."

"The silver petals turn the jungle to put the funnel where the
jungle is most dry. If everything gets too dry, then the funnel
spits hot steam."

"So?"

"Clave, it's time to put the fires out. I must tell the others.
I'll be back."

Minya followed Dloris through twisting, branching tunnels.
Minya's grip on Jinny's arm was relaxed; it would tighten if Jinny
tried anything foolish. But the treemouth, and any chance to
leap into the sky, were farther away with every step.

The way the tunnels twisted, Minya wasn't sure where she
was. Near the midbranch, she thought; and the tuft would be
narrowing toward the fin. She couldn't see solid wood, but from
the way the spine branches pointed, the branch was below and
to her left. Earlier she had passed a branching tunnel and heard
children's laughter and the shouting of frustrated adults: the
schools. She could find this place again.

The mouth of a woven hut showed ahead. Dloris stopped.
"Minya. If anyone asks . . . you and Jinny both think you're pregnant. So the Scientist's Apprentice will examine you both. Jinny,
I'll take you to your sister, and what happens then is none of *my*
business."

They had reached the hut. Dloris shooed them in. Two men
waited inside, one in Navy blue, the other—"Who are you?"
Dloris demanded.

"Madam Supervisor? I'm Jeffer, the Scientist's Apprentice . . .
other apprentice. Lawri is otherwise engaged."

To meet both Minya and Jinny was more than the Grad had
hoped for.

He introduced his Navy escort to the women; Ordon was
clearly interested. Ordon and Dloris stayed while the Grad ques-

tioned Jinny. She couldn't be pregnant, the timing was wrong, and he told her so. She and Dloris nodded as if they'd expected that and departed the hut through the back.

He asked Minya the appropriate questions. She hadn't menstruated since a dozen sleeps before Dalton-Quinn Tree came apart. He told the Navy man, "I'm going to have to examine her."

Ordon took the hint. "I'll be right outside."

The Grad explained what was needed. Minya stepped out of her poncho's lower loop, lifted it and lay down on the table. The Grad palped her abdomen and her breasts. He tested the secretions of her vagina in plant juices Klance had shown him how to use. He'd practiced such an examination in Quinn Tuft, with the Scientist supervising, as part of his training. Once.

"No problem. A normal pregnancy," he said. "It's anyone's guess when it happened."

Minya sighed. "All right. Dloris said so too. At least it gives me a chance to see you. Could it be Gavving's?"

"The timing's right, but . . . you've been available to the citizens, haven't you?"

"Yes."

"Minya, shall I tell Gavving it's his?"

"Let me think." Minya ran faces past her memory. Some were blurs, and she liked it that way. Did they resemble Gavving at all? But the arrogant dwarf had claimed two of her sleeptimes— "No. What's the truth? You don't know?"

"That's right."

"Tell him that. We'll just have to see what the child looks like."

"All right."

Jinny and Dloris had gone down to the pregnant women's complex, a good, safe distance away. Luckily the Grad's guard was male. A woman might not have given them privacy during the examination. With her poncho hiked up and her legs apart, Minya said, "Stay where you are in case Ordon peeks in. Grad, is there any chance of getting us out of here?"

Keeping his head clear wasn't easy under the circumstances, but he made the effort. "Don't move without me. I mean it. We can't do *anything* unless we can stop them using the carm."

"I wasn't sure you were still with us."

"With you?" He was startled...though he had had doubts. There was so much to *learn* here! But what was it like for the others, for Gavving or Minya? "Of course I want to break us free! But no matter what we do, they can stop us while they've got the carm. And have you seen a dwarf around?" *Like Harp*, he thought, but Minya hadn't known Harp.

"I know him. Mark. Acts like he's three meters tall, but he's less than two. Thick-bodied, lots of muscles, likes to show them off." Bruises healing on her arms helped her to remember.

"He's important. He's the only one who can use the old armor."

"We'd like him to meet with an accident?"

"If it's convenient. Don't do anything till we're ready to move."

She laughed suddenly. "I admire your coolness."

"Really? Look down."

She looked, and blushed and covered her mouth. "How long—?"

"Ever since you pulled up your poncho. I'm going to have a serious case of lover's plaint."

"When I first met you I thought...no, don't move. Remember the guard."

He nodded and stayed where he was. She said, "Grad...my guest...I hope it's Gavving's, but it's already there, no matter whose. Let's—" She sought words, but the Grad was already moving. She finished in a breathless laugh. "—Solve your problem."

The poncho was ludicrously convenient. It need only be pulled aside. He had to bite hard on his tongue to hold his silence. It was over in a few tens of breaths; it took longer to find his voice. "Thank you. Thank you, Minya. It's been...she's...I was afraid I'd be giving up women."

"Don't do that." Minya's voice was husky. She laughed suddenly. *"She?"*

"The other apprentice is a citizen who treats me like a thieving copsik. Either I'm dirt for the treemouth or I'm a spy. Anyway, it's my problem. Thanks."

"It wasn't a gift, Grad." She reached down to squeeze his hands. "I'm sick of being treated like a copsik too. When do we get *loose*?"

"Quick. It has to be. The First Officer has spoken. We move the tree as soon as possible."

"When's that?"

"Days, maybe less. I'll know when I get back to the Citadel. Lawri's up there counting-down the carm's motor systems. I'd give either testicle to be in two places at once, but I *couldn't* miss the chance to talk to you. Can you pass a message to Gavving?"

"No way at all."

"Okay. There's a cluster of huts under the branch, and that's where the women stay when they carry guests, for more tidal pull while the baby's developing. So. Is there anyone at the treemouth that you want fighting beside you?"

"Maybe." She thought of Heln.

"Maybe isn't good enough. Skip the treemouth. If something happens, grab Jayan and anyone else you think you need and go up. A lot of the men spend their time at the top of the treemouth. We can hope Gavving and Alfin are there. But wait till something drastic happens."

Chapter Seventeen

"When Birnham Wood..."

THE HUGE SILVER PETALS WERE RISING, FOLDING INWARD. THE funnel at their center faced east and out, and the sun was moving into line with the funnel. Gold was eastward and seemed close. The sluggish whorl of storm was a strange sight, neither mundane nor scientific, but mind-gripping.

Clave and Kara were alone. The other fire-tenders had gone elsewhere after the fires were quenched. The Sharman asked, "Do you know the law of reaction?"

"I'm not a baby."

"When the steam spits from the funnel, the jungle moves in the opposite direction. That would be back to moister surroundings, back into the Smoke Ring, if we weren't . . . meddling. Afterward something must be regrown: fuel, perhaps. It takes twenty years."

"That's why they've been getting away with the raids."

"Yes. But no more."

The petals stood at thirty degrees from vertical. The sun shone directly into the funnel, and the petals were shining into it too. The funnel cupped an intolerable glare.

Kara said, "The jungle-heat spits when the sun shines straight into the blossom. It's not easy to make it spit at a chosen time, but . . . this day, I think."

It came as if by the Sharman's command: a soft, bone-shaking *fumf* from the funnel. Clave felt heat on his face. The jungle shuddered. Kara and Clave clung tight with hands and feet.

A cloud began to form between himself and the sun. A column of steam, racing away from him. He felt a tug, a tide, pulling him toward the sky.

"It works," he said. "I didn't . . . How long till we reach the tree?"

"A day, maybe less. The warriors are gathering now."

"*What?* Why didn't you tell me?" Without waiting for an answer, Clave dove into the foliage. His thoughts were murderous. Had she cost him his place in the coming battle? *Why?*

Four copsiks were running the elevator lines with their legs, and the Grad's eye caught Gavving among them. The elevator had almost reached its cradle. Was there no way to tell him? *Minya's with the pregnant women. She's fine. I'm in the Citadel—*

Ordon said, "So you couldn't wait for the Holidays."

The Grad jumped violently. For a moment he was actually floating. Ordon bellowed laughter. "Hey, forget it, it's nothing. With a chance like that, how could you not? That's why Dloris got a little upset when she saw you weren't Lawri."

The Grad grinned a sickly grin. "Did you watch the whole time?"

"No, I don't need to get my kicks that way. I can visit the Commons. I just poked my head in and saw what you were poking and pulled it back out again." He put the Grad into the elevator with a friendly, forceful shove in the small of his back and followed him in.

He seemed friendly enough, but first and last he was the Grad's guard. The Grad was not to be harmed; the Grad was not to escape. He liked to talk, but . . . They had come to the pregnant women's complex the long way round, by way of the Navy installation on the fin. They had returned by the same route. Presumably Ordon had some business on the fin. The Grad had asked about it. Ordon had become coldly suspicious. He would not talk to a copsik about his work.

The tuft sank away. This was far easier than the four-day climb up Dalton-Quinn Tree. A flock of small birds was veering wide of the trunk. "Harebrains," Ordon said. "Good eating, but you have to use the carm to chase them down. The old Scientist used to let us do that. Klance won't."

A streamer of rain was blowing across the out tuft. Was that why the First was so eager to move the tree? Wet citizens?

A mobile tree: it boggled the mind. Find your own weather!

A fluffy green bauble hung east of the out tuft, with a strange spreading plume of white mist behind it. Within a day or two London Tree would have put it from sight. The Grad wondered if he was being unreasonably antsy. The carm could reach Carther States across any distance. If he couldn't capture the carm, he would be here forever; and if he could, what was the hurry?

But time had a choke hold on his throat.

Life was not intolerable for the Scientist's Apprentice. In a hundred sleeps he might grow into this new life. When the time came he feared he would move too slowly, or not at all.

Clave found Merril in the Commons. She was dipping the points of crossbow bolts in the evil-smelling brew the Carthers made from poison fern.

The increasing tide caught Clave jumping toward her. He paused, then floated back, laughing. "It's real! I sure wasn't going to call her a liar, but—"

"Clave, what's *happening*?" Merril was drifting too, arrows all about her. She managed to catch the poison pot and cap it before it spilled.

"We're on our way. The warriors are on the surface." Clave jumped to his pack against the pull of the strange tide. He had readied it some sleeps ago.

Merril barked, "*What*? How long have we got?"

She had spent her days learning how to make arrows, twist bowstrings, shape a crossbow and fire it. Clave had watched her at target practice. She was as good as most of the Carthers, and her powerful arms were faster at resetting the crossbow.

He said it anyway. "Merril, you're in Carther States whether you go or not. A lot of Carthers aren't citizens."

"So?"

"You don't have to go."

"You can feed that to the tree, O Chairman!"

Clave shoved a handful of the freshly poisoned bolts into his quiver. "Then grab your gear and go!"

The tide was about like that in Quinn Tuft. Using the tunnels was almost like walking. But it was *strange*. Every branchlet and foliage tuft had the tremors.

Clave pulled himself through crackling branchlets and soft green turf, through to the sky. A column of cloud raced outward from beyond the jungle's horizon. The surface was nearly vertical. He took care for his handholds.

Skeletal warriors emerged like earthworms out of the green billows. Fifty or sixty Carthers had already chosen and boarded pods. Clave was annoyed. The Sharman had told him late, and nobody had told Merril. Why? To give them a chance to back out? "Sure I'd have fought, but I didn't get the word in time—"

Maybe the Carthers needed copsiks more than citizens.

He helped Merril through the foliage. The light of battle was in her eye. She said, "The copsik runners left us behind. Not worth their time."

"I had a broken leg." Clave got it then, and hid his grin. "They made a terrible mistake leaving you, though."

"They'll find out. Don't you laugh!" She shook a harpoon; its point was stained with evil yellow. "This goop will drive you crazy if it doesn't kill you."

The sky was a vast sheet of cloud. Lightning flashed in dark rifts. Clave searched the western fringe until he found a thin line

of shadow. London Tree was too big to hide in a cloud: fifty
klomters or so, half the length of Dalton-Quinn, but five times
the long axis of this puffball jungle.

The Comlink's chosen leader, Anthon, already had his legs
wrapped around the largest pod. Anthon was brawnier than the
average Carther man, and darker. To Clave he might have had
a fragile look, with long bones that could be snapped at whim.
But he was festooned with weaponry, crossbow and bolts and a
club with a knot on the end; his nails were long and sharp; scars
showed here and there on his body; and in fact he looked savage
and dangerous.

The stem-ends of the jet pods had been pierced by wooden
stakes that now served as plugs. A warrior would nestle into the
inner curve of the pod and move his weight to guide it. Clave
had used up a few pods practicing.

There were more pods than warriors, a hundred or so spaced
wide apart and tied down with light line. Merril chose one and
boarded it. Clave asked, "Shall I tether you?"

"I'll handle it." She swung her coil of line below her and
caught it coming up. Clave shrugged and chose his own pod. It
was bigger than he was but less massive: thirty kilos or so.

Men outnumbered women, but not by a lot. Merril said,
"Notice the women? You *fight* for citizenship in Carther States.
A citizen makes a better wife. The family gets two votes."

"Sure."

"Clave, how are they *doing* this?"

"Classified." He grinned and ducked the butt of her harpoon.
"I can't tell you everything. The Sharman says the jungle will
pass the tree at an angle, about midpoint, with a klomter to
spare. By then we'll have launched. We'll match speed with the
tree and come in while they're still terrified."

"How do we get back?"

"I asked that too." Clave's brows furrowed. "Lizeth and Hild
are bringing extra pods. They'll hover in the sky till they see the
battle's over... but they'll just be caught with the rest of us if
the copsik runners use the carm. We've *got* to take the carm."

"What are we trying to do, exactly? I mean you and me."

"Gather Quinn Tribe. We want to look good to Carther States, but Quinn Tribe comes first. I wish I knew where they all are."

Mist was drifting over them, seeping into the foliage. A wind was rising. Storm blurred the sky. He kept his eyes on the faint, shadowy line of London Tree...which was nearer and growing.

The out tuft was nearest: the citizens' tuft. Citizens would be first to see the oncoming terror: a green mass klomters across flying at the trunk, green warriors coming out of the sky. Not much chance of surprise here. The jungle too was too big to be hidden.

Realistically, they hadn't a ghost of a chance of rescuing any-body. They would do as much damage as possible and die. Why not attack the out tuft first? Kill some citizens and they'd re-member better.

Too late now. The Sharman was klomters away, tending a pillar of fiery steam, aiming it to send the jungle a fingernail's width from the tree. Fat chance of getting to her with a change in plan!

The line within the fog had solidified into a tremendous in-tegral sign tufted at the ends. Every Carther now held a sword. Clave drew his.

"Warriors!" Anthon bellowed. He waited for silence, then cried, "Our attack must be remembered! It's not enough to break some heads. We must *damage* London Tree. London Tree must remember, for a generation to come, that offending Carther States is dangerously stupid. Unless they remember, they will come when we cannot move.

"Let them remember the lesson!

"Launch!"

Sixty swords slashed at the lines that tied them to the jungle. Sixty hands pulled the plugs from the stem-ends of sixty jet pods. Pods jetted away in a wind that smelled of rotted plants. At first they clustered, even bumping into each other. Then they began to separate. Not all jet pods thrust alike.

Clave clung with arms and legs, tight against the screaming

pod. He was wobbling a little, more than the others. Unskilled. Blood was draining from his head. The tide was ferocious.

The sky was dark and formless, and lightning flashed nearby. They were approaching the center of the tree, as planned. There at the midpoint was the carrier, its nose against the trunk. Its tail was on fire.

Lawri tapped the blue button in a row of five.

Blue numbers flickered and steadied in the bow window. Blue lights appeared in the panel below: four clumps of four little vertical dashes each, in diamond patterns around a larger vertical bar. The array tickled at the Grad's memory. Lawri's hands hovered like Harp about to play.

"Strap in," Klance said. Lawri looked back in annoyance, then tapped rapidly. The Grad got it then. He was in a chair when the carm roared and trembled and lunged.

Tide pulled the Grad back in his seat, then eased off. (It hadn't mattered in Quinn Tuft, but the Scientist had drummed it into his head. Not tide! This was thrust! It might feel the same, but causes and consequences were different. The dead Scientist's legacy: *thrust*!)

The bow window nestled snug against the trunk. A breeze had sprung up; eddies swirled through the airlock doors. The Grad couldn't see anything of import through the side windows.

Lawri activated green patterns and tapped at them. Within the bow window appeared a smaller window in which an edge of sky peeped around a glare of white light. An aft view within the forward view: disconcerting.

Klance was going for a better look. He made his way to the airlock, gripping chair backs as he went. The Grad followed. A few kilograms of tide... of thrust took the vibrating walls forward, past him, till he hit the aft wall with a solid thump.

Klance was braced in the outer door, all of his fingers and toes gripping the rim. "I'll let you see in a minute, Jeffer. Don't fall out. You might not get back." He craned his head out. "Damnation!"

"What is it?"

"It's the jungle. I had no *idea* they could move the jungle! Hah. We'll give them a surprise. We'll just move away from them." Klance grinned over his shoulder. He saw the Grad brace himself, too late.

The Grad's foot lashed out and caught the Scientist above the hip. Klance yelled and flew outward. Long fingers and toes still clung. The Grad's heel smashed at a hand and a foot. Klance disappeared.

He moved into the outer door and leaned out. The drive screamed in his ears.

The tree was massive, but it was moving. Klance drifted slowly aft, thrashing, trying to reach the nets on the carm's hull. In his terror he seemed to have forgotten his line. He saw the Grad leaning out and shrieked at him: curses or pleading, the Grad couldn't tell. He looked away.

The tree now had a slight curve to it, like Minya's bow. The carm thrust in the center, and the tufts trailed behind, not very far. A stronger thrust might break the tree in the middle. But the carm was so much tinier than the tree; it was probably thrusting at full power now.

Klance was a thrashing black shadow against a brilliance like Voy brought close. The carm's main motor sprayed blue-white fire, pushing the carm forward against the mass of the tree. Klance was floating into the flame.

Ordon, halfway to the elevator, had seen them.

The jungle had become half the sky. Scores of objects moved alongside it: shapes like those he'd seen before the bark raft crashed into the jungle. Jungle giants on jet pods! But they wouldn't arrive if the carm continued to push the tree away. He had to turn off the main motor, now!

So he *hadn't* been premature, *hadn't* murdered Klance for nothing.

Lawri! He reentered the carm and leapt toward the bow. Lawri hadn't seen him. She stiffened suddenly and half rose, staring aghast at the rear window display. A shadow was thrashing in the flame, dissolving.

She whirled about. She was staring him in the eye when the Grad lashed out at her jaw.

Her head snapped back; she bounced against her straps and hung limp. The Grad used his line to tie her to one of the chairs. He sat down at the controls and studied them.

Yellow governed life support systems, including interior lights and the airlock. Green governed the carm's senses, internal and external. Blue had to do with what moved the carm, including the motors, the two flavors of fuel supply, the water tank, and fuel flow. White read the cassettes.

What had Lawri done to activate the drive? His mind had gone blank. He tapped the blue button. No good: the blue displays disappeared, but the motor's roar continued. He restored the display.

Through a side window he glimpsed patches of Navy blue cloth moving across the bark. *No time. Think.* Blue vertical bar surrounded by blue dashes . . . in a pattern like the motors at the stern. He tapped the blue bar.

The roar and the trembling died to nothing. The tree recoiled: he felt himself pulled forward. Then it was quiet.

Kendy was prepared to beam his usual message when the source of hydrogen light disappeared.

That was puzzling. Normally the CARMs main motor would run for several hours. That, or the attitude jets would send it jittering about like the ball in a soccer match. Kendy held his attention on a drifting point within the Smoke Ring maelstrom, and waited.

A dozen Navy men were making their way toward the carm, using lines and the lineholds, wary that he might start the drive again. Ordon was far ahead of the rest, mere meters from the window. There was murder in his face.

Quick, now! Hit the yellow button. The display was too cluttered: turn off the blue. Yellow display: interior lights showed *dim*, internal wind *on*, temperature shown by a vertical line with numbers and a notch in the middle; here, a complicated line drawing of the carm's cabin seen from above. The Grad closed lines that should represent the doors, with a pinching motion of his fingertips. Behind him the airlock sealed itself.

Lawri stirred.

He heard muted clanging from the doors.

The Grad began playing with the green displays, summoning different views from the carm's cameras. He had precious little time to learn to fly this starstuff relic. He felt Lawri's eyes on him, but would not look.

The clanging stopped, then resumed elsewhere. Ordon snarled through a side window. He must be clinging to the nets, pounding at the glass.

The Grad moved to the window. He spoke a word. Ordon reacted—puzzled—he couldn't hear. The Grad repeated it, exaggerating the motions of his lips the word that would justify murdering his benefactor Klance, assaulting Lawri, betraying his friend Ordon, leaving London Tree helpless against attack.

"War, Ordon! War!"

Chapter Eighteen

The War of London Tree

CLAVE WAS BEING LEFT BEHIND. THE CARTHERS HAD JUDGED him a novice, and he was: he hadn't known how to choose among these strange pods. They had let him pick a slow one. He'd flown past the trunk; his path was curving back now. He would be among the last half-dozen to land.

Lines ran along the trunk of London Tree, and wooden boxes were rising toward the center from both ends. Clave saw both boxes break open almost simultaneously, spilling men in blue, eight to a box. The copsik runners seemed to know what they were about. They rapidly oriented themselves and fired small jet pods to send them toward the midpoint of the tree, on the eastern face.

Toward the carrier. Twenty-odd copsik runners already surrounded it. The flame at its tail had died, for whatever that might mean.

The Carthers had passed the trunk in a gust of jet pods. Now they were returning, coming up on the western side of the trunk, drastically spread out. Feathered harpoons flew from the copsik runners' long footbows. The Carther warriors sent crossbow bolts among them. They outnumbered the enemy almost two to one.

The jungle was tremendous, a green world passing less than a klomter away. Clave had wondered if it would actually hit the tree, but it seemed to be going past. The steam jet had stopped firing. The jungle trailed a curdled line of cloud and a storm of birds trying to catch up, and two dark masses: Lizeth's and Hild's clusters of twenty jet pods each.

This close to the tree, the curve of the trunk hid the ancient carrier and its mooring; but both gusts of enemy reinforcements seemed to be converging on the carrier. They would know its value too. They flew behind a thicket of feathered harpoons.

The jet from Clave's pod died away.

Curses ran through his mind while he clambered around the pod to put it between himself and the harpoons. He was still approaching the trunk. Others were there first. Carthers were using lineholds about the clustered buildings to dodge the feathered harpoons or tearing up sheets of bark for shields. The copsik runners preferred to fire on them from the sky, where their limbs were free to work their huge bows.

Anthon and a dozen warriors were firing at the carrier, using the curve of the trunk as cover.

Merril's pod struck a wooden hut with Merril behind it. She'd used the pod as a shock absorber: good technique. Some of the copsik runners were trying to reach that building. Merril shot two from behind the building, then abandoned the shelter when the rest came too close.

Something valuable in that building? The copsik runners seemed to want it. Clave put an arrow among them and thought he hit someone's foot.

They wanted the carrier more. Clave could see it now: they were all over it, hanging on the nets and the bark.

Most of the Carther warriors had reached the trunk. Clave would touch down inward from the battle, presently. For now he could only watch. From the chaos of battle, patterns began to form:

The copsik runners were outnumbered. They hung back, for that reason and another. In close work they couldn't use the bows. They had swords, and so did the Carthers; but the taller Carthers had more reach. They won such encounters.

The copsik runners had small jet pods, the kind that would grow on an integral tree. They preferred to stay in the sky.

Clave watched Carthers leap into an eight-man gust of blue ponchos. The copsik runners used their jet pods, left Carthers floundering in the sky behind them, and fired back with the footbows. Then two Carthers were among them, slaying, and two more joined them. In free-fall the copsik runners fought like children. The Carthers robbed the corpses of their jet pods.

Clave drifted, and Carther States was winning without him!

In along the trunk, a wooden box was rising slowly. It spilled reinforcements: six blue-clad footbowman and a bulky silver creature. There was a terrible familiarity to that shape... but they wouldn't arrive for a kilobreath yet.

A copsik runner spotted Clave, a sitting target. He carefully fired a harpoon through Clave's pod, then moved in along the trunk. He'd have a clear shot when Clave came nearer. Clave fired at him. No good; the copsik runner dodged and waited. Clave could see his grin.

The grin vanished when Merril shot him from behind. The bolt protruded below the kidney. He could have fought on... but his face was a silent scream; he clawed at the bolt, then went into convulsions. That poison-fern brew must be terrible stuff.

The pod bumped wood with Clave behind it. He turned it loose, clutched bark, and made his way toward Merril with his crossbow ready. He saw blue against storm cloud sky, fired a bolt through one man, and drew his harpoon as the other came at him with a sword.

The copsik runner came too fast. Clave batted him in the face with the crossbow handle and, as he recoiled, stabbed him in the throat.

Merril was making her way around the curve of the bark. He followed her. She stopped and crouched a moment before he saw the carrier, outward along the trunk. Copsik runners were all over it.

He moved up beside her. She said, "All right, why aren't they killing us with that scientific thing?"

"Good question." Clave watched Anthon's team launching crossbow bolts from around the curve of the wood. The carrier's guardians fired back, not very successfully.

He said, "Forget it. They *aren't* using it. They *are* using those wooden boxes to get reinforcements. Let's—"

"Cut the lines."

"Right."

Two lines as thick as Clave's arm ran parallel along the trunk. The last box was on its way in, nearly gone from sight. Another box must be rising. Clave and Merril made their way to the nearest line and began to chop at it.

Six men and a silver thing were coming into footbow range. Clave and Merril set bark sheets to protect themselves. Clave stared at the silver man. It was as if he were trying to remember a nightmare: a man made of starstuff, with a blank ball for a head. Clave fired at it until he saw a crossbow bolt strike and bounce away.

There were feathered harpoons in his shield and Merril's. Clave saw three tiny things like thorns strike her shield in a line aimed at her bare head.

He yelled. She ducked. Thorns spat into the trunk. She said, "Oh. The silver man."

"You know him?"

"Yes... keep chopping... he was with the copsik runners in Carther States. We don't have anything to breech that armor."

Another box had come into sight when the line parted. That box began to drift. Men spilled loose and flew in curves, pod-propelled, making for the trunk. They seemed too far in to do anything useful. The other line had gone slack. Merril said, "It's a loop. We don't have to cut the other one."

"Then let's get out. There was a cable running outward—"

"No. Let's go join the victory party. Quick, or we'll be left behind."

"Victory—?" Then Clave saw what she meant.

Green-clad warriors clustered round the carrier. Some were crawling into the doors. Men in blue floated about it with the looseness of dead men. Live copsik runners had retreated around the curve of the trunk to wait for reinforcements.

It looked like the war of the carrier was over. But other copsik runners were coming too near. Clave had made a lucky shot: there were five now, plus the silver man.

Ordon died with a bolt peeking through his chest. The Grad saw his face through the window...but even if Ordon could have heard him, there was nothing left to say. He turned back to the yellow display.

He had five floating rectangles in the bow window: aft view, dorsal, ventral, and both sides. He caught glimpses of men in blue, men and women in green; impossible to tell who was winning.

Three Navy men moved into the cover of the drive motors. The Grad touched blue dashes. Flames burst near them. They yelled, threw themselves clear, floundered to orient themselves...and one had a bolt through his hip.

Lawri screamed, "Murderer!"

"Some of us don't like being copsiks," the Grad said. "Some of us don't even like copsik runners."

"Klance and I never treated you with anything but kindness!"

"That's true enough. What have you done for the rest of Quinn Tribe? Did you forget that I had a tribe?"

"Your tribe is dead! Your tree is torn apart! *We* could have been your tribe, you treefeeding mutineer you!"

The Grad had no patricular urge to stop her mouth. Lawri's accusations only echoed those in his own mind. He had made his decisions.

So he spoke without heat. "Do you know what's been happening to our women? Gavving might have had permission to visit his wife thirty-odd days from now, but any male citizen had rights to her any time he liked. Now she's pregnant. She doesn't know who the father is, and I don't either."

Lawri said, "They'll kill you. Shall I tell you what the penalty is for mutiny?"

"Feel free, but I notice the line of argument has shifted."

She told him anyway. It sounded dreadful enough: good reason to keep the doors closed.

He had found the infrared display. It showed him red dots in along the trunk. He cut the infrared out and recognized Clave and Merril, and Navy chasing them... including what had to be a dwarf in a pressure suit.

Clave and Merril! Then the Carthers were actually on his side. He had wondered.

The green-clad warriors rushed the carm. When the Navy retreated he was able to wrap one in flame, not as a casual killing but as a signal to the Carthers. *I'm with you!* For it was Carthers who now swarmed the carm, and Navy who retreated around the trunk.

The Grad opened two yellow lines with his fingertips. He turned to greet the tall, bloody jungle giants.

Gavving was on his feet, held upright by two men, before he even started to wake up. He said, "What?"

"We need pedalers," someone said.

Four Navy men helped three sleepy copsiks out of the barracks and up through the tuft. Gavving held his temper and Horse took it with typical docility, but Alfin was still protesting as they broke through into sunlight. "I'm the treemouth tender's assistant! Not a treefeeding pair of legs—"

"Listen, you. We're sending men up to the Citadel as fast as we can. We've worked the regular team half to death. You'll take your place and pedal with the rest!"

"And carry out my regular duties too? *I'll* be half-dead! What do I tell the Supervisor?"

"You board that bicycle or you'll be telling your Supervisor where your testes went. Just before the Holidays too!"

The copsiks on the platform were sheathed in sweat; it drifted in droplets from their hair; they panted like dying men. The

Navy men helped three of them down, wincing at the soggy touch. Other Navy men were boarding the elevator.

Half the sky was textured green.

The jungle! The jungle had come to London Tree!

Only three Navy men remained. One was an officer; Gavving recognized him, and he carried a piece of old science, a talking box. The rest had entered the elevator. Gavving was lifted into the saddle. He started pedaling. The elevator rose.

The jungle had attacked London Tree. The jungle was mobile. Who would have guessed? The green cloud was awesomely close . . . and receding.

He should be doing something! But what? Armed men were watching.

The elevator was tens of klomters above him now, and Gavving was gasping. He felt the change before he saw it. Suddenly it was easier to pedal. The grating whine of the bicycle gears rose half an octave. He looked up.

The elevator box was turning, falling. Blue shapes spilled out and made for the trunk. One was too slow. When he reached the trunk he was moving too fast; he bounced away, spinning like a broken thing, and continued to fall. But the box was falling faster.

"Stop pedaling. Hold your places," the officer ordered.

The invaders had cut the cable. Now what? *In takes you east.* The box wouldn't hit here; it would strike farther east along the branch, but where? Gavving pictured the massive wooden structure smashing through diffuse cottony foliage. "Officer? Suppose that thing hits the pregnant women's complex?"

"It's under the branch," the man said. "Mmm . . . it could hit somebody, though. Damn, there's the school complex! *Karal!* Move east along the top of the branch and get everyone underneath. Don't miss the examination hut. Docking section too. Then get under yourself, if you're fast enough."

"Sir." A Navy man—wounded, with one arm bound across his chest—darted awkwardly away. Two left.

The officer spoke to his talking box. "Squad Leader Patry here.

The enemy has cut our elevator cables. What's your status?"

The answer was almost unintelligible with static. Gavving let his chin droop and his eyes half close (poor exhausted copsik, clearly too tired to think of mutiny) and listened hard. He heard, "Elevators running. We . . . ing troops. Enemy numbers for *garble,* repeat, forty to fifty. *Garble* outnumbered. They're gentling us. They garble the carm, but even . . . can't use . . . tethered."

"I see two dark masses west of here."

"Forget them. . . . trouble enough. We are sending more men to the Citadel."

"Patry out."

The Grad recognized the long-limbed woman, Debby, by her long, straight brown hair. The two men with her were strangers. The crossbows aimed at him didn't bother him as much as their fear. They didn't like the carm at all.

He spread open hands to the sides. "I'm the Quinn Tribe Scientist, the only one who can fly this thing. Good to see you, Debby—"

Lawri broke in with, "Feed it to the tree, mutineer! You'd lose us in the sky or smear us all over the trunk."

"—and this is Lawri, the copsik runner."

One snapped out of it. "I'm Anthon. This is Prez. Debby told us about you, Grad. Can we leave immediately? Pile all our warriors on the nets and go? The silver man is coming."

The Grad said, "We're tied to the tree. Cut those lines and we're free to go. But I don't leave without Clave and Merril, and I think there's time to get one more thing."

He pointed into the dorsal window display. Anthon and Debby very gingerly moved up behind him. All this scientific stuff must be daunting.

"That hut is the Lab. Debby, you'll find some cassettes and the reader inside, on the walls. You remember what they look like?"

Debby nodded.

"Go get them. Anthon, get some warriors to cut the carm loose." He looked into the displays. Clave was towing Merril as he jumped along the bark, his legs serving both while she fired bolts at their pursuers. One Navy man was dropping back, hurt. The silver man came on. The Grad said, "See if you can give them some covering fire."

Anthon said quietly, "You're not the leader here, Scientist."

"Here, I *am*. And I have had enough of being a copsik!"

"Debby, go get that treefodder for the Scientist. Take a team. Prez, get those cables chopped." Anthon waited until they were through the doors before he spoke again. He wanted no witnesses to this discussion.

"Grad, have you fought in war?"

"I captured the carm."

"You? *I* cap—" He trailed off. "Never mind."

"How many are you?"

"Forty or less, now. We won't fit inside, but we can hang on to the nets."

"I want to set the rest of Quinn Tribe free. They're in the in tuft, and I can find them. The carm's got plenty of what makes it go. We've got the small motors for spraying fire. It should be easy."

Anthon was in no hurry to make a decision. Into the silence Lawri said, "He can't fly the carm. I can. I'm the Scientist's Apprentice."

"Why haven't you killed this one?" Anthon demanded.

"Hold it! She's what she says...and I did have to kill the Scientist himself. Lawri has a great deal to teach us, if she can be talked into it. She's harmless as long as she's tied up."

Anthon nodded. "She lives, then. But *I* lead Carther States."

"*I* captain the carm."

Anthon stepped into the doors and began to shout orders. He'd let the word pass. *Captain*. He who violated the Grad's orders aboard the carm would be a mutineer!

Carthers chopped at the lines that tethered the carm. Crossbow bolts flew among the blue men who followed Clave and Merril. Those dove for cover on the bark. The silver man came on alone. He wasn't using jet pods. There must be something on the pressure suit itself.

The carm was drifting free.

Lawri spoke in an angry whisper. "They'd kill me, wouldn't they?"

"They don't have my reasons for liking you," the Grad said without overt sarcasm. "Keep your opinions to yourself for a while, if you can. Did you really think a jungle warrior would let you at the controls?"

Clave and Merril and Debby entered like a storm. Debby was gashed and bleeding along the ribs. Merril flew into the Grad and hugged him. "Grad! I mean Scientist. Good work. I mean, glorious! Can you run this thing?"

The Grad felt huge relief. Let Clave play these dominance games with Anthon! The Grad would captain the carm and hope Lawri was wrong... "I can fly it."

Clave asked, "Can you find the rest of us?"

"They're all in the in tuft. Gavving's at the top, where we can get at him. Jayan and Minya are with the pregnant women. Jinny and Alfin should be in the Commons. We may have to leave the carm to get to them."

"Then, it's going to work. I can't believe it."

The Grad grinned. "So why'd you come? Never mind. Debby—"

"I got these. We had to fight for them." Seven cassettes. "We couldn't find the reader."

"Maybe Klance had it... it doesn't matter. Get into a chair. You too, Clave, Merril, *strap down!*" He looked into the displays. "In a few breaths we can..."

"What?" Clave saw the displays floating in the bow window. "This place is too strange for me. Those pictures make my eyes cross! I... Grad, have you got anything to take out the silver man?"

"Not unless he crawls into a motor. That's a starman's pressure suit."

"Well, he's killing all our allies."

"That spitgun only puts you to sleep and makes you feel wonderful. Doesn't matter to us, though. They're still out of action. Anthon, good timing. Get into a chair."

Anthon was panting; his crossbow was on line with the Grad's eyes. "You waited too long! That goddam silver—"

"Get into a chair and strap down! And tell me how many we've got left." The Grad was trying to watch all the displays at once. Carthers were disappearing over the trunk's horizon. Too many floated limp; some were being towed by others who hadn't been hit. The man in the pressure suit was hovering over the carm, firing darts.

The glazed look left Anthon's eyes. He worked himself into a chair. "We can't hurt him. I was the only one who even got to the carrier. The rest won't come anyway. They're afraid of it."

"We can't leave them."

The silver man darted down at the doors. The Grad pinched his fingers together. The silver man shied back as the doors closed in his face, then moved back into view in the dorsal display. Now he was gripping the nets on the hull.

"He's on the carm," said the Grad.

"Take off," said Anthon.

"Leave?"

"We can leave my citizens if we take the silver man with us. I've got spare jet pods coming."

"Good enough." The Grad's fingers tapped. The silver man was still hanging on the nets when the carm backed away from the trunk and started down.

Chapter Nineteen

The Silver Man

THE LAUNDRY VAT WAS A TALL GLASS CYLINDER. IT HUNG FROM the underside of the branch, from lines pounded into the black bark over Minya's head. Around it ran an extensive wickerwork platform woven from live spine branches. A layer of rocks beneath the vat supported a bed of coals. A pipe ran all the way from the treemouth reservoir to supply the water: an impressive achievement, had Minya not been too tired to appreciate it.

Minya and Ilsa stirred dirty clothing in a matrix of foaming water with a paddle two meters long. It took skill and fine attention. Left to itself, the laundry-soup would have foamed right out of the vat, clothing and all. The supervisor Haryet kept popping out to see how they were doing.

Minya wasn't feeling awkward yet, but there was the sense of a guest building inside her. Ilsa's pregnancy looked ludicrous, a bulge on a straight-edge. Like the others, she seemed to have adjusted to her new status with little difficulty. Once she had told Minya, "We know all our lives that the copsik runners might come for us. Well, they came."

A chain of huts ran along the underside of the branch. Most of the women preferred to stay inside. They weren't all pregnant.

Some were nursing their erstwhile guests. They all had work: knitting, sewing, preparation of food to be cooked at the tree-mouth.

The quiet was broken by a hurried rustling.

Then four people burst from the tunnel that led down from the examination hut: Jayan and Jinny, the supervisor Dloris, and a Navy man with his arm in a sling. Karal spotted her, ran to her, gripped her arm. She shied from his wildness.

"You're all right." He was gasping. "Good. Minya. Stay under the branch. Don't let anyone... *anyone* else go wandering."

"We don't tend to. We're too awkward. I thought men weren't allowed...?"

"I'm not staying. Minya, it's both elevators and at least one man, they're falling from thirty klomters up, and we don't know just where they'll hit. I've got to warn the children in the school complex." He pointed a finger at the tip of her nose. "Stay here!" And he sprinted for the tunnel, wobbling, chest heaving.

If something happens, the Grad had said. Something was happening, all right, but what? Would Dloris know?

Minya guessed where the supervisor would be. She moved down the line of huts and entered the last one as Dloris came through with Haryet. "We've been counting," Dloris said. "Gwen's missing. Have you seen her? Three meters tall and pale as a ghost, with a year-old guest?"

"Not lately. What's happening?"

"Get those clothes out and drying and then put the fire out. Do you have lines? Good. Keep them handy." The two supervisors moved on.

Minya turned to Jayan and Jinny. "Give us a hand. Jinny, we're lucky you were around. We're all together now. Do *you* know what's happening?"

"No. Karal looked scared stiff."

"Is it war?"

"Better stick to our task till we're sure," Ilsa said.

They pulled the clothing from the vat in a gelid mass, manipulating it with poles. Some water remained. They inverted the vat and moved back while the water-glob flowed sluggishly out onto the fire. Live steam didn't rise fast enough in London Tree's feeble tide. It tended to expand in an invisible globe, scalding hot.

Minya had never seen that fire go out. Dloris must be expecting something drastic!

They continued to work. They set the laundry in the press and cranked two great wooden slabs together. Water squeezed out around the edges of the wad of clothing, then began to slide downward.

Something smashed through foliage, somewhere nearby.

They froze. Then Minya plunged into the branchlets with Jinny and Ilsa behind. They made their way toward the sound. Minya angled above where she thought it had stopped.

There, a trail of broken branchlets. She followed it down to the broken and twisted remains of what had been a Navy officer. The corpse wore a sword, scabbarded, and a quiver that was still full, though the bow was missing.

"*Now* it's war," Minya said.

"We'll have to kill the supervisors," Ilsa said.

Minya jumped. "What?" It was as if a stone had spoken. "Never mind, you're right. I thought you were . . . I thought you'd given up."

Ilsa only shook her head.

West takes you in. In takes you east. At first the Grad held the bow window pointed straight down. They dropped smooth-ly . . . faster . . . he swung the carm to point west and fired aft jets to correct as it drifted away from the trunk.

His passengers were rigid with terror, save for Lawri, who was rigid with fury.

They still had a passenger on the hull.

Anthon's voice wanted to stutter. He wouldn't let it. "I want to point out that we could go back to Carther States *now*. We've got the silver man and the carm. These copsik runners don't own anything they value more. We can trade for your copsiks."

That actually sounded sensible. The Grad said, "Clave?"

"Feed it to the tree."

Anthon said, "You want to kill some copsik runners. All right, I can underst—"

"I want to rescue them myself! I am the Quinn Tribe Chairman. They are entitled to my protection." Clave spat the word: "Trade! They attacked us, we attacked them. We've got the carm and we'll have our people too. All right, Grad—Scientist—have you got an opinion?"

They were dropping too fast. The Grad swung the carm nosedown and fired forward jets. He said, "Nice of you to ask. We've got the Scientist's Apprentice and the silver suit and the only man alive who can fit into it. Maybe they would trade. We keep the carm."

"Never," said Lawri. "Trade with *copsiks!*"

Anthon and Clave looked at each other. The Grad said, "Never mind," and they laughed. Lawri's tone of voice said it all.

Minya stopped and looked out through a screen of branchlets.

The supervisors had found Gwen. Haryet was scolding her as they led her toward the huts. Haryet was second-generation copsik, shorter than Minya; she looked tiny beside her very pregnant captive.

They'll have heard us coming, Minya thought. Jinny must have realized that too. She stepped out through the crackling foliage, ten meters east of Minya's position. *Good! They'll think they heard one, not two—*

Dloris came toward Jinny with thunder in her face. Breaking new paths was strictly forbidden.

Minya emerged behind Haryet and stabbed her.

Gwen turned with her baby in her arms and shrieked. Dloris whirled and stared. Perhaps this place of mothers and babies had given the supervisor a false sense of safety. She reacted slowly. Before she could reach her truncheon, Jinny was pinning her arms and Minya was running at her in long, low leaps.

Dloris flipped forward. Jinny flew over her back and came

spinning at Minya, who lost a moment sidestepping. Then Dloris held half a meter of hardwood at guard; but she faced a Navy sword.

"Wait," she said. "Wait."

"My child will not be born a copsik!" Minya screamed and lunged.

Dloris danced backward. The tunnel was behind her, and Minya knew she had to stop the supervisor from reaching it. She ran at her, ready to bat the truncheon aside. Then Jayan and Ilsa were moving into place behind Dloris. Jayan held the big paddle well up the haft, blade first, like a two-handed sword.

Dloris dropped her truncheon. "Don't kill me. Please."

"Dloris, tell us what's happening."

"Carther States is all over the trunk. I don't know who's winning."

"Have they got the carm?"

"The *carm*?" Dloris showed nothing but astonishment.

They tied her with line. Ilsa wanted to do more; Minya knew Dloris too well to allow it. She wouldn't have killed Haryet either, if . . . if.

Gavving watched the carm descend in fire. Patry was talking to his box, too far away for Gavving to hear; but the Navy officer looked furious and frightened.

He caught Gavving watching him. "You! All of you! Stay where you are! Move and you'll be shot. Do you understand? Arny, take cover."

The two Navy men disappeared into the foliage. Presently Alfin said, "We're bait."

"There's only two."

Horse asked, "Do you really think your friends have the carm? What will they do with it?"

"Rescue us," Gavving said with more assurance than he felt. "Alfin, when it comes down, jump for the doors and hope they open."

Alfin snorted. "You've got to be out of your mind. *Look* at that thing, you want to *ride* in it?"

"I'll ride anything to get out of here, if I can take Minya."

"You don't have Minya. Listen, Gavving. I remember you with your eyes red and half-closed and crying in rivers. They make their own weather here! Nobody starves, nobody goes thirsty. It's a good, healthy tree with a good crop of earthlife. I've got a responsible position—"

"You *like* it here?"

"Oh...treefodder. Maybe I don't really like it anywhere. I took orders in Dalton-Quinn too. I'm seeing a supervisor, a nice woman even if she towers over me. I didn't have that in Quinn Tuft. Kor's a year or two old for the citizens, but we get along...and I don't like that box."

"I do." It was Horse who had spoken. "Gavving, cede me Alfin's place."

The carm was falling straight at them. Those had better be friends aboard! He could only die fighting if they were not. He told Horse, "It's not my decision. Just do what I do, and we'll see what Clave says."

"Done."

"Alfin. Last chance—"

"No."

"Why?"

Alfin met his eyes. "There's tide here."

Gwen's shriek of terror had started her baby screaming. He was quieter now. Gwen's awareness was in the hands that stroked and patted the child. There was none in her eyes.

The conspirators ignored Gwen as she ignored them. Ilsa led her back, once, when she tried to return to the huts. They didn't want Gwen talking to the others.

Jayan asked, "Ilsa, are you sure you want in on this?"

Jinny wasn't pregnant; Jayan and Minya were not obtrusively so. Ilsa was. She said, "My baby won't be born a copsik either."

The branch shuddered with the force of a tremendous blow. Ilsa said, "The second elevator. Karal said two."

Jayan said, "Minya, you've talked to the Grad. What did he say?"

"The Grad said to go up. He'll try to capture the carm. If he can't get the carm—"

"Then he's dead," Ilsa concluded, "and all the Carther States warriors are going to die, and we'll never get loose at all. So he's *got* to have the carm. He's got the carm and as many Carther States warriors as he can get aboard, and he's trying to reach us. Who goes with us?"

Nobody suggested a name. Jayan said, "We're the only new copsiks. Let the rest run their own revolt."

"You can't go up."

They turned, surprised. Dloris's eyes shied from their potentially lethal attention. She repeated doggedly, "You can't go up. The tunnels lead to the fin and the treemouth. There isn't any connecting tunnel to the top of the tuft; that's where the men live. None of you are in shape to tunnel through foliage, and if you got to the top you'd stand out like so many mobies in a stewpot."

"Then what?"

"Stay here till your friends come for you."

Ilsa shook her head. "The children's complex? Karal must have the upper reaches evacuated by now."

"Ilsa, it's big and complicated and it doesn't connect to the top. The most you'd do is get lost."

"What's your stake in this, Dloris?"

"Let me live. Don't tell anyone I helped."

"Why?"

"I wanted to escape once myself. Now I've been a supervisor too long. Somebody would be sure to want me dead. But you can't go up. Stay here and wait."

They looked at each other. Minya said, "You did that. For thirty years? No. I think I know what we have to do."

The Grad tapped at the motor controls...tricky. They had to be used in pairs and clusters or they'd spin the carm. He dropped into the foliage several meters from the platform, with a horrendous crashing, and opened the doors at once.

Three men jumped toward the door. Gavving gripped an older

man's arm. The third man wore blue, and he was swinging a
sword. Debby took careful aim and put a crossbow bolt through
him.

Gavving and the stranger pulled themselves inside. The older
man was gasping. "Get us moving," Gavving said. "This is Horse.
He wants to join Quinn Tribe. Alfin isn't coming. He likes it
here."

A feathered harpoon ricocheted through the doors. The Grad
closed them. He said, "I left Minya and Jayan in the pregnant
women's compound—"

"What? Minya?"

"She's carrying a guest, Gavving. Your child. And men aren't
permitted there." Later the Grad would tell him the truth... part
of it. For now, for witnesses and the record, *Minya is carrying her
husband's child.* "Ilsa's there too, Anthon. I told Minya to gather
them all and go up. We'll have to wait for them."

Clave nodded. Gavving stared with open mouth. He said,
"Grad, don't you know the men's tunnels don't connect to the
women's?"

"What?"

"They'd have to go all the way to the fin or the treemouth,
and back! Or break trail—Grad, they're sure to be captured!"

Clave had a hand on Gavving's shoulder. "Calm down, boy.
Grad, where would they go?"

The Grad tried to think. It was Horse who spoke. "Not the
fin. That's Navy. Maybe nobody would notice some extra women
at the Commons or the schools. Or maybe they'd just stay where
they are and wait."

"Jinny'll be at the treemouth anyway. Okay." The Grad fired
the forward motors.

The carm lifted tail-first from the tuft, leaving fires in its
wake. Lawri screamed, "You're setting the tree on fire!"

She was ignored. "I've been to the pregnant women's complex,"
the Grad said. "I haven't been in the Commons."

"Alfin has," Gavving said. "It's big, and it reaches to the
treemouth. If we can get the carm into the treemouth—"

Lawri writhed. "You can't! You can't burn the treemouth,

what *are* you? This isn't mutiny anymore, it's just wanton destruction!"

Anthon asked mildly, "Will London Tree trade with copsik mutineers?"

Lawri was silent.

"Lying wouldn't have helped. You were too convincing before. We'll go get our people."

The carm moved sideways above the tuft, accelerating sluggishly. Then there was clear sky below, and the Grad swung the carm around.

They were dropping past the treemouth. The carm slowed, hovered. The Grad touched paired yellow dots. Light flared into the Commons in twin beams, as if the carm were a tethered sun.

Women were running... away. Jungle giants all, leapfrogging across the woven spine-branch floor. None were the right size, nor dark enough, to be Jinny.

"Drop it," Clave said as if his voice hurt him. "Go for the pregnant women's compound. How do we get there?"

The Grad let the carm sink. They were below the tuft now: blue sky below, green passing above. "It's under the branch. I think our best move is to go up into it. I may not hit it exactly, and the Navy may have figured out what we're doing by now. Are you ready for a fight?"

"Yes," said several voices.

The Grad grinned. "Maybe I can scrape off the silver man too. I notice he's still with us... Now what's *that?*"

Things were falling from the foliage. A bundle of cloth tied with line. Long loaves of bread. A bird carcass, cleaned and skinned. Then the green sky was raining women. Jayan, Jinny, and a jungle giant: Ilsa?

"They jumped," Gavving said in wonder. "What if we hadn't come?"

"We did," Merril said. "Get 'em!"

Two big leather bags fell, and then another woman, leaping head-down to catch up with the rest: Minya.

The Grad cut the motors and took a moment to think. He

was aware of voices yelling at him but was able to ignore the intrusive noises.

Got to catch them in the airlock. What about the silver man? He was still clinging to the dorsal surface. The Grad rotated the carm to put it between the pressure-suited dwarf and the falling women.

They were separating. It would be three operations. Jayan and Jinny first. They faced each other across clasped hands, as they had after Dalton-Quinn Tree came apart. They seemed calm enough under the circumstances. The carm eased toward them.

The silver man was crawling around to the airlock.

"Hang on," the Grad said, and he started the carm spinning. Faster. His head spun too; he could see sickness in the faces behind him. The silver man, caught rounding a corner, was hanging by his hands. The Grad used the motors again, against the spin, and slapped the silver man hard against the hull. He flew free.

The Grad opened the doors. The twins were flying at him. He jetted flame to slow the carm; stopped just alongside them, backed and moved sideways. Then they were crawling into the carm.

Blue shapes crawled within the green sky. Armed Navy men, carrying jet pods and footbows and a massive thing that took three men to handle.

The reunion would have to wait. "Get 'em into chairs," he called back to Clave. Minya next. He was flying the carm like he'd done it all his life. He got a little careless; Minya thumped the hull, then came in with a bloody nose. "Sorry," he said. "Gavving, never mind that, get her to a chair! Who's the other one?"

"It's Ilsa," Anthon said. "They're shooting at her! Grad, get her!"

"I'm doing that. Do we need the food and other stuff?" He was alongside Ilsa now, between her and the falling Navy men. Voy glared behind her. Footbow arrows *tick*ed off the hull . . . but that *thump* had no place in his scheme. What—?

Ilsa's look of terror and determination faded into blissful sleep. He knew before he looked: the silver man was back, spitgun and all. He was on the dorsal surface, out of reach of the doors, and Anthon had thrown a line round Ilsa's waist and was pulling her in.

"Get her into—" The chairs were full. "Get her against the back wall and stay with her. Don't turn any fixtures. Debby, put a tethered bolt in that carcass and we'll pull it in."

Anthon said, "The silver man—"

"These are close quarters. If he gets through the door, swarm him. The spitgun doesn't kill, but if he shoots us all, he owns us."

Jinny called to the Grad, "We brought a stack of clean laundry and a water supply."

"We've got water. Laundry . . . why not? Hey, I told Minya to go *up*. You did it right, we'd never have found you—"

Minya said, "If you had the carm, you could find us in the sky. So we grabbed what we could and went down."

The Navy men had not left the branch's green underside. Hardly surprising. If they failed to capture the carm, how would they reach the tree again? They would have looked futile, the Grad thought, were it not for the bulky starstuff thing they handled like a weapon.

The salmon bird carcass was a black silhouette with Voy painfully bright behind it. Anthon and Debby had to squint . . . but their tethered arrows nailed it and they reeled it in. Maybe the silver man was hoping someone would show his head; none did. He tried to enter with the stack of ponchos, and the Grad almost managed to catch him in the closing door. That left the laundry outside too, and a red border around the yellow diagram. "I never saw red before. What's it mean?"

Lawri deigned to answer, contemptuously. "Emergency. Your line's holding the airlock open."

The Grad opened the door (the red warning disappeared) and Debby pulled the mass in. The silver man didn't try to follow. The door may have scared him. It was his last chance: the Grad closed the doors and sighed with satisfaction.

His sigh chopped off when his ventral view flared pure, dazzling red, then disappeared from the bow window.

From other displays he caught glimpses of painfully bright scarlet. "Can that thing hurt us?" Anthon demanded, while Lawri cried, "Now you'll see! They'll cut us in half!" and Clave said, "They're almost on us. We'll have them all over the hull if—"

"Feed it to the tree!" the Grad shouted at them all. He couldn't think. What *could* that light do to them? Neither Klance nor Lawri had ever mentioned such a thing.

We've got what we need. Forget the bread, forget the water. Get out! They'll never catch the carm.

Lawri saw his hand move and screamed, "Wait!" The Grad didn't. He tapped the center of the big blue vertical bar.

Chapter Twenty

The Position
of Scientist's
Apprentice...

THE AIR SIGHED OUT OF THE GRAD'S LUNGS. HE WAS BEING crushed flat. His left arm had missed the arm rest; it was behind him, being pulled gradually from the shoulder socket. The chair was too low to support his head. His neck hurt savagely. Above the muted shriek of the main motor he heard his passengers fighting for breath.

This must be killing the jungle giants.

London Tree dwindled like a dream in the aft view. They were in the storm now, and blind. The Grad tried to raise his right arm, to touch the blue bar, to end the force that flattened him. Up, up...farther...his arm fell back across his chest with a jolt that smashed the last sipful of air from his lungs. His sight blurred.

Lawri's chin was tucked down against her collarbone. She was sure that if she relaxed her neck the tide would snap it.

She watched Jeffer trying to turn off the motor and knew he couldn't make it. And Lawri's arms were bound.

This will kill some mutineers, she thought with alloyed satisfaction. *And I did it to them.* The com laser would burn or blind at close range, but almost certainly it would not have hurt the carm. She'd lied in hope that the mutineers would panic. She'd succeeded beyond her ambitions. *But it's killing me!*

The screen of clouds swept past and away.

Gold was to left of center in the bow window. The Smoke Ring trailed left of Gold. They were accelerating east and a little out.

East takes you out . . .

They were leaving the Smoke Ring.

I knew it. That crazy Jeffer's killed us all.

With his head pulled far back, with the points of what should have been a neck rest digging savagely into his shoulder blades, Gavving looked along his nose and tried to make sense of what he was seeing.

The sky flowed away at the edges of the bow window. A triune family split and fluttered and were gone before they could move. A small, flattish green jungle drifted close, accelerated, whipped past. A fluffy white cloud showed ahead. Closer. White blindness, and the carm shuddered and rang with the impact of water droplets. Something tiny struck the bow window a terrific blow and left a pink film a quarter meter across. In a breath the rain had pounded it clear.

The cloud was gone, and the sky ahead was clear of further obstructions. Gold and the Smoke Ring showed like a puffball on a stem, against blue sky . . . a deep, dark blue sky, a color he'd never seen in his life.

He rolled his head to look at Minya. The agony in his neck shifted . . . the pressure was easier to take this way. She looked back at him. Lovely Minya, her face fuller than he remembered. He tried to speak and couldn't. He could barely breathe.

She sighed, "Almost."

The light of the CARM's main drive was back, and blueshifting!

A shift in its spectral line, and he'd caught it. Lucky. Kendy aborted his usual message. The CARM's time-eroded program would be busy enough without distraction. For the CARM was in flight. It must have been accelerating for some minutes already. By the frequency shift, it was building up enough velocity to take it out of the Smoke Ring... within a few thousand kilometers of *Discipline* itself!

When the light went out, Kendy began his message. The air was already thinning around the CARM. Reception should be good. "Kendy for the State. Kendy for the State. Kendy for the State."

The sound stopped, the terrible tide was gone, all in a moment. Bodies bent like bows recoiled. Citizens who had not had the breath for screaming, screamed now.

As the reflexive screams died to groans, the Grad heard Lawri say, wearily, "Jeffer. Never use the main motor unless you're pushing the tree."

The Grad could only nod. He'd captured the carm, he'd... treefodder, everyone he knew, if he hadn't murdered him he'd put him aboard the carm! And *then* he'd touched the blue bar. He said, "Lawri, I'm open to suggestions."

"Feed it to the tree."

The Grad heard full-throated laughter aft... from Anthon. Debby swatted him hard across the belly. The blow snapped him into a U, but he kept laughing, and she joined him.

They had reason! They had been flat against the back wall, protecting Ilsa from what should have been mild jolting. The killer chairs would have snapped their backs, but none of the jungle giants had been in them.

Others were groaning, stirring, moving from pain to fear. Ilsa was beginning to wake up. Merril—vacant-eyed, hypnotized by the peculiar sky rushing at the bow—seemed to snap out of it. "Well, *somebody* do something!"

Clave's voice was a carrying one, and it filled the carm's cabin to overflowing. "Calm down, citizens. We're not in *that* much trouble. Remember where we are."

Other sounds stopped. Clave said, "The carrier was built for this. It came from the stars. We know it operates inside the Smoke Ring, but it was built to operate *anywhere*, wasn't it, Grad?"

That simply hadn't occurred to him. "Not anywhere, but . . . outside the Smoke Ring, that's certain."

"Good enough. What's our status?"

"Give me a breath." The Grad was ashamed. It had taken Clave to get his mind working again. *We're not in trouble*—Luck, that Clave didn't have the training to know what nonsense *that* was.

The blue display was on. *Thrust*: 0. *Acceleration*: 0. The big blue rectangle had a border of flickering scarlet: *main motor on, fuel exhausted*. He tapped it off, for what that was worth. O_2: 211. H_2:0. H_2O: 1,328. "Plenty of water, but no fuel. We can't maneuver. I don't know how to find out where we're going. Lawri?"

No answer.

"But we're bound to fall back sooner or later." Green display: "Pressure's way down outside. We're—" This could start a riot; but they'd have to know. "We're leaving the Smoke Ring. That's why the sky's that peculiar color." Yellow display: "Life support looks okay." Window displays: "Oh, my."

In the aft and side views, all detail had become tiny: integral trees were toothpicks, ponds were drops of glitter, everything seemed embedded in fog. Gold had become a bulge within a larger lens of cloud patterns that trailed off to east and west: a storm pattern that spread across the Smoke Ring. The hidden planet seemed indecently close.

"Grad?"

"Sorry, Clave, I got hung up. Citizens, don't miss this! Nobody's seen the Smoke Ring from outside since men came from the stars."

Others were craning forward to see the displays or peering out through the side windows. But Gavving said, "I think Horse is dead."

Horse? The old man Gavving had brought with him. Horse certainly looked dead enough; small wonder if the tide had stopped an old man's heart. *Poor copsik*, the Grad thought. He had never met Horse, but what human could have wanted to die before seeing *this*? "Check his pulse."

Lawri said, "Port view, Jeffer."

Something in her voice . . . the Grad looked. Off to the edge: a flash of silver? "I don't—"

"It's Mark! He's still out there!"

"I don't believe it."

But the silver pressure suit was crawling into view. The dwarf must have clung to the nets throughout that savage acceleration.

"Jeffer, let him in!"

"What a man! I . . . Lawri, I can't. The pressure's too low outside. We'd lose our air."

"He'll die out there! . . . Wait a minute. Open the doors one at a time. Hah! that's why Klance calls it an airlock! So did the cassettes—"

"Sure, two doors to lock the air in. Okay." Muffled thumps sounded aft. The silver man wanted in. "Anthon, Clave, he may be dangerous. Take the spitgun away from him when he comes in." The Grad cleared all but the yellow display. No fast decisions from now on. He pinched both lines together—make *sure* they're closed tight!—then opened the outer door with a forefinger.

The silver man disappeared from view, into the airlock.

Good. Now close the outer line, *wait*—no red borders? Open the inner. Air *shush*ed into the airlock. The silver man stepped into the carm, handed the spitgun to Anthon, and reached for his helmet.

In her heart of hearts, Lawri may have hoped for a last-breath countermutiny from the Navy's toughest warrior. She gave up that hope when she saw his face. Mark was a dwarf, of course, and the bones of his face were massive, brutal; but his jaw hung slack and his breath came fast and his face was pale with shock. His eyes wavered about the cabin, seeking reassurance. "Minya?"

A dark-haired woman answered. "Hello, Mark."

Her voice was flat and her face was hostile. Mark nodded

unhappily. Now he recognized Lawri. "Hello, Scientist's Apprentice. What now?"

"We're in the hands of mutineers," Lawri said, "and I wish they were better at flying what they've stolen."

The mutineers' First Officer said, "Welcome to Quinn Tribe, as a citizen. Quinn Tribe doesn't keep copsiks. I'm Clave, the Chairman. Who are you?"

"Navy, point man, armor. Name's Mark. Citizen doesn't sound too bad. Where we going?"

"Nobody seems to know. Now, we don't quite trust you, Mark, so we're going to tie you to a seat. That must have been quite a ride. Maybe you really are made of starstuff."

Mark was letting himself be led forward, to an empty chair. "All things considered, I'd rather ride inside. I was too mad to let go. We're not really going to *hit* Gold, are we?"

He's turned docile! Lawri thought in disgust. *He's given in to the mutineers! Are they really going to win?*

And then she saw that they were not.

She kept her silence.

Clave counted ten seats and thirteen citizens, one dead. Horse didn't need a chair. Neither did the three jungle giants. Quite the contrary! But even with the wide cargo space aft, the carm was crowded.

The citizens seemed calm enough. Exhausted, Clave guessed, and too awestruck to feel fear. He felt a touch of that himself. Most of them—even the silver man—were looking out the windows.

The sky was nearly black and scattered with dozens of white points. The Scientist's Apprentice broke her angry silence to say, "You've heard about them all your lives. The stars! You say it without knowing what you're talking about. Well, there they are. You'll die for it, but you've seen the stars."

Real they were, and impressive enough, but they were just points. It was the Blue Ghost and Ghost Child that held Clave's attention. He'd never seen them either. The paired fans of violet light were vivid and terrifying. They were entirely outside the Smoke Ring, flowing out along the hole in the ring.

Anthon and Debby were keeping busy. They had moored the ponchos and the smoked and cleaned carcass of a salmon bird to fixtures along the cargo hold walls. Now they were carving thin slices from the bird.

Clave remembered feeling like this when the tree came apart. He didn't know enough to make decisions! Then, he had been ready to strangle the Grad for withholding information. Now—

The Grad was watching him uneasily. Did he think Clave would attack their prisoners? Clave smiled back. He made his way aft and helped the jungle giants pass curls of meat forward.

Now was different. Clave was not Chairman here. If they died it would not be Clave's fault.

Probably the jungle giants found the carm more frightening than most—than Clave!—yet they were acting to make it their home. Squeezegourds of water were passing up and down the chairs...three squeezegourds, looking somewhat flat. Clave wondered about the carm's water supply.

He was about to ask when the Grad spoke first. "Gavving, would you come here for a moment?"

There was secret urgency in his voice. Anthon noticed and continued what he was doing. So did Clave. If their help was needed it would be requested.

Gavving squeezed between Lawri and the Grad. The summons was something of a relief. Minya's news had startled him, and he did need time to compose his face.

The Grad pointed. "See the red border blinking around that number?"

"Sure."

"Red means emergency. That number is the air in the cabin. How do you feel? Allergy attack coming on?"

"Actually, it was the last thing on my mind." Gavving listened to his body. Ears and sinuses were unhappy...eyes scratchy ..."Maybe."

The yellow number dropped a digit behind the decimal point.

"Scientist's Apprentice, any comments?"

"Fix it yourself, Jeffer the Scientist."

"Mmm."

"Grad, what does it *mean?*"

"Oh, sorry, Gavving. There's no air outside. The air inside must be leaking out into the, um, universe. You know, I talk to you when I get confused. Maybe you'll come up with something."

Gavving chewed it over. "What Clave said—"

"Clave did *not* say that the carm is almost four hundred years old and maybe falling apart."

"Like all those bicycle gears...okay, what's your opinion of the Scientist's Apprentice?"

Lawri bore their considering stares with her lips pressed tight and her eyes full on Gavving's. The Grad smiled and said, "Better you ask her opinion of us."

Gavving didn't have to. "Four enemy warriors, six copsiks caught in mutiny, one corpse, and a Navy man who surrendered his weapon." Her expression flickered. Had she forgotten the silver man? This wouldn't be easy, guessing at a stranger's thoughts. Try anyway. "I only wondered if she's good enough to save us if she wanted to. We could waste too much time on that."

The Grad nodded. "Lawri, if the Scientist were here, could he save us?"

"Maybe. But he wouldn't!"

"Klance wouldn't save the carm?" The Grad smiled.

She shrugged as best she could within her bonds. "All right, he'd save the carm if he could."

"How?" She didn't answer. "Can you save us?"

She raised an eyebrow at him. Gavving found that admirable, but what he said was, "Bluff. Grad, we'll have to fix it ourselves. The Scientist told you things about gases, didn't he?"

"Both Scientists did. Come to that...oxygen? We must be getting air from the oxygen tank. It's the hydrogen tank that's empty. And . . . we'll have more fuel pretty soon. The carm splits water into the two flavors of fuel. The one flavor, the oxygen, it's what we breathe. At least we'll have some time."

Gavving studied the blonde girl's face. What did she know? What did she *want*? If she only wanted everybody dead, then dead they were. But there was something she might hate even more than mutiny.

It depended on getting the Grad moving, which was a good idea anyway. How? Ask stupid questions; that worked sometimes. "Can we find the leak? Set something smoldering and watch the smoke?"

"Yes! It'll tell the others what's wrong, though, and burn up air too. Mph?"

"Inspiration?"

"Molecules of . . . bits of air move more slowly when they're cold." The board was already alive with yellow numbers and drawings. The Grad touched an arrowhead on a vertical line, then moved his fingertip slowly toward him. The arrowhead became two arrowheads, and one followed his finger.

"I never even wondered if we could make the cabin warmer or cooler, but it *has* to be true. That oxygen is liquid. Cold! It'd be freezing our lungs out if something wasn't keeping the cabin warm. Okay, now it'll be cold in here, but we'll live longer. I think you'd better tell Clave what's on and let him make the announcement. They'll have to know now, because we'll have to pass out the extra ponchos. Then we'll try the smoke—"

Lawri spoke. "Just let me at the damn controls!"

Gavving turned from her. Hide the smile. Lawri might want their deaths, but she *couldn't* let the Grad save them without her help. He asked, "Is it too complicated to tell the Grad?"

"No. But I won't!"

"Grad? Try the smoke?"

"Worst she can do is kill us. Besides, Lawri always wanted to fly the carm. Lawri, the position of Scientist's Apprentice is now open."

* * *

Lawri flexed her arms and looked about at her captors. Her hands prickled; her arms hurt. Her urge was to strike out at the mutineers. But the look on Jeffer's face: considering . . . like Klance waiting for the right answer to some stupid rote question . . .

The sky was black as charcoal. The stars were white points, like tiny versions of Voy, but *thousands* of them. And if they roused fear in Lawri, what must they be doing to these savages? She watched them nibbling on rolled slices of raw meat, and suddenly smiled.

She reached past the Grad and tapped the white key. "Prikasyvat Voice." *Hear this, you treefeeders!*

"Ready," said a voice belonging to nobody in the carm. "Identify yourself."

The lunchtime conversation went dead silent. The jungle giant male cocked his crossbow. She turned her back on him. "I am Lawri the Scientist. Give us your status."

"Fuel tanks nearly empty. Power depleted, batteries charging. Air pressure dropping, will be dangerously low in five hours, lethal in seven. Displays are available."

"Why are we losing air pressure?"

"All openings are sealed. I will seek the source of a leak."

Lawri tapped the white switch again. "That's what will kill us. We'll strangle without air. Too bad. It would have been quite a show, but you won't see it," she flashed at the Grad.

"Why did you turn off the display?"

"Voice can't hear us till I tap it again. It can do almost anything if you say the wrong thing, just talking."

"Would it talk to me?"

"You're a . . ." Her scorn became something else. "It wants you to identify yourself, and it remembers. Hmm. Try it." She tapped the talk button.

"Prikazyvat Voice," said the Grad.

"Identify yourself."

"I'm the Scientist of Quinn Tuft. Do we have enough fuel to get back into the Smoke Ring?"

"No."

For a moment the Grad forgot how to breathe. Then, "We have a water supply. Won't it be separated into fuel?"

Voice paused. Then, "If the flux of sunlight maintains its intensity, I will have fuel soon enough to affect a return. I note a mass near our course. I can use it as a gravity sling."

"Would that be Gold?"

"Rephrase."

"The mass, is it Goldblatt's World?"

"Yes."

The Grad tapped the switch before he began laughing. "Go for Gold! If we live that long."

The whispering aft had become obtrusive. With the air turning icy and Voice speaking from the walls, luncheon was sliding over to panic. Jeffer said, "Gavving, you'd better tell them about the pressure. We don't have time to brief Clave."

Lawri asked, "Shall I do it?" She knew more about what was going on.

Jeffer seemed appalled. "Lawri, they'd think *you* started the leak!"

"Savages—"

"Anyone would."

She couldn't decide if he meant it.

Gavving was telling the rest of the mutineers about the leak. He told it long, including what they planned to do about it. Jeffer tapped the white button. "Prikazyvat Voice. Have you found the leak?"

"I find no point of leakage. Air is disappearing."

"Will we live long enough to get back into the Smoke Ring?"

"No. The course I've programmed would take twenty-eight hours. Air pressure will have dropped to lethal levels in ten hours. Times are approximate."

Lawri couldn't remember how long an hour might be. Still . . . ten hours? It had been seven before the cabin got so cold. She wondered why Voice hadn't taken it into account. Sometimes Voice could be such a fool.

She said, "Display the areas where you have looked for a leak."

The yellow line diagrams of the cabin sprouted green borders along two-thirds of the interior. Red dots blinked elsewhere. "Those are sensors that have died," Lawri told Jeffer. "Voice, implement your course correction."

Jeffer added, "Prikazyvat Voice. Do not use the main motor at any time!"

"I will fire as I have fuel," Voice said. "First burn in ten seconds. Nine. Eight."

"Everybody grab something," Jeffer called.

Mutineers were pulling the extra ponchos over their clothing. They stopped to strap themselves in. The jungle giants moved against the aft wall and grabbed fixtures—

"Two. One."

But only the attitude jets lit. The carm's nose swung toward the Smoke Ring and stayed there while the aft motors fired. It lasted several tens of breaths. They would pass closer to Gold . . . which had become huge, a spiral storm seen edge-on, whose rim was already below them.

If Mark weren't tied, Lawri thought, *and if the main motor fired, nobody would be able to move except Mark.* It was something to keep in mind. Jeffer didn't seem to realize that the thrust could be controlled, by touching the top or bottom of those rectangles to raise or lower the fuel flow.

Meanwhile . . . how could the leaks be blocked? If there was a way, Lawri was damned well going to find it before Jeffer did.

Chapter Twenty-One

Go For Gold

"KENDY FOR THE STATE. KENDY FOR THE STATE. KENDY FOR the State."

The response came almost instantly, sharp and crisp through near-vacuum and dwindling distance. The CARM was out of the Smoke Ring. Kendy had clear sending for the first time since the mutiny. He sent: "Status?"

The motors were functional, all of them. Fuel: a few teacupsful. Water: a good deal. Solar power converters: functional. Batteries: charged, but running down as they changed water into liquefied hydrogen and oxygen. Sunlight flux from T3 would be steady in vacuum. There *would be* fuel.

The CARM was on manual. CO_2 flux indicated a full load of passengers. The carbon dioxide was accumulating slowly; the life support system could almost handle it...and the cabin was leaking air. Oh shit, they were dying!

"Course record since initiating burn."

It came. The CARM was rising. It would have passed near the L2 point—Kendy's own location, the point of stability behind Goldblatt's World—were it not for Goldblatt's World itself. And were it not for Goldblatt's World, the CARM would presently fall back to safety... but the core of an erstwhile gas giant planet was pulling the CARM's orbit into a tilted near-circle entirely outside the Smoke Ring.

"Switch to my command."

Massive malfunction.

"Give me video link with crew."

"Denied."

And the cabin pressure was dropping. Something had to be done. Kendy sent, "Copy," and waited.

The CARM computer thought it over, slowly, bit by bit; geared up; and began beaming its entire program. It took twenty-six minutes. Kendy looked it over—a simplified Kendy, patched with subsequent commands and garbled by time and entropy—while he sent, "Stand by for update programming."

"Standing by."

Kendy didn't believe it. The long-dead programmer would have embedded *protect* commands. He simply hadn't reached them yet... unless they had deteriorated too? Kendy didn't *have* an update program, he'd been so sure. He'd have to assemble it from scratch.

The speed with which a computer can think was Kendy's triumph and tragedy. Always he was freshly surprised by the boredom of his eventless life. It stayed fresh, because Kendy was constantly editing his memories. The storage capacity of his computer-brain was fixed. He was always near his limit. He had edited his memory of the mutiny, deleting the names of key figures, for fear that he might later seek vengeance against their descendants. He regularly deleted the memory of his boredom.

Once he had examined the solution to the Four-Color Problem in topology. The proof submitted in 1976 by Appel and Haken could not be checked except by a computer. Kendy *was* a computer; he had experienced the proof directly and found it valid. He remembered only that. The details he had deleted.

He had used a simplified program for the CARM computers, then deleted it. But now he had the CARM's program as a template. He ran through it, sharpening everywhere, correcting where suitable, updating his own simplified personality . . . leaving intact the CARM's own memories of the time of mutiny, because he was determined to ignore them. He looked for a way to plug the leak in the cabin. It was hopeless: the life support sensors had failed, not the program. He almost deleted the command that barred use of the main motor. The main motor was more efficient. He didn't understand that command . . . but it was input, and recent. He left it alone.

Now: a course program to bring them here, to study them . . .

He barely had time to hope. Kendy apprehended orbital mechanics directly. He saw instantly that the fuel wasn't there, nor the sunlight to electrolyze enough water in time. His own pair of CARMs, which fed him power via their solar collectors, didn't have fuel to meet and tow the savages' CARM even if he were willing to risk them both.

Forget it and try again . . . He could get them back into the Smoke Ring via a close approach past Goldblatt's World. In fact, the CARM's computer had already worked out a course change. It didn't matter. They'd be dead by then.

He left that part of the program intact. He deleted the barriers that barred him from communication. He beamed the revised program to the CARM at the snail's pace the CARM could accept.

The CARM filed it.

It had worked! At least he could look them over, get to know them a little, before they were gone. After five hundred and twelve years!

The cold had gotten to the jungle giants. Anthon and Debby and Ilsa were curled into a friendly, cuddling, shivering ball, with the spare ponchos pulled around them.

The other passengers were taking it better. There were ponchos for everyone but Mark, and two to spare. One they tore into scarves. Jinny wound a scarf around Mark's neck and tucked the ends into the collar of the silver suit. "Comfortable?"

The silver man seemed cheerful enough, despite the lines that held him immobile in his chair. "Fine, thanks."

"Is that suit thick enough?"

"Damn it, woman, you're the one who's shivering. This suit keeps its own temperature, just like the carm. If anyone needs my scarf...you want it?"

Jinny smiled and shook her head.

"Of course, I'd be even better off with my helmet closed," Mark said, and they laughed as if he'd said something funny. It didn't need saying: if they couldn't plug the leak, or if Lawri chose to kill them somehow, Mark would die with the rest.

The Grad had made a torch from one of the scarves plus fat scraped from the skin of the salmon bird. He was about to light it when he noticed mist before his face. He blew...white smoke. Everyone save Horse was breathing white smoke, as if they were all using tobacco.

"If you think something's leaking, breathe on it!" he announced. "Watch your breath. No, Jayan, forget the doors. Voice has sensors there."

Lawri did something to the controls. "I'm turning up the humidity...the wetness in the air. More fog that way."

Citizens took their turns at the control panel to find the blank spots in the yellow diagram. The Grad began the uncomfortable job that others might miss: he crawled between the seats, edging around the cold corpse of Gavving's friend, blowing mist where the floor joined the starboard wall.

Merril called, "I've got it. It's the bow window."

A crowd of citizens crawled around the rim of the bow window, blowing, watching the pale smoke form streamlines where the window joined the hull. The window was loose around the ventral-port corner.

"Keep looking," Lawri ordered. "There may be more."

She herself made her way aft. The Grad joined her at the back wall. "What have you got in mind? Is there a way to plug the leaks?"

Voice began a countdown. Lawri waited while small jets fired. The cluster of jungle giants sagged against the aft wall without falling apart. Ilsa giggled. She must be still floating from the spitgun drug.

The burn ended. Lawri said, "Maybe. Have we got something to hold water?"

The Grad called, "We need squeezegourds!"

They found three. Merril collected them and brought them back. Jayan and Jinny were blowing on the side windows, which seemed all right. Gavving and Minya moved along the rim of the bow window, blowing and watching. Mist formed outside and vanished immediately, along a curve of window as long as the Grad's arm, shoulder to fingers.

Lawri turned a valve. Brown water oozed from the aft wall, formed a growing globule.

"It's *mud*!" Merril said in disgust.

Lawri said, "We put pond water in. The carm breaks the pure water into hydrogen and oxygen, but it leaves the goo behind. Every so often we have to clean it out. That's why there's an *eject* system, and you can be damn glad of it."

"We can't drink that stuff. We should have picked up Minya's water supply."

"Say that if we live long enough to get thirsty." Lawri took the gourds and filled them from the brown globule. Merril winced, watching each of their water gourds become fouled.

Lawri went forward with the gourds. Would she plug the leak with mud? He could do it himself, now, if Lawri balked; but he wanted her on his side, as far as that was possible.

Lawri squeezed muddy water along the rim of the bow window.

Mist showed outside. The glass began to frost. The water stayed where she put it, in a long brown bubble. Over the next several minutes—while Lawri alone watched the controls—the water dwindled and thickened to a darker brown. Presently it began to turn *hard*.

Clave said, "Grad? Is it working?"

The Grad had read of ice. It was no more real to him than the liquefied gases in the tanks. He looked to Lawri.

Lawri met his eyes and said, "I will not accept the position of Scientist's Apprentice."

After such a performance, was she quitting on them? Clave

spoke first, and in haste. "I'm certain there's room in Quinn Tribe for two Scientists. Especially under the circumstances."

"I've saved you. Now I want to go home to London Tree. That's *all* I want."

She's earned it, the Grad thought, *but*—

Clave said, "Point to it."

The carm was nose-down to the Smoke Ring. Closest was the storm pattern that surrounded and cloaked Gold, a turbulent spiral of cloud, humped in the middle. The whole pattern drifted west at a speed that looked sluggish, but must be quick beyond imagination. The arms of the Smoke Ring reached away in both directions. They could see the flow of cloud currents, faster toward Voy, drifting backward near the carm. Minor details—like integral trees—were invisibly small.

"You're the Scientist," Clave said. "Could you get us back to London Tree?"

Lawri shook her head. She began to shiver; and once begun, she couldn't stop. Minya got her the last of the ponchos and they wrapped it around her, then tied a strip of cloth round her head and throat. She said, "We're not losing air anymore. Leave the humidity up and we won't get thirsty so fast. Jeffer, I'm cold and tired and lost. I can't make decisions. Don't bother me."

They weren't human.

Kendy had watched them for a bit. They had the temperature turned far down. Kendy was going to fix it, until he realized that the lowered temperature had slowed the leak.

They must have kept some of the old knowledge. But the cold was killing them too. He watched the *really* strange ones succumb first and crawl into a ball to wait for their deaths.

The CARM's medical sensors indicated a corpse and twelve citizens, not one of them quite normal. One had no legs. If lethal recessive genes were appearing in the Smoke Ring, it might point to inbreeding. Otherwise they seemed healthy. He saw no scars or pockmarks, no sign of disease—which was reasonable. *Discipline* had carried none of the parasites or bacteria that had adapted over the millions of years to prey on humanity. They didn't even show the sores that came with insufficient bathing.

The abnormal height, the long, vulnerable necks and long, fragile fingers and long, *long* toes, must be evolution at work, an adaptation to the free-fall environment.

He would have his problems, bringing *these* back into the State. In its way this small group was a perfect test sample. He could make his mistakes here and never pay a penalty. In time the CARM would be found by other savages.

Time to make his appearance.

Lawri was eating raw salmon bird, clearly hating it, but eating. Jayan and Jinny had gone aft to join the clustered Carther States warriors. It looked like fun, the Grad thought wistfully; but he was needed here.

Something was happening to the bow window: a pattern like a colored shadow, occluding the view.

"Lawri? Have you done something?"

"Something's wrong...I've never seen anything like..." she trailed off.

The carm was silent. A ghostly face filled the bow window. It took on color, huge and transparent, with the storms around Gold showing through.

It was brutal, with bushy brown hair and brows; thick brow ridges and cheekbones; a square, muscular jaw; a short neck as thick in proportion as a man's thigh. A face that resembled Mark's or Harp's. A gigantic dwarf. It spoke in Voice's voice.

"Citizens, this is Kendy for the State. Speak, and your reward will be beyond the reach of your imagination."

The passengers looked at each other.

"I am Sharls Davis Kendy," the face said. "I brought your ancestors here to the Smoke Ring and abandoned them when they made mutiny against me. I have the power to send you into Gold, to your deaths. Speak and tell me why I should not do so."

Too many were looking at the Scientists. Was this some trick of Lawri's? The Grad could feel the hair rising in a halo around his head . . . but *somebody* had to speak. He said, "I am the Quinn Tribe Scientist—"

"And I am the London Tree Scientist," Lawri said firmly. "Can you see us?"

"Yes."

"We are lost and helpless. If you want our lives, take them."

"Tell me of yourselves. Where do you live? Why are you of different sizes?"

'The Grad said, "We are of three tribes living in two very different places. The three tall ones—" He kept talking while his mind sought a memory. *Sharls Davis Kendy?*

Lawri broke in. "You were the Checker for *Discipline*."

"I was and am," said the spectral face.

"'The Checker's responsibility includes the actions, attitudes, and well-being of his charges,'" Lawri quoted. "If you can help us, you must."

"You argue well, Scientist, but my duty is to the State. Should I treat you as citizens? I must decide. How did you come in possession of the CARM? Are you mutineers?"

The Grad held his breath . . . and Lawri said, "Certainly not," contemptuously. "The carm belongs to the Navy and the Scientist. I'm the Scientist."

"Who are the rest of you? Introduce me."

The Grad took over. He tried to stick to lies he could remember, naming the copsiks of London Tree—Jayan, Jinny, Gavving, Minya—as London Tree citizens; Clave and Merril as refugees who had become copsiks; himself as a privileged refugee; the jungle giants as visitors. Too late, he remembered Mark tied motionless in his chair.

Go for Gold—"Now, Mark *is* a mutineer," he said. "He tried to steal the carm."

Would the dwarf brand him a liar? But the rest would back him up . . . except Lawri . . . Mark let his eyes drop. He looked sullenly dangerous.

Sharls Davis Kendy began to question Mark. Mark answered angrily, belligerently. He created a wild tale of himself as a copsik barred from citizenship by his shape; of trying to steal the carm by activating the main motor, hoping to immobilize all but himself, then finding that the ferocious thrust left him as helpless as the rest.

The face seemed satisfied. "Scientist, tell me more of London Tree. You keep some who are barred from citizenship, do you?"

Lawri said, "Yes, but their children may qualify."

"Why does a tree come apart?" the face asked, and "How does London Tree move?" and "Why do you call yourself *Scientist*?" and "Are many of you crippled?" and "How many children do you expect to die before they grow to make children?" It wanted populations, distances, durations: numbers. Lawri and the Grad answered as best they could. With these they could stick close to the truth.

And finally the voice of Kendy said, "Very well. The CARM will reenter breathable atmosphere in eleven hours. The air will slow it. Keep the—"

"Hours?"

"What measure do you use? The circuit that Tee-Three makes around the sky? In about one-tenth of a circuit, you'll be falling through air. Air is dangerous at such speeds. Keep the bow forward. You'll see fire; don't worry about it. Don't touch anything at the bow. It will be hot. Don't open the airlock until you've stopped. By then you'll have fuel to move about. Do you understand all of that?"

Lawri said, "Yes. What are our chances of living through this?"

The face of Kendy started to answer—and froze with its mouth half-open.

Update: Cabin pressure has returned to normal.

They had blocked the leak! *How?* A man without glands might naturally feel curiosity and duty as his strongest emotions. For Kendy these were now in conflict. And the CARM was about to pass out of range.

Kendy had never intended to tell them that they would not live to see reentry. Medical readouts implied that they had lied to him too...and he dared not accuse them of it.

This changed everything. The savages might actually return

to describe Kendy and *Discipline*. He could stop them, of course, by beaming some wild course change to the CARM. Or he could spend the next few minutes... indoctrinating them into the State? Impossible. He could take one trivial step in that direction, then try to impress them with the need to talk to him again.

And when they did that—years from now, or decades—he could begin the work that had waited for half a thousand years.

The face said, "You have stopped the leak. Well done. Now you must kill the mutineer. Mutiny cannot be tolerated in the State."

Mark went pale. Lawri started to speak; the Grad rode her down. "He'll face trial on our return."

"Do you doubt his guilt?"

"That will be decided," the Grad said. At this point he probably became guilty of mutiny himself, but what choice did he have? If Mark didn't talk to save himself, Lawri would. *And I captain the carm!*

"Justice is swift in the State—"

The Grad countered, "Justice is *accurate* in Quinn Tuft."

"Our swiftness may well depend on instant communication, which you clearly do not have." The face began speaking louder and more rapidly, as if in haste. "Very well. I have a great deal to tell you. I can give you instant communication and power that depends on sunlight instead of muscle. I can tell you of the universe beyond what you know. I can show you how to link your little tribes into one great State, and to link your State to the stars you now see for the first time. Come to me as soon as you can..."

The voice of Kendy died in a most peculiar fashion, blurring into mere noise, as the brutal face blurred into a wash of colored lines. Then the voice was silent, and the storm pattern around Gold glowed blue and white through the bow window.

Chapter Twenty-Two

Citizens' Tree

KENDY'S READINGS WERE BEGINNING TO BLUR. FRUSTRATINGLY, the CARM's aft and ventral cameras worked perfectly. He had two fine views of the stars and the thickening Smoke Ring atmosphere. Plasma streamed past the dorsal camera, and Kendy sought the spectral lines of silicon and metals: signs that the CARM's hull was boiling away. There was some ablation, not much more than he would have expected when the CARM was new.

Inside the cabin the CO_2 content was building. The jolting looked bad enough to tenderize meat. The passengers were suffering: mouths wide, chests heaving. Temperature was up to normal and rising. A blurred figure snapped its safety bands loose and struggled to tear its clothing away. Kendy couldn't get medical readings through the growing ionization, but the pilot had been under terrific tension earlier...

It looked chancy, whether the CARM would live or die. Kendy wasn't sure which he preferred.

He had bungled.

The principle was simple and had served the State before. To further the cause, a potential convert was ordered to commit some

224

obscene crime. He could never repudiate the cause after that. To do so would be to admit that he had committed an abomination.

The caveat was simple too. One must never give such an order unless it would be obeyed.

Kendy was ashamed and angry. He had attempted to bind their loyalty to him by ordering an execution. Instead, he had almost turned them all into mutineers! He'd had to back down gracefully and fast. He'd had no chance to recover from that, with the ionosphere building up around the CARM, cutting communications. His medical readings told him that they had lied to him, somewhere. He shouldn't have forced them to do that either! He didn't know enough even to guess at what they were hiding.

Too late now. If he sent some lethal course correction now, ionization would garble it. If they lived, they would tell of a Kendy who was powerful but gullible, a Kendy who could be intimidated. If they died . . . Kendy would remain a legend fading into a misty past.

The forward view was a blur of fire as the CARM plowed deeper into atmosphere. He was losing even the cabin sensors . . .

There was flame in front of them, transparent blue, streaming to the sides. The Grad felt the heat on his face. They'd be losing air again: the black ice around the rim of the bow window had turned to mud . . . mud that bubbled. He'd been wrong. The screaming flame-hot air massed before the bow was coming *in*.

Things came at them. Little things were hopeless; they hit or they didn't. Blood spots turned black and evaporated. Larger objects could be avoided.

His hands strangled the chair arms. Trying to steer the carm through this would have been bad enough. Watching Lawri steer was distilled horror. From her rigid posture, the knotted jaw and bared teeth, she was just at the edge of screaming hysterics. Her hands hovered like claws, reached, withdrew, then tapped suddenly at blue dashes. His own hands twitched when she was slow to see danger.

The chairs were full. Citizens had objected, but the Grad had simply kept yelling until it got done: the corpse of Horse moored to cargo fixtures; Mark the silver man in back, gripping cargo moorings with his abnormal strength; Clave beside him, swearing that his own strength was enough; everyone else strapped into seats that would give *some* protection, even to jungle giants, against thrust from the bow. Reentry wasn't like using the main motor. It was an attack. The air was trying to pound the carm into bits of flaming starstuff.

Lawri had lived half her life with the carm. She *had* to be better at this than the Grad, she'd insisted, and she was right. He gripped the chair arms and waited to be smashed like a bug.

The carm fell east and in. Integral trees showed foreshortened, as three...four pairs of green dots, hard to see...she'd seen them: jets fired. A bit of green fluff, dead ahead...Lawri fired port jets...the carm swung sluggishly around, shuddering as the flaming air blasted the nose off-center. Forward jets: the carm eased backward, too slowly, while the fluff swelled to become an oncoming jungle.

A grunt of pain, aft. Clave had been jarred loose. The silver man was holding him in place with a hand on his chest.

The Grad saw birds and scarlet flowers before the jungle was past. Lawri let the bow face forward again. A pond a klomter across just missed swatting them; droplets of fog in its wake rang the hull like a myriad tiny chimes. The debris was growing ever thicker.

And it was moving past them more slowly.

Something barred their path like a green web. It might have been half of an integral tree with the tuft gone wild, the foliage spreading like gauze, the trunk ending in a swollen knob. Small birds played in the slender branches. Swordbirds hovered at the edges. He'd never seen such a plant...and Lawri was steering clear of it.

The Grad said, "Lawri?"

"It's over," she said. "Damn, I'm tired. Take the controls, Jeffer."

"I have it. Relax."

Lawri rubbed her eyes fiercely. The Grad touched blue dashes to slow the carm further. A fingertip touch set the cabin warmth control to normal. The cabin was already warm. If it hadn't been lethally cold when they entered atmosphere, they might well have roasted.

He looked back at his passengers. Six of Quinn Tribe remained. Twelve total, to start a new tribe... "We're back," he said. "I don't know just where. Are we all alive? Does anyone need medical help?"

"Lawri! You did it!" Merril chortled. "We lived long enough to get thirsty!"

The Grad said, "We're low on fuel and there's no water at all. Let's find a pond. Then pick a home."

"Open the doors," Jayan said. She released her straps and moved aft, with Jinny following.

"Why?"

"Horse."

"...Right." He opened the airlock to a mild breeze that smelled fresh, clean, wonderful. The carm's air stank! It was stale, a treefodder stink, fear and rotting meat and too many people breathing in each other's faces. Why hadn't he noticed?

The twins released the corpse from its mooring, wincing at the touch. They towed it through the doors. The Grad waited while they sent the bones of the salmon bird after it.

Then he fired the aft motors. *If I met his ghost, he wouldn't even recognize me. How can I say I'm sorry? Never use the main motor unless*—Horse dwindled into the sky.

The pond was huge, spinning fast enough to form a lens-shape, fast enough to have spun off smaller ponds. The Grad chose one of the smaller satellites, no bigger than the carm itself. He let the carm drift forward until the bow window just touched the silver sphere.

What happened then left him breathless. He was looking into the interior of the pond. There were water-breathing things shaped like long teardrops with tiny wings, moving through a maze of green threads. He turned on the bow lights, and the water glowed. There was a jungle in there, and swimming waterbirds darting in flocks among the plants.

Lawri roused him. "Come on, Jeffer. Nobody else knows how to do this. Pick two mutineers with good lungs."

He followed her aft and didn't ask her about lungs until he'd figured it out himself. "Clave, Anthon, we need some muscle. Bring the squeezegourds. Better than lungs, Scientist."

"Squeezegourds, fine. If you'd planned your mutiny better, you'd have dismounted the pump and stored it aboard."

He laughed and thought, *Should I have asked your advice too?* and didn't say it. After all Lawri had been through, it was good to hear her joking, even in treemouth humor.

While she mounted the hose to the aft wall, the Grad carried the other end outside. He saw no sign of the nets that had covered the hull. Even the char had been burned off. He tethered himself before he jumped toward the water a few meters away. Clave came after him, also properly moored, carrying squeezegourds, followed by Jinny and Jayan.

Everyone was coming out. Mark was out of his pressure suit and tethered to Anthon. Merril, Ilsa, Debby... In a tangle of lines they plunged into the water and drank. The Grad hadn't let himself think of his thirst. Now he surrendered to it, submerging head and shoulders and doing his best to swallow the pond. The carm's headlamps lit the water around him.

It was playtime. Why not? He tugged on his line, pulled himself out before he drowned. The rest of the citizens were drinking, splashing, washing themselves and each other.

Was Lawri alone in the carm?

Alone with the controls of a vehicle that could hover near the pond, spraying fire on men and women who would have to choose between burning and drowning—He saw Lawri emerge with Minya and Gavving behind her. He'd been careless; they hadn't. The Grad kept an eye on her thenceforth to be sure she didn't return alone.

She splashed in the water. She and the dwarf washed each

other and talked a little, in earshot of Anthon. Her motions were jerky, twitchy. She looked wire-tense in the aftermath of reentry. His suspicions seemed silly; she was in no shape to contemplate a countermutiny. He wondered if she would have nightmares.

They took turns pumping. The technique was to shove the neck of a squeezegourd into the hose, warily, because there were three gourds in motion; squeeze; duck it under water, squeeze, wait while it filled; into the hose, squeeze...

"My arms just quit," Minya said and handed her gourd to Merril. With her archer's muscles she had lasted longer than most. Gavving was some distance from the others, motionless in the water. He'd already speared four peculiar, supple, scaly waterbirds. She watched him and wondered how he really felt about the guest growing in her.

How did she feel? Her impregnation was part of her past. The past was dead for anyone, but stone dead for these citizens, with hundreds of thousands of klomters and the storms of Gold itself between them and their homes. She would have a child. Time was when she had given up hope of that...but how did Gavving feel?

Merril said, "Nobody's talking about Sharls Davis Kendy."

"What for?" Debby wondered. "He never bothered us before and he never will again."

"Still, it's something to have seen the Checker, isn't it? Something to tell our children. Someone that old must have learned a lot—"

"If he wasn't lying, or crazy."

"He had the facts right," the Grad said. "We did take him at his word, didn't we? Maybe he only had cassettes, like me. A dwarf Scientist, stuck out there in a carm, like we almost were. He's not all that bright, either. He swallowed Mark's story—"

"Come on, I was brilliant!" the silver man bellowed.

"You tell a fine story. Mark, why did you back me up?"

It was a breath or two before the dwarf answered. "You understand that I can't support a bloody copsik revolution."

"Okay. *Why?*"

"It was none of this Kendy's business. Whoever he is. Whatever he is."

"Yeah . . . He did have some interesting machinery. Maybe he got stuck aboard *Discipline* itself, somehow. I'd have liked to see *Discipline.*"

Lawri hadn't even tried pumping. She flexed her fingers, wondering if they would heal. She had smelled the stink of fear on herself. That at least was gone.

She said, "I wouldn't deal with Sharls Davis Kendy if he *gave* me *Discipline.* Ugly, arrogant treefeeder. He wanted Mark dead like you'd kill a turkey, because it's time. Convenient. And he ordered us around like copsiks!"

They laughed at that. Even Mark.

At the end of three hours their forearms were distilled pain. The blue indicator inside read H_2O: 260. The Grad asked Lawri, "Enough?"

"For what we've got in mind—"

"We wondered about going home," Debby said.

Clave snorted, but they waited for Lawri's reply. She said reluctantly, "I'd never find London Tree again. Carther States is even smaller, and they're both on the wrong side of Gold. We'd have to accelerate west, drop in from the Smoke Ring, and let Gold pull us around. Do you want to go for Gold again?"

She smiled at their reactions. "Me neither. I'm tired. We can get to another tree and moor the carm. We'll build a pump before we need more water than that."

"We'd prefer a jungle, of course," Ilsa said.

One of the women bristled. "Nine of us and three of you! If—"

Clave said, "Hold it, Merril. Ilsa, are you sure? You can move a jungle, and that's good, right?"

Ilsa nodded cautiously. Anthon said, "That's *one* of the things we like about jungle life."

"But you can only do it every twenty years or so. We can moor the carrier . . . carm to the middle of an integral tree and move it when and where we like."

"Why not do that with a jungle?"

"Where would you mount the carm?"

Anthon thought it over. "The funnel? No, it might suddenly blow live steam—" He smiled suddenly. "There are more of you than us anyway. Sure, pick a tree."

There was a grove of eight small trees, thirty to fifty kilometers long. The Grad chose the biggest, without asking. He hovered on the forward jets at the western reach of the in tuft.

It was a wilderness. A stream ran down the trunk and directly into the treemouth. He looked for the rounded shapes of distorted old huts, and they weren't there. The foliage around the tree-mouth had never been cut; there were no paths for burial cere-monies or moving of garbage. No earthlife showed, not even as weeds.

It was daunting. He said cheerily, "It seems we're the first here. Lawri, have you thought of a way to land this thing?"

"You have the helm."

He'd thought it through in detail. "I'm afraid our best move is to moor at the trunk and go down."

"Climb?"

"We did it before. Clave could lead most of us down while, say, Gavving and I wait. We'd have the carm for rescue opera-tions. After the rest of you get down, Gavving and I can follow. We've climbed before—"

"Hold it," Clave said. "This is taking too treefeeding *long*. Grad, quit fooling around and just land in the treemouth."

"We might set it on fire!"

"Then we try again with another tree!"

Lawri had gone berserk at the suggestion of landing in the treemouth of London Tree. Now she just rubbed her eyes. Tired...

They were all too tired. They'd had enough of shocks and strangeness. Clave was right, delay would be torment, and there were trees to waste.

There was no kind of landing site in that wilderness. Every-thing he saw was green; there was no drought here. Would it burn?

Go for Gold.

He went in over the treemouth and rammed the carm into the foliage hard enough to stick. Still shaken by the impact, they forced their way through the doors, fast, and flailed with ponchos at the smoldering fires until they went out.

Then, finally, they had time to look around.

Minya stood panting, grinning, her black hair wild and wet, the blackened poncho trailing from her hand. She snatched at his hand and cried, "Copter plants!"

Gavving laughed. "I didn't know you liked copter plants."

"I didn't either. But in London Tree they weeded out the copter plants and flowers and anything else they couldn't use." She tapped at one, two, three ripe plants, and the seed pods buzzed upward. Suddenly she was looking into his eyes, close. "We did it. Just like we planned, we found an unoccupied tree and it's ours."

"Six of us. Six out of Quinn Tuft . . . sorry."

"Twelve of us. More to come."

She had fought the fire with a predatory grace unhampered by the thickening around her hips. *Mine*, Gavving thought. *Whether it looks like me or some copsik runner . . . or Harp, or Merril! Mine; ours.* He'd tell her when the mood was right. But that was too serious for now. "Okay, everything you see is ours. What shall we call it?"

"The thing I like best . . . I can say *citizen* and mean *all of us.* I'm no copsik and I'm not a triune. Citizens' Tree?"

The foliage tasted like Quinn Tuft in the Grad's childhood, before the drought. He lay on his back in virgin foliage and sucked contemplatively.

He became aware that Lawri was watching him from the dappled shadows. She looked cold, or just twitchy, hugging her elbows, cringing as if from a blow. He snapped, "Can't you relax? Eat some foliage."

"I did. It's good," she said without inflection.

It was irritating. "All right, what's got you worried? Nobody's ever going to call you a copsik runner. You saved our lives and everyone knows it. You're clean, fed, rested, safe, and admired. Take a break, Scientist. It's *over*."

Now she wouldn't meet his eyes. "Jeffer, how does this sound? There are only two London Tree citizens for at least ten thousand klometers around. Doesn't it stand to reason that we'd...get along best together?"

He sat back on his haunches. Why ask him? "I suppose it does."

"Well, Mark thinks so too."

"Okay."

"He didn't have to say so. We talked a little about building huts, that's all, but he looks at me like he *knows*. Like, he's too polite to broach the subject yet, but where else can I go, who else is there? Jeffer, don't make me marry a dwarf!"

"Uh...huh."

She turned, convulsively, to see his face. He held up a hand to stop her from speaking. "In principle, two Scientists ought to make good mates too. Does *that* make sense? But you watched me murder Klance. I didn't warn him. I didn't make any speeches about copsiks and freedom and war and justice. I just killed him the first good chance I got. I'd have killed you too to get us free of that place."

She didn't nod, she didn't speak.

"You could put a harpoon in my belly while I'm sleeping. So don't push me. I have to think."

She waited. He thought. Now he knew why she irritated him with her twitchy unhappiness. He was guilty, and she had seen it. Not quite what one wanted in a mate!

Did he want a wife? He'd always thought he did, and with seven women and five men in Nameless Tuft...no chance for an unmarried man to play around in such a tiny population, but he should have his choice of wives. So who?

Gavving and Minya: married. Clave, Jayan, Jinny: a unit, and the twins seemed to like it that way. Anthon, Debby, Ilsa might all have left mates in Carther States, and they might all be looking around...but Anthon didn't seem to think so, and even if Debby or Ilsa were available...a romp might be fun, but they looked so *odd*. Which left...Lawri.

He said, being nearly sure he could get away with it, "Lawri, will you forgive me for murdering Klance?"

"I notice you said murder. Not kill."

"I'm not even claiming it was war. I know what he was to you. Lawri, I *demand* this."

She turned her back and wept. The Grad did not turn his back. He'd virtually invited her to try to kill him. *Now or never, Lawri! You can add too. There's me or there's Mark or there's nobody. I might be giving Mark another reason to kill me. Do I want to risk that?*

She turned around. "I forgive you for murdering Klance."

"Then let's go to the carm and register a marriage. We'll pick up witnesses along the way."

Clave looked down into the treemouth. "I see rocks down there. Good. We'll have to collect them for a cookfire. Cook Gavving's waterbirds. Tear out some foliage so we'll have room. Where do we want the Commons?"

He didn't see many of his citizens in earshot, and none were listening.

He raised his voice. "Treefodder, we have to get organized! A reservoir. Tunnels. Huts. Pens. Maybe we won't find turkeys, but we're bound to find *something*. Maybe dumbos. We need *everything*. Sooner or later we want elevators to the midpoint so we can moor the carm there. But for now—"

Anthon, flat on his back in the foliage with a long, long woman in each arm, bellowed, "Claaave! Feed it to the treeee!"

Clave grinned at Anthon. He did seem to represent the majority opinion. "Take a break, citizens. We're home."

For good or ill, they were alive and safe, two-thirds of the distance from Goldblatt's World to the congestion of masses and life forms around the L4 point; and they would remember Kendy.

He had promised a treasure of knowledge. A pity he hadn't had time to give them more of a foretaste; but they must have experienced exactly what he'd predicted during reentry, given that they'd survived. A savage's gods *were* omniscient, weren't they? Or were they gullible, easily manipulated? Kendy's memory had been pruned of such data.

Whatever: the legend would spread.

I can show you how to link your little tribes into one great State.

He had altered the programming in the CARM. The CARM would watch their behavior and record everything. Before the children of the State came again to Kendy, he would know them . . .

He would know one tiny enclave within that vast cloud. The Smoke Ring was roomy enough for endless variety. 10^{14} cubic kilometers of breathable atmosphere was about thirty times the volume of the Earth! Kendy wished for a thousand CARMs, ten thousand. *What were they doing in there?*

Never mind. Sooner or later there would come a man eager to carve out an empire, determined enough to take the CARM, crazy enough to trust his life to the ancient, leaky service vehicle. Kendy would know how to use him. Such men had helped to shape the State on Earth. They would again, in this strange environment.

Kendy waited.

Dramatis Personae

Discipline

SHARLS DAVIS KENDY　　Once a Checker for the State, now deceased. Also, the recordings of Sharls Davis Kendy's personality in the master computer of the seeder ramship *Discipline* and its service spacecraft.

Quinn Tuft

GAVVING　　A young warrior subject to allergies.
HARP　　The teller, or bard.
LAYTHON　　The Chairman's son.
MARTAL　　Quinn Tuft's cook (deceased).
THE SCIENTIST　　Quinn Tuft's guardian of knowledge.
THE GRAD　　The Scientist's half-trained apprentice.
THE CHAIRMAN　　Ruler of Quinn Tribe.
CLAVE　　A mighty warrior, the Chairman's son-in-law.
MAYRIN　　Clave's wife, the Chairman's daughter.
JAYAN and **JINNY**　　Twin sisters enamored of Clave.

MERRIL   An older woman, strong, but barren. Small, withered legs.

JIOVAN   A hunter.

GLORY   A woman of unwanted fame.

ALFIN   An older man, Keeper of the treemouth.

Others

MINYA   A fighting woman of the Triune Squad, of Dalton-Quinn Tuft.

SAL, SMITTA, JEEL, THANYA, DENISSE   Others of the Triune Squad.

KARA   Sharman (or Scientist) of Carther States.

DEBBIE, ILSA, HILD, LIZETH, ANTHON   Citizens of Carther States.

KLANCE   London Tree's Scientist.

LAWRI   London Tree's Scientist's Apprentice.

HORSE, JORG, HELN, GWEN   Copsiks in London Tree.

DLORIS, HARYET, KOR   Supervisors in London Tree.

KARAL, MARK, PATRY   London Tree Navy men.

Glossary

BLUE GHOST and **GHOST CHILD**—Auroralike glow patches produced by magnetic effects above Levoy's Star's poles. Rarely visible.

BRANCH—One at each end of an integral tree, curving to leeward.

BRANCHLETS—Grow from the spine branches and sprout into foliage.

CARM—Cargo And Repair Module. *Discipline* originally carried ten of these.

THE CLUMPS—The L4 and L5 points for Gold. They tend to collect debris.

COPSIK—Slave. Used as a general insult.

COPSIK-RUNNER—Slavetaker or slavemaster.

COTTON-CANDY JUNGLE or **JUNGLES**—Describes almost any large cluster of plants. A good many plants and clusters of plants look like fluffy green cotton candy. Many are edible.

DAY—One orbit about Levoy's Star, the neutron star (equals two hours for Dalton-Quinn Tree).

DUMBO—A predator of the integral trees.

FAN FUNGUS—An integral tree parasite. Parts are edible.

"FEED THE TREE"—Defecate, or move garbage, or die.

FLASHER—An insectivorous bird.

GHOST CHILD—See BLUE GHOST.

GO FOR GOLD—Rush headlong into diaster. Or battle!

GOLD—See GOLDBLATT'S WORLD. Secondary meaning: something to avoid.

GOLDBLATT'S WORLD—A gas giant planet captured after Levoy's Star went supernova/neutron. Named for *Discipline*'s Astrophysicist, Sam Goldblatt.

HUTS—Any dwelling. In the integral trees, huts are woven from living spine branches.

INTEGRAL TREE—A crucial plant.

JET POD—Some plants grow pods that may be carried for attitude control: they jet gases (of corruption, or of oxygen in plants that favor the outer fringes of the Smoke Ring). Other plants fire seeds when dying, or going to seed, or falling too far out of the Smoke Ring. There are tropisms.

LEVOY'S STAR—A neutron star, the heart of the Smoke Ring system. Named for its discoverer, Sharon Levoy, Astrogator assigned to *Discipline*.

NOSE-ARM—See DUMBO.

OLD-MAN'S-HAIR—A fungus parasite on integral trees.

POND—Any large globule of water.

PRIKAZYVAT—Originally, Russian for "command." Presently used to activate computer programs.

QUINN TUFT—The in tuft (or point nearest Levoy's Star) of Dalton-Quinn Tree.

THE SCIENTIST—Quinn Tuft's guardian of knowledge. Tribes elsewhere use the same term.

SPINE BRANCHES—Grow from the branch of an integral tree.

SUN—A G0 star orbits the neutron star at 2.5×10^8 kilometers, supplying the sunlight that feeds the Smoke Ring's water-oxygen-DNA ecology.

TREEFODDER—Used as a curse. Treefodder is anything that might feed the tree: excrement, or garbage, or a corpse.

TUFTBERRIES—Fruiting bodies growing in the tuft of an integral tree. They fruit and scatter seed only at the tuft closest to the Smoke Ring median.

VOY—See LEVOY'S STAR.

YEAR—Half of a complete circuit of the sun around Levoy's Star, equal to 1.385 Earth years.

Directions

OUT—Away from Levoy's Star.

IN—Toward Levoy's Star.

EAST—In the orbital direction of the gas torus.

WEST—Against the orbital direction of the gas torus. The way the sun moves.

WINDWARD—Into the wind.

LEEWARD—The direction toward which the wind blows.

PORT—To the left if your head is out and you're facing west, or if your head is in and you're facing east, and so forth. Direction of the Ghost Child.

STARBOARD—Opposite port. Toward the Blue Ghost.

DOWN and **UP**—Usually applied only where tides or thrust operate. The general rule as known to all tribes is "East takes you out. Out takes you west. West takes you in. In takes you east. Port and starboard bring you back." Even those tribes who no longer can maneuver within the Smoke Ring know the saying.

About the Author

Larry Niven was born on April 30, 1938, in Los Angeles, California. In 1956, he entered the California Institute of Technology, only to flunk out a year and a half later after discovering a bookstore jammed with used science-fiction magazines. He graduated with a B.A. in mathematics (minor in psychology) from Washburn University, Kansas, in 1962, and completed one year of graduate work in mathematics at UCLA before dropping out to write. His first published story, "The Coldest Place," appeared in the December 1964 issue of *Worlds of If.*

Larry Niven's interests include backpacking with the Boy Scouts, science-fiction conventions, supporting the conquest of space, and AAAS meetings and other gatherings of people at the cutting edge of the sciences.

He won the Hugo Award for Best Short Story in 1966 for "Neutron Star," and in 1974 for "The Hole Man." The 1975 Hugo Award for Best Novelette was given to "The Borderland of Sol." His novel *Ringworld* won the 1970 Hugo Award for Best Novel, the 1970 Nebula Award for Best Novel, and the 1972 Ditmars, an Australian award for Best International Science Fiction.